Copyright

The Fox: A Summer In The Dark
© 2024 Toshibooks

All rights reserved. No part of this publication may be reproduced, distributed, or transmitted in any form or by any means, including photocopying, recording, or other electronic or mechanical methods, without the prior written permission of the publisher, except in the case of brief quotations embodied in critical reviews and certain other non-commercial uses permitted by copyright law.

This is a work of fiction. Names, characters, places, and incidents are either the product of the author's imagination or used fictitiously. Any resemblance to actual persons, living or dead, or actual events is purely coincidental.

Published by Toshibooks
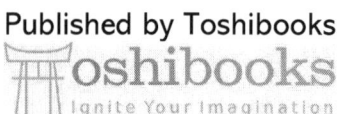

First Edition: November 2024
ISBN (paperback): 9798301260179
Printed in United Kingdom

For permissions or inquiries, please contact us on our social media accounts:
Gmail: Toshibooks2024@gmail.com
Instagram: @toshibooks_
Tik Tok: @toshibooks
X: @Toshibooks_

Dedication

To all other first-time authors hoping to make a breakthrough.

Content warning

This novel contains graphic depictions of violence and explores challenging themes, including physical and mental assault. It may be distressing to some readers.

Prologue

The summer of 1984 had descended upon England with a gentle grace. Life in Leighton Buzzard, Dunstable, and Tring, three small, provincial English towns, was placid and uneventful. Nestled in the embrace of the Chiltern Hills, these scattered towns that formed a quaint triangle seemed to exist in a different world - one where time moved slowly, and the summer days stretched luxuriously, inviting residents to linger on their porches, swap stories over fences, and savour the lingering warmth of the evening sun. It was an area where everyone knew everyone, and the night, soft and warm, was something to be trusted.

Hardly the setting for major crime - or so it seemed.

Part One: The Terror Begins

Chapter 1

The tranquil façade of these sleepy towns masked a sinister reality. High above in the Ivinghoe Hills, a lone man clad from head to toe in black stood atop Ivinghoe Beacon, a popular spot for hikers, dog walkers and model aeroplane enthusiasts. His silhouette was unadorned against the early evening sky, a stark contrast to the idyllic scene below. He was motionless, peering through binoculars with a cold intensity, his eyes narrowing as he surveyed the homes scattered around the region below him. The scene unfolding in the streets was of little concern to him; his focus was singular, his purpose darker than the shade of his outfit. He was observing a home that stood alone, bordered by open land, offering the perfect route for a swift, unseen escape.

As the final light of dusk began to pierce the horizon, the area beneath him was stirring. The daily routine of the townsfolk unfurled with the predictability of a well-rehearsed play: doors were locked, curtains drawn, children tucked away in their beds. There was a comforting rhythm to it all - an unspoken agreement that each day would pass as the last had. But today, that routine was about to be interrupted.

The lone man was about to execute his plan with a chilling precision. With Leighton Buzzard's inhabitants blissfully unaware of the danger lurking so close to home, he slipped into the Chambers' cottage while Lizzie and Alan Chambers were out at a friend's house having dinner. The back door lock popped open with relative ease. The lock was old and no match for the man's trusty screwdriver. He knew that as he had been watching and observing the property for several days.

The cottage, a quintessential representation of country charm, was quaint and well-loved, its floral sofa a testament to the comfort of home. The man had chosen this particular home with care; it was perfect for his purposes.

He moved with the precision of a surgeon. His hands gloved and steady, he grabbed food from the fridge, poured a glass of water and took his stash into the living room. There he worked a thin blade through the fabric of the sofa's back, carefully slicing it open. Sweat beaded on his forehead, but he was methodical, thorough. The room was silent, save for the slow rip of fabric giving way. He pulled at the foam, hollowing out a space big enough for his wiry frame. He removed the evidence, hiding it in an outside bin. Then he wriggled inside the sofa, pulling the fabric back into place, sealing himself in like a spider waiting in its web.

And then, he waited.

Time stretched on, the only sound his own shallow breathing. The man knew how to make himself disappear. How to become part of the furniture. He focused on each breath, his body tense but still, like a lion crouched in the tall grass, waiting for the perfect moment to pounce on its prey.

He could feel the stiffness settling in his muscles, the ache creeping up his spine. Still, he didn't move. His eyes stayed wide open, staring into the darkness of his makeshift hiding spot.

The couple returned home just after ten o'clock, the front door creaking open, and slamming shut, the sound echoing through the quiet house. The man's heart quickened, but his breath remained even. He listened carefully to the soft thud of bags hitting the kitchen counter, the rustle of paper, and the murmur of their voices. He imagined the scene in his mind's eye - Lizzie laughing as Alan tried to juggle too many things at once.

They had no idea. No idea that their cosy, little home had been breached. No idea that a stranger lay coiled like a snake, hidden right beneath their noses.

"Do you want tea, love?" Lizzie's voice carried from the kitchen, light and pleasant, blissfully unaware.

"Yeah, that'd be good. I'll get the milk," Alan replied. The man could hear the refrigerator door opening, the clink of bottles. He imagined the couple, so comfortable in their routine, so assured in their safety. They were wrong. So, so wrong.

The man felt a twisted thrill deep in his gut as he listened to them go about their lives, his pulse a steady thrum in his ears. The ordinary sounds of domesticity – teacups clinking, the faint hiss of the kettle, soft laughter - became a symphony of ignorance. They were living their lives, clueless that a stranger was hiding inside their sofa, listening, waiting.

Alan eventually settled into his sofa, the familiar rustle of the newspaper folding open. The man's ears pricked up at every sound, every word exchanged between them. His breathing was measured, his body numb and sweaty from hours in the cramped hollow of the sofa, but his mind was razor sharp. Lizzie hummed softly as she moved about, her footsteps light, her movements graceful.

The man imagined her delicate hands making tea, pouring milk, unaware that they could so easily be turned into instruments of something far darker. His fingers twitched involuntarily. The thought of it - the power he held - sent a shiver of excitement through him. He was in control. They were his to toy with, to decide their fates.

Minutes ticked by and still, he remained hidden. Lizzie's laughter bubbled up from the kitchen, mixing with the clinking of dishes. She was telling Alan a story, something about an old school friend. The man didn't care about the details; he focused on her voice, its rise and fall, the way it wove a sense of normalcy around the room.

Alan muttered something in response, his voice a low rumble. The man's body tensed, his fingers curled tighter around the blade in his hand, just in case.

"Do you hear that?" Alan's voice broke the rhythm of the evening. The man's pulse quickened. For a moment, his breath hitched, his eyes widening in the dark.

"Hear what?" Lizzie asked, her voice distant, still in the kitchen.

Alan paused; he was sat directly above the man's hiding place. "I don't know. Thought I heard something, that's all."

A moment of silence hung in the air. The man could hear his own heart pounding in his ears, the tension crackling around him. He pressed his body even flatter against the hollowed-out sofa, barely daring to breathe. Sweat trickled down his spine.

"You're always hearing things, love," Lizzie chuckled. The sound of water running in the sink drowned out the stress for a moment. "Probably the house settling or something."

Alan hesitated, then muttered, "Yeah, must be." The friction ebbed, and he settled back into his sofa with a soft groan. Oblivious to the danger, he picked up his newspaper once more.

Meanwhile, the man exhaled silently, his lips bending into a slight, twisted smile. How easy it would be to reach out, to make them know he was there. To make them see. But that wasn't his plan - not yet.

He needed more. More time, more control.

Midnight approached, and the cottage was darkened, albeit for a lamp in the living room, its soft, yellow glow barely reaching the man's hiding spot. Alan yawned loudly, his body sinking further into his sofa. "Must be time for bed" he conceded.

Alan stood up and turned off the television, while Lizzie switched off the lamp. The couple started their nightly routine, brushing their teeth, whispering in hushed tones. The man listened to every word, every breath.

Lizzie, always cautious, checked the front door lock with her usual ritualistic accuracy. She glanced toward the living room with a hint of unease. "You think I'm paranoid, but I'd rather be safe than sorry," she muttered to herself, her fingers lingering on the latch. Lizzie was a woman in her sixties, her life a blend of practicality and affection. Tonight, something about the quiet felt off, a prickling discomfort that she couldn't quite shake.

Alan, dismissive as ever, grumbled from the bathroom. "Nothing ever happens around here, Lizzie. We're in the middle of nowhere, for God's sake."

But something *was* happening. Inside his hiding place, the man was a coiled spring, every nerve ending attuned to the subtle shifts in the atmosphere.

When Alan and Lizzie had finally retired in their bed, the man waited - counting the seconds, then minutes. The house settled into a deep silence, the only sounds now the distant hum of the refrigerator and the occasional creak of the building.

Upstairs, Lizzie had left her bedside lamp on. Her unease grew with the quiet of the house, an unsettling feeling that gnawed at her. She pulled the blankets up to her chin, and slowly her eyes began to rest. Alan had sunk into the mattress with a sigh, his weariness quickly overcoming him. Within minutes, his soft snores filled the room, a regular counterpoint to Lizzie's anxious thoughts.

The man's body ached as he slowly manoeuvred himself out of the hollowed sofa, each movement calculated, every shift of weight deliberate. He slipped out silently, like a phantom emerging from the shadows.

The room was dark, but his eyes had adjusted. He could see the silhouettes of the furniture, the glint of a knife left carelessly on the counter. He crept through the living room, his footsteps silent, his breath steady.

He pulled out a balaclava from his pocket and slipped it on. He was ready. He stood at the bottom of the stairs, listening to the soft snores coming from above. His hand tightened around the handle of his blade. The man smiled in the dark, feeling the cold thrill of terror simmering just beneath the surface, and he waited a few more minutes.

He crept up the stairs, each step measured and cautious. He avoided the squeaky spots with practiced ease, the darkened house now his domain. At the top of the stairs, he paused, listening intently. His heartbeat was steady, his breath slow and controlled. The thrill of the hunt, the invasion of their personal space, was an intoxicating rush. He pushed the bedroom door open just enough to slip inside, his gloved hand brushing against the cool metal of the door handle.

The bedroom was bathed in the pale, wan glow of the lamp. Lizzie lay in bed, her back turned, her face partially hidden by the pillow. Alan was snoring softly beside her, oblivious to the danger that was now inches away. The man moved closer, each step calculated, until he was standing directly over Lizzie's side of the bed. His gloved fingers reached out, brushing gently against her cheek.

Lizzie's eyes snapped open, terror flooding her features as she registered the figure looming over her. Before she could scream, the man's hand clamped over her mouth, his touch cold and unyielding. "Not a word," he whispered, his voice a chilling whisper that sent shivers down her spine.

Alan stirred, sensing the disturbance, his eyes fluttering open to see the dark figure towering over his wife. Panic surged through him as he bolted upright, but the man was quicker. In a swift, practiced motion, he brandished his knife, its handle catching the dim lamplight and casting a menacing gleam.

"Stay quiet, both of you," the man hissed, his voice low and threatening. "Or it gets worse."

Alan's hands trembled as he raised them in a gesture of surrender, his voice a trembling whisper. "Please...we don't have much. Take whatever you want."

The man's lips curved into a malevolent smile beneath his balaclava. He savoured the fear, the trembling of their bodies, the wide, terrified eyes. It was a perverse pleasure, seeing them so vulnerable. But just as he was about to escalate his threats, a noise cut through the oppressive silence.

Two late night dog walkers, Victor and Philippa Smith stood chatting outside the cottage while their dog did its business against the white picket fence running along the front of the garden.

The man's eyes darted to the open window, his expression darkening with a mixture of frustration and alarm. As he opened the curtain and peered out of the window, Victor looked up. Their eyes met catching Victor by surprise.

"Hey, why's there a man wearing a balaclava in Lizzie's bedroom?" he quizzed.

"A what?" replied a surprised Philippa.

The man quickly stepped away from the curtain. This wasn't part of the plan. The sudden interference, the unexpected scrutiny - it was too risky. Without a second thought, he bolted down the stairs, his movements frantic as he dashed through the kitchen and out the back door, over the back fence and into the dark of the fields.

Lizzie, her face pale and her hands trembling, burst out crying, her mind racing with fear. "Alan are you alright?" she gasped, her voice barely more than a whisper.

Alan, his breath ragged and his mind still in shock, nodded weakly. "He had a knife...I thought..."

Lizzie's steady voice cut through the panic. "Stay calm," she said urgently. "We need to call the police. Now."

By dawn, the quiet town was wide awake, the fear spreading like wildfire. The man had breached the sanctity of one of their homes, hiding inside a sofa, and the sense of security that had once blanketed the town was shattered. The Chamber's cottage, once a symbol of peaceful domesticity, had become the scene of an intrusion that would forever alter their perception of safety.

The community gathered, whispers of the intruder's presence mingling with the rising sun. The man had been among them, watching, waiting, hidden in their very midst. As the sun rose over the Chiltern Hills, the townsfolk faced a new reality: an evil buzzard was flying high, and no one knew if or where he would strike next. The once unassuming tranquillity of their lives had been disrupted, leaving behind a lingering sense of unease that would take more than just time to heal.

Chapter 2

Two days later, the warm afternoon sun gently filtered through the lace curtains of a small, secluded bungalow, on the outskirts of Tring, casting intricate patterns of light and darkness that danced across the room. The air was heavy with the comforting scents of old wood and lavender, blending with the faint aroma of blooming roses that drifted in through the open window. Donna Rutland, a seventy-four-year-old woman with a graceful air and a face etched with the lines of a life well-lived, moved around the cosy living room humming softly to herself. She adjusted a stack of books on a small, round table, straightened a framed photograph on the mantelpiece, and dusted off a ceramic figurine with tender care.

Her husband, Arthur, sat in his favourite armchair by the window, his head tilted back slightly, and eyes closed. His newspaper, which he had been reading only moments before, was now draped across his chest. The corners of his mouth twitched upward, perhaps in response to a pleasant dream or simply the contentment that comes with a peaceful afternoon nap. His thinning white hair caught the sunlight, giving it a soft, almost angelic glow. A light breeze fluttered the lace curtains, and the room was filled with the sounds of birds chirping in the distance and the faint chatter of neighbours from down the lane.

It was a scene that could be painted on a canvas, a moment of pure, tranquil domesticity. But inside this serene little bungalow, something was terribly wrong. Lurking within the cosy confines of their living room, hidden away deep within the back of the old leather sofa, an intruder lay in wait, his presence unseen and his intentions unknown.

Earlier that day, the man had slipped into the bungalow with the stealth and precision of a seasoned criminal. He had observed the occupants' comings and goings from his vantage point in the Chiltern Hills. Nobody had suspected him, he was just another naturist, gazing at the wildlife through his binoculars.

He was a man of lithe build, his movements almost unnatural in their quietness, a shadow in the daylight. With the quick flick of his blade, he had sliced open the back of the sofa, creating a hollow space just big enough for him to crawl into and hide. He had chosen his hiding spot well. From there, he could hear every movement without being seen himself, concealed within the very fabric of the Rutland's' everyday life.

He listened intently to the tempo of the couple's day: the soft drone of Donna's song, the rustle of Arthur's newspaper, the faint clink of teacups as they enjoyed their afternoon tea. He lay still, waiting for the right moment to strike.

As the hours crept by, the sun began its slow descent in the sky, and the day transformed into early evening. The golden hues of the afternoon light gradually gave way to the muted tones of dusk, casting longer, softer shadows throughout the room. Donna, her energy seemingly endless, moved into the kitchen to prepare dinner, the comforting clatter of pots and pans adding a homely background noise to the evening. Arthur, now awake and stretching the stiffness from his limbs, switched on the radio, and the gentle strains of a classical symphony filled the bungalow, soothing and melodic.

The man remained perfectly still, his body cramped from the tight confines of his hiding place, but his mind was focused, his senses heightened. He was accustomed to discomfort; in fact, he thrived on it. Each muscle that ached, each cramp that seized his body, only sharpened his resolve. He knew he had to bide his time. Tonight, he was going to strike. He had decided that much already, and he was a man who always saw his plans through.

The Rutland's dinner time passed slowly, and the couple began to wind down, their routine practiced and predictable. Donna glanced at the clock on the wall, a simple piece with a soft, rhythmic tick that marked the passing of time. She yawned softly, stretching her arms above her head, and turned to Arthur with a gentle smile. "Time for bed, love," she said softly, her voice warm and tender as she placed a comforting hand on his shoulder. They loved an early night.

Arthur nodded, his eyes crinkling at the corners as he smiled back at her. He folded his newspaper neatly and set it aside, the rustling of the paper breaking the calm stillness of the room. The two of them shuffled slowly toward their bedroom, their movements slow and tired but full of a quiet contentment. The living room fell into darkness as they left, save for the dim glow of the streetlight outside that seeped through the window, casting faint lines of light on the walls.

For a moment, an almost tangible silence settled over the bungalow. All that could be heard was the soft ticking of the clock and the distant buzz of the world outside. Then, like a wild bear emerging from hibernation, the man began to move. He slipped out from his hiding place, emerging from the darkness of the sofa with a smooth, almost feline grace. He stretched his limbs carefully, feeling the pressure ease from his muscles, but his eyes remained concentrated, his mind alert. He put on his balaclava and gripped his knife tight.

Each step he took was slow and calculated. He knew the layout of the cottage well, having observed the Rutland's conversation and movements. He moved like a silhouette, gliding silently across the floorboards, making his way down the hallway toward the bedroom where Arthur and Donna now lay. Inside, Arthur was already asleep, his breathing steady and deep, while Donna, with her back to the door, was still drifting in and out of consciousness.

The man reached the doorway and paused, his breath steady and controlled. His eyes gleamed with malice, cold and calculating. This was it - the moment he had been waiting for. He took another careful step forward, his hand tightening around the handle of his knife.
A floorboard screeched under his weight, the sound piercing the silence like a needle through cloth.

Donna stirred, her instincts pricking at her sleep-dulled senses. "Arthur, did you hear that?" she whispered, her voice barely a breath as she turned slightly toward him.

The man reacted instantly. He lunged forward, his movements swift and menacing, his voice low and threatening. "Not a word," he hissed, brandishing his knife. The blade caught the faint light from the window, gleaming with a cold, deadly promise.

Donna froze, her heart pounding in her chest like a drumbeat. She could see his masked face, partially shrouded in shadiness, and her breath caught in her throat. There was a darkness in his eyes, a malice that sent a shiver down her spine.

Arthur jolted awake, his eyes snapping open as he tried to comprehend what was happening. "What...who are you?" he croaked, his voice hoarse and trembling with fear.

"Shut up," the man growled, his tone dripping with danger. "You make a sound, and I swear-"

He stepped around to Arthur's side of the bed, moving with a chilling calm. In one swift motion, he pulled a length of coarse rope from his pocket and tied Arthur's hands together, his grip firm and unyielding. "Don't move, or she gets it," he snarled, his eyes never leaving Arthur's face.

Arthur's breath came in shallow, panicked gasps, his eyes wide with terror. He nodded slowly, understanding the gravity of the situation, his heart pounding in his chest.

Without breaking his gaze from Arthur, the man moved back to Donna's side of the bed, his demeanour shifting. There was a new glint in his eyes, one of cruel intent. He reached down and pulled back the duvet covers, revealing Donna's legs beneath her light nightgown.

Donna's breath hitched in her throat, her eyes darting to Arthur, who lay helpless beside her. She was paralysed with fear, her body stiff and trembling. Tears welled up in her eyes, spilling down her cheeks in silent streams.

The man ran his left hand slowly up Donna's leg, his touch cold and invasive. "Ssh, don't make a sound," he whispered, his voice a soft, sinister murmur in the darkness. Donna's body was rigid with terror, her heart beating so loudly she was sure he could hear it. She squeezed her eyes shut, trying to block out the reality of what was happening, her tears falling faster now.

As the man's hand reached inside her underwear, Donna sobbed uncontrollably. The man showed no remorse, he smiled from underneath his mask. The assault lasted only a few minutes before the sound of a car's engine approached from the distance, its headlights suddenly sweeping across the bedroom window. Bright beams of light cut through the darkness, casting sharp, moving shades across the room. The man's eyes flicked toward the window, his grip on the knife tightening instinctively. For a moment, panic flashed across his face. Another disturbance.

In that split second, Donna saw an opportunity. Summoning every ounce of courage she had, she acted.

"Arthur!" she shouted, her voice breaking the strain like a lightning strike. It was louder than she intended, but it was enough. The sudden burst of noise startled the man, his head snapping back toward her, eyes wide with surprise.

Outside, a dog began barking, its frantic yaps growing closer and more insistent. The man's eyes darted to the window again, calculating his options. The risk was too high now. Too many variables. Too much noise. He wasn't here to get caught.

"Damn it," he muttered under his breath, taking a step back, his gaze shifting rapidly between Arthur and Donna. "You got lucky tonight," he spat, his voice filled with frustration and anger. And then, just as quickly as he had appeared, he turned and bolted out of the bedroom. His footsteps were hefty and rapid as they pounded down the hallway, a stark contrast to his earlier stealth. Arthur and Donna could hear the back door slam open, and a gust of warm night air swept into the bungalow, bringing with it an unexpected chill as their intruder fled into the darkness of the nearby fields.

For a moment, the bungalow was engulfed in silence once more, broken only by Donna's shaky, uneven breaths and Arthur's stunned murmurs. The fear still lingered, deep and suffocating, as the reality of what had just happened began to sink in.

"Donna are you-" Arthur started, his voice a trembling whisper, his eyes wide with concern.

"I'm fine," she interrupted, her voice barely audible, her body still trembling. "We're fine. But he...he was in our home, Arthur."

Donna untied Arthur and pulled him in close. His heart raced with a mixture of relief and horror, his mind struggling to process the events that had unfolded.

After a few minutes, Donna plucked up the courage to call the police, while Arthur surveyed the crime scene.

They both stared in disbelief as they noticed the torn back of the sofa, the leather sliced open, revealing the hollow where the man had hidden for hours.

The terrible truth settled over them like a dark, oppressive cloud. They hadn't just been visited by the man; he had been with them all day, lurking in the corners of their own home, waiting for the right moment to strike.

The realisation left them cold, a deep, unsettling chill settling into their bones. But as they held each other in the dim light of their living room, they knew one thing for certain: they were alive. And sometimes, in the face of darkness, that was enough.

Chapter 3

The following evening, the sun began to set over the small village of Cheddington, its low arc painting the quaint streets with a warm, golden hue. The last of the spring flowers bobbed gently in the breeze, their colours vivid against the backdrop of a serene evening. The village, accustomed to its cadenced quiet, seemed to have settled into its habitual lull. In a place where little ever happened, the pervasive sense of calm was both a comfort and a façade.

Beneath this veneer of peace, a sinister reality was taking shape.

The man, an outline in the twilight, moved silently through the creeping dusk. All day he had been observing the cottage on the corner of Tring Road, his keen eyes tracking its every movement. He was a meticulous predator; he knew the owner's routines and vulnerabilities. Tonight, Benjamin Young, the owner of the cottage - a solitary bachelor in his mid-thirties - was out for the evening, leaving behind an opportunity the man was determined to seize.

"Time to move," he muttered to himself, the words barely more than a hiss in the growing darkness. He approached the back of the cottage with the stealth of a practiced infiltrator. The window he had selected days before, now weathered and worn, yielded to his touch. The lock, old and feeble, surrendered with a soft click that barely disturbed the stillness of the night.

Inside, the man paused, letting his senses adjust to the dim interior. The cottage was enveloped in darkness, its silence profound and almost oppressive. It was perfect.

He slipped through the small kitchen, his eyes scanning every detail with a rapacious focus - the hum of the fridge, the faint clink of a loose floor tile beneath his boot. His gloved fingers brushed over the countertop, grazing a pile of unopened mail. He glanced into the living room; it was empty. He moved down the narrow hall, his steps silent and calculated. He passed a closed door and halted, sensing something behind it. With a slight twist of the handle, he pushed the door open, revealing a tidy bedroom. The room was modest, with a narrow bed neatly made, but it was the gleam of metal propped against the wall that drew his attention - a twelve-bore shotgun. His heart quickened with a dark thrill.

"Well, well," he whispered, a twisted smile creeping across his face. He picked up the gun, feeling its weight, the power it represented. Moments later, he found gun shells, and some cash stashed in a drawer, hidden beneath some clothes. "Won't be needing those anymore, mate," he uttered.

Pocketing the shells, he moved back into the living room, his eyes now fixed on the small television set. Next to it, a collection of pornographic tapes lay scattered. He leaned in, tracing the crude handwriting on one of the labels *'Debbie Does Dallas'.* An aggressive grin spread across his face as he selected it. He slipped the tape into the VCR player, turned on the television, and watched as the screen flickered to life, bathing the room in a ghostly glow.

The man grabbed some dining room chairs, some nearby blankets and made himself a den. He then had the audacity to make a cup of tea and a sandwich from the contents of the fridge.

Time passed slowly, each minute stretching into an eternity as the video played. The man lounged in his den, the shotgun resting on his lap, the £300 cash he had found stuffed into his coat pocket. His breathing was controlled, his eyes fixed on the screen, anticipation building with each passing moment. He checked his watch; the man would be home soon.

Just after ten o'clock, the soft glow of headlights swept across the front window. The man's pulse quickened, a rush of adrenaline sharpening his focus. He rose slowly from his den, the television's glow casting an eeriness across the room. He turned off the television, slipped on his balaclava and melted into the darkness, his senses acutely tuned to the sounds outside. He heard the soft crunch of gravel, the jingle of keys. The front door creaked open.

"Bloody hell, another late one," came Benjamin's weary voice, oblivious to the danger that lurked inside. The door closed behind him. The man tensed, listening to the approach of footsteps growing closer, each step a harbinger of what was to come.

As Benjamin stepped into the living room, the man struck. He lunged out of the darkness, smashing the cold barrel of the shotgun into Benjmain's ribs, drooping him to his knees.

"Don't move," the man hissed, his breath hot and rancid. Benjamin's eyes widened in shock, his mouth opening in a wordless gasp of terror.

"Wh-what do you want?" he gasped, his hands trembling uncontrollably.

"Take whatever you need, just-"

"Shut up," the man cut him off, his voice a sharp, harsh whisper. He picked Benjamin up and shoved him toward a dining room chair. "Sit. Now."

Benjamin, his breath coming in short, ragged bursts, complied, collapsing into the chair. The man kept the shotgun levelled at him, the weapon a constant, menacing presence. Reaching into his pocket, he pulled out a tie, one from Benjamin's collection. Benjamin's eyes widened even further in fear.

"Please...please don't do this," he begged, his voice breaking as he tried to offer anything to delay the inevitable. "I have money. I can-"

"Quiet," the man snapped, his patience wearing thin. He moved behind Benjamin, looping the tie around his wrists and pulling it tight. Benjamin whimpered as the tie dug into his skin, the fear evident in every shuddering breath.

The man tied the knots efficiently, securing Benjamin to the chair. His face twisted into a grotesque smile, a twisted semblance of friendliness. "There now. We're just going to have a little chat," he said, his tone almost playful. He walked back to the television, turned it on again, and resumed the tape. The screen flickered with grainy, explicit images that cast a sickly glow across the room. The man undid his jeans, slid down his underpants, and slowly caressed himself.

Benjamin's face drained of colour as he realised what was playing. "Oh God," he whispered, the gravity of his situation sinking in.

"Like to watch, do you?" The man asked, his voice a low growl. He crouched down in front of his captive, their faces inches apart. "Well, tonight's your lucky night. Because so do I."

Benjamin twisted in the chair, his eyes darting around the room, desperately searching for something, anything, to help him. "Please...whatever you're thinking...you don't have to do this."

The man's expression darkened behind his balaclava. Without warning, he slapped Benjamin hard across the face, the sound echoing sharply through the small room. "Did I say you could speak?"

Benjamin went silent, his lip trembling as a thin line of blood trickled from where his teeth had cut the inside of his cheek. The man straightened, pacing slowly around the room. The shotgun, now casually slung over his shoulder, seemed almost an extension of him.

"I've been watching you," the man murmured, more to himself than to his captive. "Watching this place. Studying it. Studying you. And I know your type. Thinks he's safe out here in his little village, locked up in his little cottage. But no one's ever really safe, are they?"

He stopped in front of the television again, his eyes fixed on the screen. "You just never know what might be lying in wait."

The minutes stretched on, each second a slow, torturous tick of the clock. Benjamin tried to control his breathing, to avoid looking at the screen, to steel himself against the horrors he could only imagine. But he could feel the man's gaze on him, a substantial, oppressive presence that seemed to suffocate the room.

Without warning, the man moved closer, his lips brushing against Benjamin's ear as he whispered, "Time to have some fun."

Benjamin closed his eyes, bracing himself for the worst. The man's cold, low chuckle was the last sound he heard before the terror that was to follow.

The man knelt before Benjamin; his gaze fixated on the young man's tear-streaked face. His left-hand moved with a disturbing intimacy, pressing against Benjamin's body, an act laced with menace. Benjamin's sobs grew louder, trembling under the weight of his fear, but the man remained unmoved, his tongue darting out to wet his lips as he savoured the fear in his captive's eyes.

As the man toyed with the fabric of Benjamin's clothing, methodically undoing his trousers, the atmosphere grew increasingly charged. Benjamin's silent sobs echoed through the room. The man was focused, driven by a dark intent that consumed the moment, indifferent to the terror etched in Benjamin's eyes.

The sexual assault that followed was ferocious and forceful. Benjamin stared up at the ceiling as the man attacked him with his hands and his mouth. With every intimate stroke, the man let out a groan of grotesque pleasure.

The assault continued all night, each touch from the man followed by the sound of Benjamin's pain and anguish. The man revelled in the power he wielded, drawing out the suffering with a perverse satisfaction. The cottage, once a symbol of quiet domesticity, was now a stage for an unspeakable horror.

By the time the man had ended Benjamin's torture, the first light of dawn was breaking. Benjamin lay bound to the chair, shaking uncontrollably, his breath ragged and uneven. His face was a mask of trauma.

The echoes of the man's footsteps faded into the early morning mist, as he made his escape through nearby woodlands. The darkness that had invaded the cottage would linger long after the man had disappeared, leaving behind a haunting presence that would overshadow the village's peaceful façade for years to come.

The man knelt in the dense woodland; his hands caked with dirt as he carefully buried the shotgun beneath a thick tangle of roots. The soft earth gave way easily, swallowing the weapon that had served him well on this occasion, but it was too dangerous to keep close. He patted the soil down, his eyes scanning the area to mark the spot in his memory - a fallen log, a cluster of ferns. Confident that the shotgun was hidden from prying eyes, he continued his getaway.

Three days later, when he returned to retrieve it, a cold panic gripped him. The familiar landmarks blurred together, and no matter how much he dug or searched, the shotgun seemed to have vanished, lost to the very earth he'd thought would keep it safe.

Chapter 4

The following day, the first light of dawn crept slowly over the newly dubbed 'Triangle of Terror' - Leighton Buzzard, Dunstable, and Tring - its pale fingers stretching across the quiet streets and casting long, skeletal shadows. The early morning calm, usually a comfort, was now steeped in a tangible sense of unease. Curtains remained tightly drawn, and inside their homes, residents spoke in hushed, anxious tones. The news of the sexual assault on Benjamin Young had travelled fast. And now, another assault had occurred.

Detective Inspector Peter Hargreaves, a twenty-two-year veteran of the Leighton Buzzard police force, stood at the back door of a small cottage; his gaze fixed on a set of footprints half-hidden in the dewy grass. They trailed off toward the back fence and the woods, disappearing into the dense undergrowth like a bad memory that refused to be forgotten. He glanced back at his partner, Detective Sergeant Linda Collins, who had served alongside him for nearly a decade, who was speaking with the homeowner - a frail, elderly man, named Mike Cox, whose hands shook uncontrollably as he recounted the horrors of the night before.

"He was in my bedroom," Mike murmured, his voice breaking with the weight of his fear. "Didn't hear him come in. Didn't even see him until he was right there… standing over my bed."

Collins leaned in closer, her expression a mix of professional concern and personal empathy. "What did he look like? Anything specific?"

"Just... just his eyes," Mike whispered, his voice trembling. "Cold. Like he was looking right through me. He was wearing a mask and didn't say a word, just... stood there. Then he attacked me and was gone, like he was never there."

Hargreaves scanned the scene with a growing sense of frustration. Four houses had been hit, all in different locations but close enough to establish a connection.

Collins walked over to Hargreaves; her face lined with tension. "This is the fourth incident now. Similar description: masked intruder, broke in, made a den inside their home, had a cup of tea, ate food, looked through photo albums, watched videos, laid out belts and ties, attacked them, in and out like a ghost."

"Bloody hell," Hargreaves muttered under his breath, more to himself than to Collins. He glanced at the old man's back door, which still swung loosely on its hinges, then back at the fading footprints. "He's got a taste for fear. That's what he wants."

Collins nodded, her eyes scanning the surrounding area. "What's our next move?"

Hargreaves, his jaw set with determination, turned to face her. "It's probably just a homeless person, hungry and needing some respite from the outside world. Albeit with a sick and twisted mind. Let's search the area for homeless people. See if anyone matches the description."

Collins flipped open her notebook, her expression resolute. "The press has nicknamed him 'The Fox'." A name that suited him well. Known for his cunning and stealth, The Fox was an expert in building dens and attacking at night.

"They can call him what they want," Hargreaves said, his eyes drifting toward the woods where the footprints had disappeared. "If they contact us, tell them whatever you like. Let them run wild with it. Maybe it'll draw him out."

As he spoke, Hargreaves felt the weight of the task ahead. Whoever this intruder was, he thrived on the chaos and fright he spread. The darkness that had settled over the area was not just a physical absence of light but a creeping, pervasive menace that left everyone on edge. And Hargreaves worried that the worst was yet to come.

Across the 'Triangle of Terror', phones rang incessantly as concerned voices filled the airwaves. The quiet towns and villages were abuzz with rumours and whispered fears. "Did you hear about the break-in last night? And the sexual assault the night before?". In her modest kitchen, Mary Whitfield clutched the receiver tightly, her voice wavering as she spoke with her neighbour. "Yes, I've heard," she said, her tone anxious. "No, I don't know where he'll strike next, but I'm keeping the lights on tonight. All of them. And I'm checking my sofas, twice if I must."

Mary's hands trembled as she hung up, her mind racing with dark thoughts. The idea of someone slipping into homes without a trace and hiding inside sofas, was enough to make her feel vulnerable in her own space. She moved through her house with heightened vigilance, her gaze darting to every window, every door. The Fox could come through any of them.

Two streets away from where Benjamin Young lived, Tom Bridger, a retired constable, sat on his porch, his weathered face etched with concern. His old instincts had kicked in, the hairs on the back of his neck prickling with a sense of impending danger. He gripped his baseball bat like a lifeline, his eyes scanning the street with a mixture of hope and dread. "He'll be back," Bridger muttered to himself, his voice a low rumble. "Foxes always come back."

The day passed in a blur of activity as Hargreaves and Collins continued their canvassing efforts. Each door they knocked on, each person they interviewed, offered no real clues as to who The Fox might be.

The sun climbed higher in the sky, casting an uneasy light over the towns and villages. The chatter of frightened residents and the buzz of rumours filled the atmosphere, creating a pressure that seemed almost physical.

As their shift ended, Hargreaves and Collins had worked their way through the neighbourhoods, their every step marked by the weight of their responsibility. When they eventually returned to their car, Collins opened the passenger door and slid into her seat, her face lined with worry. "We've got a difficult task ahead of us," she said, her voice tired but resolute.

Hargreaves nodded; his eyes fixed on the horizon. "We do. And we need to be ready for whatever comes next. This Fox character is out there, watching, waiting. We've got to find a way to outsmart him."

Hargreaves words carried a weighty sense of foreboding. The Fox had demonstrated an unsettling ability to remain one step ahead, exploiting the townspeople's fears to his advantage. Each new break-in was not just a crime but a statement - a declaration of his dominance over the frightened communities.

In the newsroom of the Leighton Buzzard Observer newspaper, local journalist Claire Milford was immersed in her work, surrounded by the clacking of typewriters and the haze of cigarette smoke. She was new to the area, having been transferred from London, and the pace of life in Leighton Buzzard was a stark contrast to the hustle and bustle she had been accustomed to. But now, a story with real bite had emerged - a story that had quickly become the focal point of her reporting.

Claire's pen tapped rhythmically against her notepad as she reviewed police reports and witness statements. The picture that was emerging was one of a crafty figure who moved with a chilling precision, leaving behind only fear and confusion. She scribbled a headline on her pad: "The Fox Strikes Again." The idea of this elusive raider capturing the imagination of the public was both thrilling and terrifying.

As she envisioned the morning edition flying off the stands, Claire's excitement was tempered by a growing sense of unease. She had covered crime in major cities before, witnessed firsthand the way fear could tear communities apart, turning neighbours against each other and projecting deep-seated doubts. In these quiet rural areas, the stakes seemed even higher. The fear of the unknown was like a wildfire, spreading quickly and consuming everything in its path.

The evening brought a chill to the atmosphere, despite the blazing heat of the summer. The towns and villages, once buzzing with anxious chatter, now seemed subdued, as if holding their breath in anticipation of what might come next. The Fox had become a spectre haunting their every thought, a dark presence that lurked just beyond the edge of their comfort.

As night fell, the fear that had gripped the locals only seemed to deepen. In their homes, residents checked and rechecked their locks, their hearts pounding with a mixture of dread and helplessness. The sky outside seemed darker, the noises of the night more ominous. Despite the hot, sticky night, they were too scared to chance leaving a window open.

Hargreaves and Collins had returned to their office to review the day's findings before heading home. The frustration was evident in their voices, a sharp edge to their words as they discussed their next steps.

"We're missing something," Collins said, her frustration evident. "There's got to be a pattern, a clue we're overlooking."

Hargreaves rubbed his temples, trying to focus through the haze of exhaustion. "We need to think like him. What drives someone to do this? What's his end game?". "Let's go home and get some rest. I'll see you bright and early in the morning."

The words lingered, dark questions that neither of them could easily answer. The Fox had proven himself to be a master of evasion, who slipped through their grasp with a chilling ease.

The Fox was not just a criminal; he was a harbinger of terror; he had turned the area into a maze of anxiety and suspicion. The hunt was on, and The Fox loomed large, a dark and enigmatic force that seemed to defy comprehension.

Chapter 5

The once tranquil region encompassing Hertfordshire, Bedfordshire, and Buckinghamshire had been transformed into a realm of fear and paranoia. Windows, once left open to catch a refreshing breeze, were now bolted shut. Doors with old, rusty locks were upgraded to modern, heavy-duty versions. The change in the area was not just a reaction to the series of break-ins and assaults; it was a response to something far more unsettling.

Conversations at local pubs, hairdressers and newsagents were dominated by talk of The Fox - an intruder who seemed to slip through the night like a wisp of smoke, unseen and unstoppable. What had started as a series of seemingly random burglaries had escalated into a dark, almost mythical terror. The usual inane chatter had been replaced by fearful whispers and speculation. The Fox was no longer just a name; he had become an entity of dread.

Detective Inspector Peter Hargreaves sat at his desk in the Leighton Buzzard police station, the dim light casting clouds over the map of Herts, Beds, and Bucks spread before him. The map was a collage of red pins marking the sites of The Fox's crimes. But despite the glaring visual representation of his spree, Hargreaves couldn't distinguish any discernible pattern. No rhythm to the madness, no clue as to what drove this criminal's decisions.

"What kind of person thinks to hide inside a sofa all day, let alone actually does it," Hargreaves muttered, his voice a low growl of frustration. The walls of his office seemed to close in, laden with the weight of the investigation's mounting pressure. His eyes, bloodshot from working late into the night, flicked over the scatter of pins, each one representing a piece of a puzzle that refused to fit together.

Across from him, Detective Sergeant Linda Collins leaned back in her chair, her eyes sharp but tired. She rubbed her temples, trying to stave off the headache that came with long hours and mounting stress. "Psychological terror," she said, her voice carrying the burdensome weight of her own exhaustion. "That's what this is. Maximum fear factor."

Hargreaves nodded; his gaze fixed on the map as if willing it to reveal some hidden truth. "Last night's attack proves it. He's getting bolder. He's enjoying it."

The night before, The Fox had gone further than before, sexually assaulting an elderly couple, Michael and Louise Stamp. They lived in an isolated farmhouse in Tring, an easy target with an easy escape route.

Hargreaves and Collins set off to visit the victims, which was becoming an all too familiar occurrence.

The Fox had chosen to break in during the day when the occupants were out, a calculated move that showed his confidence and control. He had removed all the light bulbs from the property, ensuring that when the couple returned, they would be plunged into an all-encompassing darkness. The act of removing the bulbs was more than just a crime; it was a deliberate act of psychological torment.

He had stolen money and, more significantly, he had found another shotgun and gun shells. A huge stroke of luck.

Michael Stamp and his wife had lived on the farm for over thirty years. Michael, a greying man with hands weathered by decades of hard work, sat at the kitchen table, his eyes hollow and haunted. The trauma was visible in every tremor of his hands, every haunted glance.

"He was just…there," Michael whispered, his voice cracking with the weight of his terror. "I was looking for candles when the power didn't work. I didn't see him until he was standing in the doorway."

The memory seemed to choke him, his words faltering as he continued. "He just...he just stared. And then he laughed." His voice broke entirely, and he looked down, unable to continue.

Collins exchanged a glance with Hargreaves, the look on Michael's face a stark reminder of the psychological damage inflicted by their elusive adversary. It was the look of someone who had stared into the eyes of a monster and found themselves forever changed.

"Can you describe him to us, any distinguishing features?" asked Collins.

"It was hard to tell due to the darkness, but the moonlight helped a bit. I'd say he was erm, he was around five feet nine or ten inches tall, and he had a slim frame. He was wearing a mask, but I saw curly hair, and his accent-" replied Michael.

"Yes, go on-" asked Collins.

"It was northern. Soft but sounded Geordie," responded Louise.

"And did he smell, erm, like he hadn't showered in days?" Collins queried.

"Oh no, he smelled fresh." Michael retorted.

"Well then. I think we can rule out this perpetrator sleeping rough on the streets. Thank you for your help, it has been very useful." Hargreaves said, his voice firm but tinged with an undercurrent of frustration. "We will find him; I promise you that."

But as they left the farmhouse, Collins could see the doubt etched on Hargreaves's face. The weight of the case was beginning to show, and the fear that had taken root in the community seemed to be seeping into the detectives themselves.

"So, he's not homeless," Collins said, breaking the silence that had settled between them. "He's hidden in amongst us."

Hargreaves's face hardened, a mixture of determination and grim resignation. "Yeah," he replied. "And he's enjoying every bloody minute of it."

Back in Leighton Buzzard, Claire Milford, the journalist who had first dubbed the intruder 'The Fox', was feeling the pressure of the growing panic. The headlines were selling papers and fuelling the fear, but the responsibility of covering such a chilling story was taking its toll. Claire sat in her cramped office, surrounded by the clutter of police reports and half-empty coffee cups, her fingers tapping nervously on her desk as she reviewed the latest updates.

She picked up the phone and dialled Tom Bridger, the retired constable who had been keeping a close eye on the developments. "Tom, it's Claire Milford. I wanted to ask about the other night. Did you see or hear anything?"

Bridger's voice came through the line, gravelly and tense. "You mean apart from the entire town locking themselves in their houses despite the boiling hot summer? No, I didn't see or hear anything. But I heard about that poor couple in Tring. We're dealing with something different here, Claire. This isn't just some common thief."

Claire's brow furrowed, her concern deepening. "I know. It's like he wants to be seen now. He's pushing people to their limits." Bridger sighed heavily. "Fear makes people do strange things. Makes them see things that aren't there. Or miss things that are." There was a pause, a moment of grim realisation. "We need to be careful. He's playing a game, and he's winning."

The words weighed heavily on them; a chilling reminder of the stakes involved. The Fox was not just a criminal; he was a master manipulator, an umbra that danced just out of reach, feeding off the fear and uncertainty he created.

After committing three more burglaries, The Fox struck again, this time breaking into another house in Tring. The home was empty which The Fox knew having studied it for many days. The occupants informed the police the intruder had carefully removed clothing from drawers and photographs from albums The crimes were linked to The Fox, as the meticulousness spoke volumes about his intent to cause psychological damage, not just material loss.

The following night, in Wingrave, the moon hung low in the sky, a dull, misty orb barely piercing the darkness that enveloped the village. A welcome faint drizzle began to fall from the sky, coating the rooftops and streets in a slick, cold sheen. Somewhere on the outskirts, in a neighbourhood where the streetlights flickered weakly against the encroaching night, a soul destroyer crept through the alleyways. He moved with sleek elegance, disappearing smoothly into the dim surroundings.

The Fox, no one knew his real name - only the reputation that preceded him, was a silent hunter with a reputation for brutal efficiency. Tonight, he was out hunting again.

The target was a two-story house, dark and still except for a single light flickering in an upstairs window. The Fox crouched beneath the cover of an overgrown hedge, his breath steady and measured. His eyes, cold and calculating, he scanned the perimeter. He saw the slightest tremble of a curtain in an upstairs room. Someone was home.

He moved swiftly, silent as death itself. With a gloved hand, he tested the window on the side of the house. With a gentle push, it gave way. Sliding it open, he slipped inside, crouching low to let his eyes adjust to the dim interior. The house smelled of mildew and something sour - unwashed clothes, maybe. He could hear the faint ticking of a clock coming from the living room.

The Fox didn't need a weapon; but he carried his stolen shotgun for maximum fear effect. His senses were sharp, ears attuned to the smallest sounds. He crept forward, listening.

Low whispers came from upstairs. A man and a woman's voice - nervous, on edge. The Fox felt a faint smile tug at his lips. He took the stairs slowly, avoiding the spots where the wood might rasp. Each step was calculated, his weight carefully distributed to remain silent. At the top of the stairs, he paused, listening again. The voices had fallen silent.

He was close now. He could hear their breaths, smell the fear sweating off their skin. The Fox took a moment, his gloved hand slowly reaching for the doorknob. In one fluid motion, he twisted and kicked the door open with a force that sent it crashing against the wall.

Chaos erupted. The man who had been whispering, Markus Longman, a thin, wiry figure, staggered backward, eyes wide with terror. He regained his composure and charged forward, bellowing like an enraged animal. The Fox reacted quickly - too quickly for Markus. He sidestepped Markus, his movement almost lazy, letting Markus crash into the wall. Before he could recover, The Fox struck - a swift elbow to the back of the skull. Markus let out a grunt and staggered, but he wasn't down. He turned, swinging a wild haymaker. The Fox ducked under it, came up, and delivered a vicious uppercut to his jaw. There was a sickening crack, and Markus's eyes rolled back as he slumped to the floor.

Markus sat frozen, back against the wall. His eyes darted around, looking for something, anything to use as a weapon. His hand found a lamp on a nearby table. He grabbed it and swung it in desperation. The Fox caught his wrist mid-swing, twisted it sharply, and the lamp fell to the floor with a dull thud.

A single, fluid movement brought The Fox's knee into Markus's face. He doubled over, gasping for air, and then a sharp, snapping kick to the side of his head flattened him to the floor.

Silence filled the room, broken only by the heavy breathing of the two men, and the sobbing of Sara, Markus's wife. The Fox stood over them, his face unreadable. He knelt, grabbing Markus by the collar and pulling him close. His voice, when he spoke, was low and calm - a voice devoid of mercy.

"Tell the world," he said. "You just got outboxed and outfoxed."

He released Markus, letting him drop back to the floor, semi-conscious. The Fox took one last glance at the wreckage, then quietly slipped away, vanishing as silently as he had appeared.

Chapter 6

The atmosphere was dense with the smell of warm rain-soaked earth, and the village of Heath and Reach sat in an unsettling stillness, the kind that settles just before something breaks. The Fox had returned, slipping through the night like a bat on the prowl. This time, his target was a quaint little house, the kind with flowerpots on the windowsills and a white picket fence. A place of warmth and safety. A place he would turn into his lair.

The Fox moved with a cold, calculated confidence, slipping past locks and bolts as if they were mere inconveniences. The occupants of the house were out for the evening, unaware of the creeping terror that had chosen them. As he crept through the back door, he removed each light bulb, leaving the home shrouded in an impenetrable darkness, a void where light had no purchase. He rearranged the furniture with the accuracy of a chess player setting the board. Every chair, every table was moved, covered with blankets and sheets, twisted into a camouflaged nest in the centre of the living room.

The Fox's movements were fluid, purposeful. He worked in silence, as if darkness itself was his ally. In the main bedroom, he opened drawers with a calm hand, selecting dressing gown cords like a connoisseur, tucking them into his coat with a clinical grace. He reached for the telephone and cut the wires with a swift motion - one less connection to the outside world. His fingertips brushed against the buttons of the answering machine, hovering over them for a moment as if contemplating something, before he withdrew.

He moved with a cat-like agility, his senses heightened, his pulse steady. The house was his now, a temporary kingdom he had claimed for himself. He ransacked the fridge with a sense of entitlement, taking what he wanted - slices of ham, a half-eaten apple, and a carton of milk. The sound of the kettle boiling broke the silence, its whistle cutting through the darkness like a scream. He made himself a cup of tea, stirred it slowly, and savoured it. The audacity of it all - the invasion, the reordering of a life that wasn't his - was not lost on him. It was an act of psychological warfare, a game of dominance and terror.

Hours passed, and with them, a stillness that could make the skin crawl. The Fox's lair, cloaked in darkness, became a living thing - a place where the walls had eyes, and every creak of the floorboards whispered his presence. He waited in his constructed den, the silence so thick it felt as if the walls themselves were holding their breath. His heartbeat was the only rhythm in this symphony of dread. Time stretched, distorted, a trick played by the darkness.

At one o'clock in the morning, the crunch of gravel under tyres signalled the return of the homeowners. The Fox tensed, his muscles coiling like a spring. Keys rattled in the front door, and the lock clicked open. His breathing slowed, his pulse quickened, and his eyes narrowed into slits, peering through the gaps in his makeshift hideout. The door screeched open, and the couple, Antony and Antoinette Bednarek stepped inside, they were oblivious, tired, and unsuspecting.

But something must have changed in the air - a scent, a sound - Antony paused. He turned his head as if sensing the shift in the atmosphere, a subtle but undeniable wrongness. The Fox's heart drummed faster; he could feel it in his throat. A single misstep, a clang of the floor beneath him, broke the spell. The couple froze. Antony's eyes widened in horror, and in that instant, The Fox bolted from his hiding place, a swift blur of motion.

"Oi, come back here you bastard," shouted Antony.

For once The Fox had lost his cool. Panic surged through his veins as he burst through the back door. The heat of the night hit him like a hot flannel. He sprinted through the garden, vaulting over the hedges, and melted into the darkness beyond. Behind him, the shrieks of terror rose into the night like a wailing siren. He didn't look back; he didn't need to.

Antony and Antoinette shaking from the experience, called the police.

"He's been here," shouted Antony. "The Fox, he's been in my house."

The police arrived within minutes, flooding the quiet street with flashing lights and the murmur of radios. In the house, the police surveyed the crime scene. They found his lair - a still-warm cup of tea sat ominously inside his den, a chilling testament to his unsettling presence. The Fox, in his haste to leave, had also left behind £130 in stolen cash, an anorak, and a packet of peanuts, spilled on the floor like a breadcrumb trail of madness.

For Antony and Antoinette, it was as if a spirit had invaded their sanctuary, a phantasm that had sipped tea where they dined, watched them from the darkness where they once felt safe.

But The Fox wasn't done. The hunger for fear, for chaos, pulled him onward. The anger grew inside him, he rarely lost his cool. He needed to strike back instantly; prove to himself he was still in control.

He moved across the fields on foot, the darkness swallowing him whole. He emerged on the Planets estate in Leighton Buzzard. Here, another house, another life, would be drawn into his web of terror.

Ashton and Zarah Hartwig slept soundly, wrapped in the comfort of ignorance. They had locked their doors and windows, never imagining that a nightmare would manifest in their home. But nightmares have a way of seeping through cracks, of slipping under doors and through windows. The Fox crept through the blackness, his breath controlled, his footsteps silent. He prized open the back door lock with ease and snuck into the house. Inside their bedroom, the dim glow of a night-light cast a faint halo around their sleeping. The Fox stood in the doorway, his presence filling the room with a chilling malevolence. He wore a different mask than usual - a grotesque thing fashioned from a trouser leg with jagged cut-out eye holes. It was both absurd and terrifying, like something born from a fevered mind.

Ashton stirred first, his eyes opening slowly, adjusting to the darkness. At first, he thought he was dreaming, but the dream solidified into reality as his gaze fixed on the figure standing in the doorway. His breath caught in his throat, and he let out a guttural shout, instinct taking over.

The Fox reacted instantly, raising his shotgun. Whether by intent or accident, a deafening blast shattered the silence, and a spray of wood splinters flew across the room as the bullet struck the doorframe. Ashton screamed in pain, clutching his hand, blood dripping onto the floor. An index finger had been blown off. But adrenaline is a powerful thing. Even with the injury, he lunged from his bed, charging at The Fox with a primal roar.

The Fox turned and fled. He sprinted down the stairs, out the back door, over the back fence and through the night, his breath coming in ragged bursts, his feet pounding the ground like the rapid-fire beats of a drum. He was a phantom, a creature of the night, leaving behind only fear in his wake.

Ashton didn't give chase, his eyes were wide with panic, his heart racing as blood poured from his mangled hand. The pain was excruciating, but it was the shock that truly began to sink in, numbing his thoughts. Zarah, frantic and barely able to think straight, rushed into the bathroom, yanking open the cupboard and grabbing every towel she could find. Her mind raced as she ran back to Ashton's side. He was now sitting on the edge of their bed, his face pale, breathing uneven, as if his body was still trying to catch up to what had happened.

She knelt beside him, wrapping his hand as tightly as she could, though her own fingers trembled violently. Blood seeped through the fabric, staining it almost instantly. Tears welled in her eyes, but she forced herself to stay focused. She couldn't lose control now.

"My finger... it's by the door," Ashton muttered, his voice hoarse from the adrenaline surging through him. "Go to the freezer, get some ice. Hurry." He winced, struggling to stay coherent through the waves of pain. "And grab a freezer bag too - we'll need to preserve it."

Zarah, her face stricken with fear, nodded and hurried toward the stairs. Her mind spun in a thousand directions - she couldn't believe what was happening. Their home, once a safe haven, had been violated in the worst possible way.

With a deep breath, Ashton forced himself to focus. His good hand fumbled as he reached over to the telephone. His fingers trembled as he dialled nine-nine-nine.

"Hello," he rasped into the receiver. "Yes, I need the police and an ambulance. I've been shot. By The Fox." The words sounded surreal even to him. He had read about The Fox, heard the stories, but never imagined he would be a victim in his own home.

Within minutes, the once-quiet street was alight with flashing blue lights. Police cars and an ambulance arrived at the scene, their flashing lights illuminating the front of the house with an unsettling shine. The warm summer air was punctuated by the sound of sirens and urgent footsteps.

Detective Inspector Peter Hargreaves arrived swiftly; his eyes sharp as he surveyed the scene. He knew the sight too well - The Fox was becoming bolder, more violent. Inside the house, he found Zarah pale and shaking, and Ashton gripping his bandaged hand as paramedics worked around him. Blood still pooled on the floor near the door, a chilling reminder of what had transpired just minutes before.

Ashton recounted the horrifying moment in broken sentences, struggling to piece together the terror of it all. Zarah sat by his side, her face drawn and hollow. They could barely believe it themselves - The Fox had been inside their home. He had aimed, fired, and left them scarred, both physically and emotionally. The Fox had stolen more than a finger that night - he had taken their sense of security, their peace of mind. And as Ashton stared out the window of the ambulance, he knew that this wound, like the one on his hand, would take far longer to heal than anyone could imagine.

Ashton and Zarah's lives would never be the same. From that night forward, they lived in constant fear, haunted by the thought that The Fox could return. The lingering threat cast a shadow over their once peaceful lives. Ashton, a landscape gardener, was now out of work, not only because of the physical damage to his hand but because of the psychological trauma he faced daily. Every sound made them jump. Every night they wondered if he was out there, watching, waiting.

The morning after, Hargreaves sat in his office reading a report of the previous night's events, his jaw clenched, eyes burning with frustration. The Fox was out of control and becoming more violent with each attack.

The atmosphere in Herts, Beds and Bucks had turned electric. The Fox was no longer a mere criminal; he had become something else - an entity, a force of nature. Stories of his exploits spread like wildfire, each tale more terrifying than the last. He was the bogeyman, lurking in the nearby fields, hiding in every street corner.

The hunt for The Fox had transformed into something primal. It was no longer about justice or law - it was a battle of wills, a struggle to regain control over a fear that had gripped the 'Triangle of Terror' by the throat. Hargreaves knew the stakes were escalating with every passing day. This wasn't just a hunt for a man - it was a hunt for a legend, a spectre who thrived in the darkness, who revelled in the terror he sowed.

The weight of it all settled on Hargreaves' shoulders. He stared out into the hot summer sky, knowing that somewhere out there, The Fox was walking free. His presence was a dark stain on the fabric of their lives, a constant, gnawing dread that refused to fade.

The hunt was far from over, and with no new leads, a chilling realisation gripped Hargreaves. They were chasing a man who had become a myth. The Fox was out there, always one step ahead, a dark and enigmatic presence that defied capture. And so, the game continued, a game drenched in darkness, fear, and the unending echo of a shotgun blast in the night.

Chapter 7

The Fox had terrorised communities for weeks now, slipping in and out of homes leaving a trail of destruction in his wake. Each crime, a violation of both physical space and personal security, adding another layer of horror to the ever-growing mystery. His methods were unpredictable yet precise. He attacked homes that seemed vulnerable - ones where the locks were weak, the windows left open, or the inhabitants complacent.

But now, the police were fighting back, determined to put an end to his spree. Flyers appeared in neighbourhoods across the region, posted on telephone poles, in shop windows, and through letterboxes. The bold black letters screamed the urgent warning: **Beware of The Fox.** Beneath that headline, there were instructions - practical advice aimed at protecting the public.

"Do not leave windows or doors unlocked, even during the heat of the summer. If you notice anything suspicious - no matter how small - report it to the police immediately."

The message struck at the heart of the fear that had already gripped the three counties. People double-checked their doors at night, hesitated before leaving a window ajar, and scrutinised every unusual movement in the street. The sense of safety had been shattered, and the police wanted to make sure no one underestimated the threat The Fox posed.

Yet behind the public warnings, a more critical effort was underway. Deep in the heart of the police forensic labs, the case against The Fox was being built piece by painstaking piece, evidence that could one day tie this elusive criminal to his growing list of crimes. Detective Inspector Peter Hargreaves led his team with a grim determination. He knew they had to be thorough, patient, and methodical, but time was not on their side. The Fox was still out there, and every day that passed without an arrest was another opportunity for him to strike again.

A small breakthrough had come when forensic officers working at several of the crime scenes began to notice patterns - subtle ones, but patterns, nonetheless. At first, the scenes had appeared to be isolated incidents, unrelated in any obvious way. There were no clear fingerprints, no easily recognisable patterns of entry or exit. The Fox was careful, methodical. He left very little behind, and that was what made him so dangerous.

But crime scene investigators were trained to look beyond the obvious, to find the details that most would overlook. And it was in these details that they began to piece together the puzzle. One of the first clues came in the form of the forced locks. While The Fox's entry points varied - sometimes a back door, sometimes a window, other times through side entrances - the way he broke in had a consistency to it.

Using a fast-setting plastic, a specially designed material that could capture minute details quickly, forensic teams had taken impressions of the locks that had been forced open. They compared these impressions from multiple crime scenes and discovered a striking similarity. The tool used to pry open the locks left marks that matched across multiple properties.

After careful analysis, they deduced that an 8mm-wide flat screwdriver had been used. This wasn't just any screwdriver. The markings on the tool were unusual, indicating either that the blade had been modified or that it was an older, perhaps custom-made, piece of equipment. This was their first concrete link - the same tool, used again and again, leaving its unmistakable signature behind.

But that wasn't all. As they scoured the crime scenes, meticulously gathering any trace of physical evidence, they unearthed something even more useful.

Human beings shed fibres just as animals shed fur, but these fibres were so small that they can only be seen under a microscope. At one of the homes where The Fox had attacked, the forensic team had collected fibres from a bedroom, a painstaking process that required patience and expertise. When these fibres were analysed, they made a remarkable discovery: white rabbit hairs had been found on the knots tied around the victim's hands.

It was a clue that seemed almost bizarre at first. Why would there be rabbit hairs at the scene? As they delved deeper into the analysis, two possibilities emerged. Either The Fox had handled a white rabbit at some point, or he had worn gloves lined with angora wool - an expensive, rare material made from rabbit fur.

This single piece of evidence, seemingly so minor, opened up new avenues of investigation. The presence of the rabbit hair tied The Fox directly to the crimes. No matter how careful he had been, he hadn't anticipated the forensic teams discovering such a minute detail.

But they weren't done yet.

In addition to the rabbit hair, forensic officers also collected other fibres - tiny, almost invisible to the naked eye - scattered throughout the scenes. The fibres were found in odd places: on carpets, under furniture, and even embedded in the victims' clothing. It was the kind of detail that could easily be dismissed if not for the dedication of the team working the case. They analysed these fibres and found something striking.

Fibres from one of the crime scenes matched fibres from another scene, despite the two locations being miles apart and the victims having no known connection to each other. The fibres appeared to come from a woollen jumper, likely worn by The Fox. Further tests were conducted, examining the chemical composition of the fibres and the dye mixtures used in their production. The results were conclusive - the fibres were identical. The Fox had worn the same clothing during both attacks.

This was a significant find. While fibres were far from the kind of smoking gun that could directly lead to an arrest, they were another brick in the growing wall of evidence linking these crimes together. The Fox, who had worked so hard to cover his tracks, was starting to leave behind a trail that was becoming harder and harder to erase.

By now, the police had gathered enough evidence to definitively link multiple crimes to the same perpetrator. The screwdriver marks, the rabbit hairs, and the fibres from the jumper all pointed to one person - The Fox. There was no longer any doubt. These were not isolated incidents. They were all the work of the same man, moving stealthily from one home to another, leaving behind traces of his presence that, piece by piece, were building a case against him.

The scientific proof was undeniable. Each time The Fox broke into a house, he inadvertently left behind clues, no matter how meticulous he thought he had been. The crime scenes were now telling a story, and it was one the police were eager to read.

"We're closing in," Hargreaves said quietly to Collins one evening, as he reviewed the latest reports.

"Yes sir. He is starting to slip up. It won't be long before he makes a big mistake, and we get him," replied a chirpy Collins.

The team was energised by the progress. They had the evidence, and now they just needed the man. With the forensic evidence tying the crimes together, they had moved past the point of speculation. The Fox had a distinct modus operandi, one that was revealed in the fibres from his clothing, the hairs from his gloves, and the marks left by his screwdriver. He was methodical, yes, but human. And like all humans, he was leaving behind traces of his presence.

With the forensic evidence mounting, the hunt for The Fox grew more intense. The police now had a description - based on the fibres, they knew he likely wore a wool jumper, possibly grey or blue. The rabbit hair suggested he may have worn angora-lined gloves at some point. And the specific tool he used to break into homes, the 8mm flat screwdriver with unusual markings, provided another clue to his habits.

But despite these breakthroughs, The Fox was still at large. Hargreaves and his team knew that it was only a matter of time before he struck again, and the pressure was mounting. Public anxiety was growing, especially with the police's warnings plastered across towns and villages. Everyone was on edge, and every clank in the night or rustle outside a window made people jump.

Hargreaves ordered increased patrols in the areas where The Fox had been known to strike. Officers were briefed on the new evidence, and a dedicated unit was tasked with scouring pawnshops, hardware stores, and markets, looking for any sign of someone selling or buying a distinctive screwdriver or angora-lined gloves.

The team worked tirelessly; their focus sharpened by the weight of the evidence they had collected. They knew The Fox couldn't hide forever. He had grown too comfortable, too reckless. Each crime left behind another piece of the puzzle, and soon, Hargreaves was sure, they would have enough to identify him.

Chapter 8

Five years earlier, in the winter of 1979, fear had gripped the north of England. For five years, the elusive killer known as the Yorkshire Ripper had terrorised women across the region, leaving a trail of brutality and unanswered questions. The police, stretched thin by the mounting number of attacks and public pressure, were struggling to make headway. Thirteen women had been murdered, their bodies found in public spaces, all victims of horrific violence. Investigations had been plagued by missteps, false leads, and a growing mistrust from the public. The police force needed fresh leadership, someone with a reputation for methodical work and a history of successful cases. That person was Detective Chief Superintendent Mark Talbot.

Talbot, already a highly respected officer within British law enforcement circles, had earned his stripes in solving several high-profile cases, most notably bringing down notorious criminals with cunning, patience, and precision. When the Yorkshire Ripper investigation was handed to him, he took it as both a challenge and a moral duty. To him, this was not just about catching a killer but about restoring public faith in the police and protecting vulnerable women paralysed by fear.

When Talbot first assumed control of the investigation in early 1980, he was stepping into a quagmire. The case files were immense - thousands of witness statements, mountains of forensic reports, and more than two hundred thousand pieces of evidence had already been gathered. However, despite the wealth of information, the police were no closer to identifying the killer. The previous task force, overwhelmed and under pressure, had become bogged down by dead-end leads and miscommunication between various departments.

One of Talbot's first actions was to review the entire case from the beginning. He realised that the investigation had been too reactive, with the police chasing tips and suspects without a cohesive strategy. Moreover, the investigative team had been plagued by internal issues: competing egos, jurisdictional disputes, and an overwhelming sense of frustration. Talbot knew he had to centralise the investigation and bring a fresh perspective.

He set about reorganising the investigative team, bringing in officers he trusted and restructuring how information was handled. A new incident room was created where all incoming leads would be managed more efficiently. He appointed senior officers to review and re-interview key witnesses and reanalyse evidence. His goal was to establish a clear timeline of events, focusing on the most solid clues and discarding the red herrings that had derailed the investigation.

In Talbot's mind, the first major problem was the noise surrounding the case. There had been too much information, much of it irrelevant. He told his team: "We need to go back to basics. Look at the facts. The killer is out there, and the truth is hidden in these files. We just have to find it."

Unlike previous investigators who had been swayed by the emotional weight of the case, Talbot was known for his logical, methodical approach. He believed that the key to capturing the Yorkshire Ripper lay in identifying patterns in the killer's behaviour, locations, and victimology. He also understood that they had to out-think the Yorkshire Ripper, who had shown a disturbing ability to evade capture, despite being seen by witnesses' multiple times.

One of the early mistakes made by the initial investigative team was their reliance on a hoax recording and letters purportedly sent by the Yorkshire Ripper. The man in the recording, nicknamed "Wearside Jack" due to his Sunderland accent, had misled investigators, directing them away from the real killer. Talbot immediately expressed scepticism about the authenticity of the recording. He pushed for the team to focus on physical evidence and witness testimonies rather than speculative leads from unverified sources.

Talbot's sharp eye for detail led to a breakthrough when he revisited the forensic evidence from the various crime scenes. Though the Yorkshire Ripper's attacks had varied somewhat in location and time, Talbot noticed that the areas were linked by proximity to transportation hubs - particularly lorry routes and service stations. This suggested that the killer might be a travelling worker, someone who could move easily between towns and cities without drawing too much attention.

Furthermore, Talbot brought in criminal psychologists to build a more refined profile of the killer. The Yorkshire Ripper's crimes were marked by extreme violence toward his victims, most of whom were vulnerable women - either sex workers or women alone in the streets late at night. This indicated a deep-seated misogyny and a desire for power and control. The psychologists worked with Talbot to analyse the escalation in violence, theorising that the killer might be an unassuming man in public but deeply troubled in his private life, someone capable of hiding in plain sight.

As the months wore on, Talbot's commitment to the case became a personal mission. The pressure from the public and the media was immense. The public's frustration with the lack of progress was palpable, and every day the killer remained at large was a blow to the morale of the Yorkshire police. Newspapers ran scathing editorials criticising the police, while politicians made public statements calling for accountability. As the face of the investigation, Talbot bore the brunt of this pressure, but he remained resolute, never allowing the media frenzy to distract him from the task at hand.

Behind the scenes, Talbot's health and personal life began to suffer. His wife, aware of the weight her husband carried, worried about the toll it was taking on him. Friends noticed how gaunt and exhausted he looked. Talbot's sleep became more fitful as the weeks dragged on without any significant breakthroughs. However, he remained a constant presence at the investigation headquarters, rarely taking time off. The Yorkshire Ripper's victims haunted him. He often revisited the crime scene photographs, mentally placing himself in the moments leading up to the murders, trying to think as the killer might.

By December 1980, Talbot's team had narrowed their suspect list to a few hundred individuals. Among them was Peter Sutcliffe, a lorry driver from Bradford, who had been interviewed several times by the police but had slipped through the net due to a series of unfortunate administrative errors and miscommunications.

Sutcliffe's arrest came almost by accident. On the night of January second, 1981, Sutcliffe was spotted by two police officers in Sheffield acting suspiciously in a parked car with a sex worker. When questioned, he gave a false name, and the officers noted discrepancies in his story. It was only after they checked his license plate, which was found to be fake, that they decided to take him into custody. During the routine search, they discovered tools in his car that raised alarm bells: a hammer and a knife, eerily like the instruments used in the Yorkshire Ripper murders.

Talbot was immediately notified of the arrest. Although Sutcliffe initially denied any involvement in the killings, further searches of his property and vehicle uncovered additional damning evidence, including a second set of clothing hidden in a nearby yard. Under intense interrogation, Sutcliffe finally cracked, confessing to the murders with chilling detachment.

Sutcliffe's confession detailed his methodical approach to the killings, how he would choose his victims, and the psychological compulsion that drove him to kill. He admitted to hearing voices commanding him to murder women, and his confessions matched with the forensic evidence and witness statements the police had gathered over the years.

The arrest of Peter Sutcliffe was a moment of both triumph and sombre reflection for Talbot and his team. While they had finally captured the man responsible for the horrific crimes, it was not without a sense of regret that Sutcliffe had been able to evade justice for so long. Thirteen women had died, and several more had been attacked, their lives forever altered.

In the days following Sutcliffe's arrest, Talbot worked closely with the Crown Prosecution Service to ensure that the evidence was airtight. Sutcliffe was charged with multiple counts of murder and attempted murder, and the trial that followed was one of the most high-profile in British legal history. He was found guilty and sentenced to life imprisonment without the possibility of parole.

For Talbot, the end of the case brought little personal satisfaction. The investigation had consumed him for over a year, and while justice had been served, the cost had been hefty. After the trial, he gave a series of interviews to the press, expressing his admiration for the resilience of the victims' families and acknowledging the failings of the investigation in its earlier stages. "We got him in the end," he said in one interview, "but it should have been sooner."

Talbot's leadership during the Yorkshire Ripper investigation cemented his legacy as one of Britain's most skilled and dedicated detectives. His methodical approach, his insistence on revisiting evidence, and his reliance on psychological profiling were pivotal in finally capturing Peter Sutcliffe. Talbot's techniques were later studied by law enforcement agencies around the world and became standard practice in complex, multi-victim investigations.

The Yorkshire Ripper case also sparked significant changes within British policing. The failings of the initial investigation led to reforms in how large-scale investigations were managed, particularly in the handling of forensic evidence and witness statements. More resources were allocated to tracking serial offenders, and inter-agency communication was improved to prevent future breakdowns in the sharing of critical information.

In the years following Sutcliffe's capture, Talbot would often reflect on the case in private. He remained haunted by the knowledge that, had things been done differently in the early days of the investigation, lives could have been saved. He was proud of his work, but the weight of those lost lives stayed with him.

Chapter 9

The Fox's crimes had escalated to an unprecedented level, forcing law enforcement to expand their efforts to catch him. As the crimes were committed in three different police force areas, and due to their serious nature, the investigation took on the status of a national enquiry under the new command of Detective Chief Superintendent Mark Talbot. Operations were moved to Dunstable police station.

Due to the similarities of the cases, Talbot's expertise was needed to help capture The Fox. He had learned from the Yorkshire Ripper case the importance of sharing information and recording it properly.

The search team swelled to over two hundred officers, all working tirelessly to track down the elusive criminal. The police were receiving over three hundred calls a day from the public, all leads needed to be followed up. The growing scope of the investigation demanded a larger operations room to accommodate the influx of personnel and resources needed to bring The Fox to justice.

The operations room at Dunstable police station was awash in a haze of stale coffee and underlying stress. The usual murmur of low conversation was absent, replaced by the sporadic squeak of leather chairs and the occasional clatter of a pen dropping on the floor. The room was charged with an unmistakable sense of dread. This wasn't just another case - it was an insidious infection that had seeped into the very bones of the town, tightening its grip with every new attack.

Detective Chief Superintendent Mark Talbot from West Yorkshire entered the room, his presence immediately commanding attention. He carried a stack of folders under one arm, and as he stepped in, the room fell silent. Talbot's reputation preceded him - he was the man who had brought down the notorious Yorkshire Ripper, Peter Sutcliffe. Yet even he knew that this case, with its elusiveness and psychological torment, was a different beast entirely. His sharp eyes took in the faces around him, reading the fear, frustration, and simmering anger that marked his audience.

"Alright, listen up," Talbot began, his voice steady and authoritative. The weight of his words seemed to press down on the room, accentuating the gravity of the situation. "I've been brought in to lead Operation Peanut. This task force's sole mission is to catch The Fox. I know you've all been working this case tirelessly for weeks, and you have uncovered some useful forensic evidence, but it's clear that what we've been doing isn't working. We need to change tactics."

Detective Sergeant Linda Collins, who had been deeply involved in the case from the outset, spoke up. "We've got no fingerprints, no clear descriptions. He's like a ghost - he comes and goes without leaving a trace."

Talbot nodded in acknowledgment. "That's because he's smart. Methodical. He's not just breaking into homes; he's breaking into their minds. He wants people to be afraid, and he's damn good at it."

He set down the folders on the central table, spreading out a series of crime scene photos that painted a chilling narrative. Each image depicted the same unsettling scenario: open doors and windows, broken locks, rooms upended, and disturbing makeshift dens created within the victims' homes. Yet, in every photo, there was no clear image of the intruder. It was as if The Fox had deliberately blurred the lines between reality and nightmare.

"This guy knows what he's doing," Talbot said, his voice carrying the weight of grim recognition. "No pattern to his targets. No obvious motive beyond scaring the hell out of people. We're dealing with someone who understands fear, who thrives on it."

Detective Sergeant Jake Miller, known for his grizzled demeanour and sharp temper, leaned back in his chair, his scepticism evident. "So, what's the plan, boss? Are we just supposed to sit around and wait for him to strike again?"

Talbot fixed Jake with a steely gaze, his patience wearing thin. "No, Jake. We're going to get inside his head. We need to think like him. This isn't a normal investigation. We're hunting a sociopath."

The plan began to take shape as Talbot outlined the new strategy. "We are stationing officers in barns and houses around the area known as the 'Triangle of Terror' to attempt to catch the attacker. I want a psychological profile - something to help us build a picture of The Fox's character traits."

He continued with specifics. "What we know so far: The Fox is between twenty and thirty years old. He's always masked, so the exact details of his appearance are elusive. He's approximately five foot eight to ten inches tall, with a slim, athletic build, weighing between ten and eleven stones. He has long fingers and appears to be left-handed. Witnesses have suggested a northern accent, possibly 'Geordie.'"

Detective Sergeant Linda Collins nodded, her face set with determination. "We need to profile him and figure out what makes him tick."

Talbot's eyes met hers with a shared sense of urgency. "Exactly. I want every detail, no matter how small. We're going to piece together who this guy is and how he thinks. I want a list of every burglary, every break-in, every sexual assault, every reported prowler in the region for the last ten years. He didn't just appear out of nowhere."

The room erupted into a flurry of activity. Officers began rifling through files, pulling out statements and organising evidence. Talbot's energy had ignited a spark of urgency among the team, pushing them into action. But as the meeting concluded, Collins lingered behind, her gaze locked on the crime scene photos laid out on the table.

"He's changing, you know," Collins said quietly, her voice carrying the weight of her growing concern.

Talbot turned to her; eyebrows raised in curiosity. "What do you mean?"

Collin's expression was troubled. "He's evolving. The first few break-ins were simple burglaries, almost like he was testing the waters. Now he's targeting more vulnerable people and isolated homes. It's not just about getting in and out unnoticed anymore. He's breaking people."

Talbot absorbed her words, his face reflecting a grim realisation. "He's getting more confident. More dangerous. And that means he'll make a mistake eventually."

Collins looked sceptical; her eyes shadowed with doubt. "You really think so?"

Talbot offered a small, grim smile. "They all do. It's part of the nature of sociopaths. They believe they're invincible until they're not."

Later that evening, Talbot found himself alone in his dimly lit office, the walls adorned with maps of Herts, Beds, and Bucks, and numerous crime scene photos. Talbot leaned back in his chair, closing his eyes as he tried to immerse himself in the mindset of The Fox.

"He's clever," he muttered to himself, grappling with the enigma before him. "He's careful. But he's not invincible."

In his mind's eye, Talbot pictured The Fox as a cold, calculating individual - someone who meticulously observed his prey for days, perhaps weeks, before making his move. A man who thrived on the adrenaline rush and the sense of control. But Talbot knew every criminal had a weakness. His challenge was to uncover it.

His thoughts were abruptly interrupted by the shrill ring of his phone. It was Claire Milford, the journalist who had coined the moniker 'The Fox.'

"DCS Talbot," Claire's voice came through with a sense of urgency, "I've got something you might want to see. A letter arrived at the paper this afternoon. I think it's from him."

Talbot's heart raced with a surge of adrenaline. "You're sure?"

Claire hesitated. "I can't be absolutely certain, but it's addressed to me directly and mentions the nickname I gave him. No one else knew that before it went to print."

"I'm on my way," Talbot said, abruptly ending the call and grabbing his coat.

At the Leighton Buzzard Observer office, Claire handed him the letter with a tremor in her hand. The paper was cheap, and the handwriting uneven, betraying an unsettlingly casual tone. Talbot's eyes scanned the message, his face hardening into a mask of concentration as he read:

"TO THE ONE WHO NAMED ME THE FOX, YOU AIN'T SEEN NOTHING YET. I AM EVERYWHERE AND NOWHERE. I CAN SEE YOU, EVEN IF YOU CAN'T SEE ME. WHEN THE TIME COMES, YOU'LL KNOW IT'S ME. I PROMISE."

The words seemed to vibrate with an ominous energy, and Talbot's expression darkened. "If this isn't a hoax, he's taunting us," he said finally, his voice low and intense. "He's trying to get inside our heads."

Claire's face was pale, her eyes wide with a mix of fear and curiosity. "How do we know if it is a hoax or not?"

Talbot took a deep breath, his mind racing through the implications. "Well, we wait. And if he contacts you again, make sure I am the first person you call. We are going to catch him."

Milford nodded her head, while Talbot gathered his things and left the room.

The weight of Talbot's words settled heavily in the room, the promise of an imminent confrontation lingering. But deep down, Talbot knew the truth: catching The Fox wouldn't be simple. The Fox was more than just a criminal; he was an enigma, forever one step ahead. To capture him, Talbot would need to embrace the elusive nature of his quarry, becoming an evil exploiter himself in the relentless pursuit of justice. The hunt was on, and the stakes had never been higher.

The face of British law enforcement was about to change forever. It was a time of transformation, not only for society but also for the way police tackled the rising tide of crime. The United Kingdom had seen a dramatic rise in criminal activity, and with it, the complexities of policing were becoming more apparent. The traditional methods of investigation were reaching their limits. Criminal cases were becoming more intricate, with offenders leaving fewer clues behind, and the sheer volume of information officers had to sift through was overwhelming.

Detective Chief Superintendent Mark Talbot, known for his sharp instincts and dedication, was at the forefront of a revolution in policing. His career had been built on hard work, persistence, and old-fashioned investigative legwork. But now, with the advancements in technology, he was about to lead his team into uncharted territory. For the first time in British law enforcement history, detectives would use a computer to assist in solving a major case. This machine affectionately nicknamed Metal Mickey would become a silent partner in one of the most important investigations of Talbot's career.

Talbot stood in a large room inside Dunstable police station, staring at the blinking lights and whirling of Metal Mickey, a room-sized computer that looked like something out of a science fiction movie. It was massive, a monstrosity of wires, switches, and blinking screens, but to Talbot, it represented the future. This machine had the potential to do what no human could - process and organise the vast amounts of data that were pouring in from across the 'Triangle of Terror'. In the age before modern databases, this was a monumental leap forward.

The police were faced with a monumental challenge: crime was evolving, and the criminals were becoming smarter. Serial offenders moved across jurisdictions, making it difficult for local forces to link crimes. Eye-witness reports, forensic evidence, and crime scene details had to be logged manually, and any connections between cases were often lost in the deluge of paperwork. Detectives worked tirelessly, but human limitations meant that critical leads were sometimes missed.

Talbot had seen this firsthand. His team was often buried under stacks of reports and witness statements. They could only do so much, and every officer had their breaking point. Solving a case often came down to luck - whether the right officer happened to remember the right detail at the right time. Talbot knew they needed something more.

And that something was Metal Mickey.

The machine had been brought in to assist the force in sifting through criminal records, compiling data, and searching for patterns that could link The Fox's crimes across different areas. For the first time, detectives could use technology to narrow down suspects based on witness accounts, crime scene details, and known offender profiles. It wasn't perfect, and it certainly wasn't fast, but Metal Mickey could process thousands of pieces of data in a fraction of the time it would take a human team to do the same.

Talbot oversaw this new initiative, a job that came with both excitement and pressure. This wasn't just an experiment - it was a test of whether the police could evolve and meet the challenges of the future.

At first, some of his team were sceptical. After all, policing had always been about gut instinct, about knocking on doors, interviewing suspects, and following leads. The idea that a machine - a cold, unfeeling piece of metal - could somehow help them catch The Fox seemed far-fetched to many.

But Talbot, ever the pragmatist, knew they had to adapt. He called a meeting in the operations room, standing in front of his team with a sense of purpose.

"Look, I know we've all got our doubts about this thing," Talbot said, gesturing toward Metal Mickey, visible through the glass window of the adjacent room. "But we're drowning in data. We've got thousands of names, addresses, witness reports, and we're just not getting anywhere fast enough. This machine can help us cut through that. It can process information in a way we can't - not this fast, not this accurately."

There was silence in the room, some officers shifting uncomfortably in their seats. Detective Sergeant Jake Miller, one of Talbot's most trusted men, raised an eyebrow and leaned back in his chair.

"Boss, I get what you're saying, but can a machine really catch a criminal? I mean, we've always done this the hard way - talking to people, making connections."

Talbot nodded. He understood the concern. He had the same questions himself. But he also knew that times were changing.

"It's not about replacing the work we do," Talbot explained. "It's about helping us do it better. Metal Mickey's not going to interview suspects or walk the beat. That's still our job. But what it can do is help us see the patterns we're missing - connections between crimes, suspects who match The Fox's description but live in different jurisdictions. It's a tool, and if we use it right, it could make all the difference."

The room was quiet for a moment before Miller finally nodded.

"Alright, let's give it a go."

Within days, the team began feeding information into Metal Mickey. Every detail from every crime scene - addresses, times of the break-ins and assaults, descriptions of The Fox, even the types of tools used to force entry - was meticulously logged. The machine hummed and whirred, its internal systems processing the data faster than any human team could have hoped to do.

As the days went by, Metal Mickey began to spit out potential leads. The computer's algorithms analysed the data, looking for matches in known offender profiles, cross-referencing witness descriptions, and identifying similarities between seemingly unrelated incidents.

Metal Mickey provided the names of over five thousand potential suspects. It was a painstaking and time-consuming list of people for the police to work through.

Talbot and his team were astonished. The machine had done in days what would have taken them months to piece together.

Metal Mickey became a permanent fixture in the investigation. But while technology was becoming an essential part of policing, Talbot never lost sight of the human element. He knew that computers, no matter how advanced, could never replace the instincts and dedication of a detective on the ground. Metal Mickey was a tool - an important one - but it was still the men and women of the force who would ultimately bring justice to the victims.

And so, as the sun set on another long day of policing, Detective Chief Superintendent Mark Talbot stood in his office, watching the lights of the town twinkle in the distance. The world was changing, and the police force was changing with it. But one thing would never change: the fight against crime was a human endeavour, built on the backs of those who were willing to dedicate their lives to protecting others.

For Talbot, the future was bright - and he was ready to lead his team into it.

Chapter 10

Since relocating from the north of England, The Fox had lodged with his brother. His domain was a grimy, unremarkable house in Leighton Buzzard. From the outside, it was a rundown semi-detached dwelling on a nondescript street - a place that seemed to blend seamlessly into its surroundings, almost as if its very ordinariness served to obscure the sinister presence within. To the casual observer, it was just another residence in a sea of similar homes, but for The Fox, it was the perfect hiding spot. A sanctuary for someone who thrived in the shady crevices of society, it was here that he found solace in his own darkness.

It was another balmy warm summer's evening, the moonlight trickled through the bare branches of the trees outside, casting fleeting shadows that danced across the worn walls of the living room. The Fox reclined in a creaking wooden chair, a faint smile curving his lips as he contemplated the scene before him. The room was sparsely furnished, yet meticulously organised. A sense of order prevailed amid the chaos - a reflection of the man himself.

He traced his fingers along the jagged scar on his cheek, a mark of his past. The scar was more than a physical reminder; it was a symbol of the deep-seated anger and resentment that fuelled his every move. His father's voice echoed in his mind, sharp and unforgiving. "Useless boy. Can't do anything right." Those words had been seared into his memory, defining his early life and shaping his path. But those days were long gone. Now, The Fox had carved out his own existence - a stalker operating on a higher plane.

"A clever fox outsmarting the hounds," he muttered to himself, his eyes glinting with a manic light. The name the media had given him - The Fox - was more than a moniker; it was an identity he had embraced. He wasn't just a thief or a thug; he was a master of his craft. A manipulator who thrived on the fear he instilled in others. The police, the newspapers, the public - they were all merely players in his elaborate game.

The small wooden table beside him was cluttered with trophies from his conquests. A man's silk tie, a woman's leather belt, a faded photograph of a smiling couple. Each item was a piece of his legacy, a testament to his power. He picked up the tie, letting it slip through his fingers like liquid. The faint scent of perfume lingered, a poltergeist of the past. "Antoinette something," he whispered with a twisted smile. "Pretty little thing. Screamed so nicely."

His eyes darkened, and the smile faded. It wasn't about the things he took or the chaos he created. No, it was about control. He decided who lived in fear and who slept soundly at night. He dictated the rhythm of terror. With each invasion, each shattered life, he felt a deep-seated satisfaction. The police, the newspapers, the public were all dancing to his tune - and they didn't even know it.

A distant, haunting voice cut through his reverie - the voice of his mother. "You'll never be anything but trouble." She had never understood him, never recognised the potential in his cunning. But he didn't need her approval. Not anymore. "Look at me now, Mum," he said softly, a cruel twist to his words. "Look at what I've become."

A sudden rustling from outside jerked him back to reality. He peered through the grimy window, his eyes narrowing as he scanned the nighttime. A fox - an actual fox - emerged from the underbrush, its eyes glowing with an eerie luminescence. The Fox regarded the creature with a strange, reflective gaze. "Ah, my brother," he murmured. "Out hunting tonight, too?"

He rose from his chair, his movements deliberate and measured. The thrill of the hunt was something he relished - the anticipation, the creeping silence before the storm. His childhood had been spent hiding in the evenings, evading the blows of a drunken father and the cold indifference of his mother. He had learned early on that the world belonged to those who could seize it. Now, he was the one calling the shots. The hunters had become the hunted, and the hounds hadn't even begun to catch on.

He picked up a crumpled clipping from the table, smoothing it out with a rough hand. Leighton Buzzard Observer, first of May 1984: 'The Fox Strikes Again.' He couldn't read, but he could tell from the photos in the article, it was about him.

"Keep chasing your own tail, Detective Chief Superintendent Mark Talbot," he said, his voice a low, mocking whisper. He had observed Talbot from a distance, noting the way the detective barked orders and tried to project confidence. But The Fox saw through the façade - the weariness in Talbot's eyes, the subtle hesitation in his step. Talbot was close, but not close enough. "You're not ready for me," he said, almost pitying the man. "Not yet."

The thought of Talbot lying awake at night, consumed by thoughts of him, brought The Fox a perverse pleasure. It was a game - a dance of cat and mouse, or rather, fox and hound. But Talbot didn't yet grasp the rules. The Fox knew them all too well. He understood the delicate balance of pushing boundaries and retreating, the art of timing and precision. He was the master of his own clock.

"Soon," he muttered to himself, his eyes glinting with a dark promise as he sketched a crude outline of a house in his notebook. "Soon, they'll understand the full extent of my craft."

The thrill of the next break-in pulsed through him like an electric current. He envisioned the meticulous planning, the careful execution - the fear, the screams, the whispered terror that would ripple through the towns and villages. They'd see him, but they wouldn't catch him.

"Good night," he whispered to the encroaching darkness. "Sleep tight. The Fox is watching."

The Fox gathered his things and slipped out of the house while his brother slept. Tonight, he didn't have to travel far. He moved silently through the back streets of Linslade, his form a ghostly silhouette against the night. Clad in a mask fashioned from a trouser leg and armed with a shotgun that felt solid in his gloved hands, he experienced a heady mixture of fear and exhilaration. Each time he performed his dark ritual, the hunger within him grew stronger.

He approached a modest two-story house, its curtains drawn tight against the night. The soft glow of a streetlight bathed the lawn in a gentle light. The Fox's keen eyes noted the outline of a car in the driveway - evidence of a couple inside, asleep and vulnerable. He could almost taste their fear, his pulse quickening with anticipation.

"No turning back," he muttered to himself, his voice barely more than a whisper.

He slipped around to the side of the house, where a small kitchen window was left ajar. He pried it open with ease and slid inside, landing silently on the cool linoleum floor. Every sound, every grind of the house seemed amplified in the silence. His heartbeat echoed in his ears as he moved stealthily through the darkened hallway.

Upstairs, he could hear the recurring breathing of the sleeping couple. He ascended the stairs slowly, each crackle of the wood beneath him a sharp reminder of the stakes. Reaching the top, he moved swiftly toward the bedroom, where the door stood agape. The darkness of the room swallowed him whole as he stepped inside, the vague outline of the bed coming into view. He raised the shotgun, the barrel gleaming ominously in the faint moonlight filtering through the window.

"Wake up," he commanded, his voice low and menacing.

A sleepy murmur, followed by a wave of panic. The husband, groggy and disoriented, was the first to sit up. His eyes expanded in dread as they focused on the dark figure in the doorway, the glint of moonlight reflecting off the barrel of the gun. The wife's breathing quickened as she awoke, her eyes spreading in horror.

"Out of bed," The Fox ordered, his voice cold and unyielding. "Now."

The elderly couple, Mick and Liza Brierley, hesitated, fear paralysing them momentarily. The Fox's eyes narrowed behind his mask, his grip on the shotgun tightening.

"I said, get up!" he barked, his tone leaving no room for argument. The couple scrambled from the bed, their hands trembling nonstop.

He tossed a pair of shoelaces at the woman's feet. "Tie him up. Do it tight."

With shaking hands, Liza complied, her fingers fumbling as she wrapped the laces around her husband's wrists. Her breaths came in short, panicked bursts. When the knots were secure, The Fox yanked on them, ensuring they were tight. He then grabbed a belt from the closet and bound her hands behind her back.

The room was warm and stuffy, each second stretching into what felt like an eternity. Mick's eyes darted between his wife and The Fox, his voice a strangled whisper. "Please...don't hurt her. Don't hurt us."

The Fox ignored the plea, his gaze locked on Liza. His breath was hot and shallow beneath the mask. He reached out with a gloved hand, brushing her cheek. She recoiled, but he seized her hair, jerking her head back.

"Stop it!" she screamed, her voice shattering the suffocating silence of the room.

Annoyed by her resistance, The Fox slammed the butt of his shotgun into the back of Liza's head. She slumped forward. Three additional brutal blows cracked her skull open, and blood gushed from the wound. Liza, barely conscious, stopped moving. No more resistance from her – it was pure control for The Fox.

"Any noise from you, and you get the same," he growled at Mick, who sat helpless on the bedroom floor, sobbing.

Empowered by his dominance, The Fox flipped Liza onto her back and yanked down her pyjama bottoms. With no mercy, he forced her legs apart and sexually assaulted her, all while keeping the shotgun aimed at Mick. Each violent thrust was answered by Mick's choked sobs.

The Fox's heart pounded with a sickening blend of dread and satisfaction. Once the physical torture was over, he pulled up his trousers and walked out of the bedroom and the house, leaving behind another scene of utter desolation - a couple bound, broken, and terrified.

Four days later, he struck again.

This time, the bungalow in Wing was isolated, surrounded by tall hedges that obscured it from prying eyes. Inside, a husband and wife, Jimmy and Selena King lay asleep, their two children in the room next door, blissfully unaware of the nightmare approaching. But The Fox had other plans.

He eased the back door open, his senses sharpened and his mind focused. He moved through the kitchen and into the hallway, his movements precise and calculated. The flicker of a small nightlight from the children's room served as a reminder of the delicate balance he had to maintain. He preferred not to have an audience.

He pushed the main bedroom door open and stepped inside. Selena stirred first, her eyes blinking in the darkness until she saw him - a slim figure in a black balaclava, a shotgun aimed directly at her husband's head.

"Don't scream," The Fox said calmly. "Or your children will wake up without a mother."

Selena's breath hitched, her eyes wide with fear. Jimmy was already awake, his face a mask of terror. "What do you want?" he asked, his voice trembling.

"Tie him up," The Fox replied, tossing a cord to Selena. Her hands trembled nonstop as she wrapped the rope around Jimmy's wrists, the cord biting into his skin. The Fox's eyes burned through the mask, his gaze a vulture's scrutiny.

Once she had finished, The Fox pushed her onto the bed and leaned in close to Jimmy. "Don't move," he warned, his voice grim and hostile. Jimmy's face twisted in helpless rage as he struggled against his bonds.

"Leave her alone!" he shouted; his voice hoarse with desperation. The Fox responded by swinging the shotgun like a club, striking him across the face. Blood splattered onto the sheets as Jimmy collapsed, dazed and bleeding.

Selena's scream was a strangled, terror-filled cry as The Fox leaned over her. His breath was hot and menacing against her skin.

"Open your mouth." he demanded.

Selena shook her head at first. A swift blow to the face from The Fox's shotgun ensured she soon changed her mind. A solitary trickle of blood seeped from her cut eyebrow down her cheek and onto her neck.

"I said open your mouth." The Fox demanded again.

Selena, unsure as to what his demands would lead to, slowly complied. The Fox, staring deadpan at Selena, moved his shotgun towards her mouth.

"Wider. Open wider." He requested, as he slowly forced the barrel of the shotgun into her mouth.

The sexual violence that followed was ferocious and lasted what felt like a lifetime, the shotgun never leaving her mouth. Selena, her tears now combining with the blood streaming down her face, struggled to breath, struggled to comprehend how her life was being turned upside down by such a wicked act of brutality.

When he was done, without another word, The Fox pulled up his trousers, turned around, and slipped back into the night, leaving behind a nightmare that would haunt the family forever - a shattered existence, irrevocably scarred.

The Fox's hunger was insatiable, and as he disappeared into the nighttime, he knew that he would strike again. The thrill of the hunt, the power he wielded - these were his driving forces.

Chapter 11

The Fox's neighbours saw him as a quiet man, polite but distant. He didn't socialise much, but he wasn't rude either. He was the type of man people forgot about minutes after a conversation. This anonymity was his greatest weapon.

Each day, he woke up early - before the sun had risen - to get a head start on his day. He'd pack his tools into the back of his van, a battered white Ford Transit that had seen better days, and drive to wherever the next job took him. Some days he'd be cutting hedges for an elderly couple, other days he'd be fixing a broken gate for a young family. His work was spread across the three counties - Hertfordshire, Bedfordshire, and Buckinghamshire - which gave him a wide range of areas to scout for potential targets.

He had learned early on that it was in the mundane details of life where people were most vulnerable. He listened intently as clients talked about their upcoming holidays, mentioned which neighbours they trusted to water the plants or when they expected delivery of an expensive item. They never thought twice about telling him such things. After all, he was just a labourer - a working man, like so many others. Harmless. Reliable. That was his secret: people saw only what he allowed them to see.

One particularly warm summer morning, The Fox was tasked with repairing a stone wall at a large estate in Hertfordshire. The owners, a wealthy couple in their fifties, were planning a three-week holiday to the south of France. As he worked, the wife, Carol, brought him a glass of water and chatted about the trip, casually mentioning that the house would be left empty during that time. Her husband, Quentin, had state-of-the-art window and door locks installed, but she was still worried about leaving it unattended.

"Don't worry," The Fox had said with a reassuring smile. "These new locks are top-notch. You'll be fine."

But even as he said the words, his mind was working out the details. He'd already noticed the flaws in the locks when he walked past the front and back doors. He had also noted the positioning of the neighbour's house, slightly obscured by a dense line of trees. A perfect setup for a job.

Carol smiled, reassured by his calm demeanour, and left him to his work. To her, he was just another nameless tradesman who would be gone by the end of the day. She had no idea that in just a few weeks, after their departure, The Fox would return to her home in the dead of night to strip it of its valuables. He didn't rush jobs like these. Planning was key.

The times between his crimes were just as important to The Fox as the actual acts themselves. He was methodical, careful not to act too soon after finishing a job. If he broke into a house the same week he worked on it, suspicions would naturally point in his direction. Instead, he played the long game. Weeks might pass before he returned to a property. By then, the connection between him and the crime was buried under the passage of time and memory.

When he wasn't working on jobs or scouting out potential targets, The Fox kept to himself. He had no real friends, only his brother to keep him company. He floated through the everyday world without leaving a trace. On occasion, he'd visit a local pub, nursing a pint and listening to the idle gossip of the locals. Pubs were great places for gathering information. People talked freely, especially after a few drinks. He'd hear stories of neighbours who had just bought new cars or gone on shopping sprees, boasting about their latest purchases.

There were moments when the monotony of his cover life wore on him. Moving from job to job, always pretending, always watching, it could be tiring. But he knew it was necessary. To slip up now - to give in to impatience - would risk everything. So, he played the part of the hard-working labourer, putting in long hours and doing quality work. If people liked him, they wouldn't suspect him.

Occasionally, his clients would recommend him to their friends and neighbours. These referrals were pure gold. It meant more access, more opportunities. The tight-knit communities in Hertfordshire, Bedfordshire, and Buckinghamshire were built on trust, and once you were in, you were in for good. The Fox used this to his advantage, becoming a familiar face in the area without drawing any unwanted attention.

It wasn't just homes The Fox targeted. Vulnerable people were often the easiest prey. He learned to identify them quickly: the elderly, living alone; women who had recently lost their husbands and were struggling to cope; young couples with children who left their doors unlocked, thinking nothing bad would ever happen to them. These were the people he could exploit without a second thought.

One job took him to the home of an elderly woman named Maeve Harrington in Newport Pagnell. She had recently lost her husband and was struggling to keep up with the maintenance of her large, old house. The Fox had been hired to fix a broken gutter, but as he worked, he took note of everything. Maeve was frail, her movements slow and unsteady. She lived alone, relying on a local care worker who visited twice a week to help with the shopping and cleaning. The house itself was a goldmine - old, with original fixtures that could fetch a small fortune if sold to the right buyers.

He'd bide his time with this one. It would be too easy to take advantage of her vulnerability immediately. No, he'd wait until the care worker was away on holiday, or until Maeve mentioned some other detail that would ensure there were no unexpected visitors. For now, he played the role of the helpful handyman, coming back every few weeks to do small jobs and build her trust.

One day, when the timing was perfect, The Fox would return, and no one would ever suspect him. After all, Maeve had spoken so highly of him to her neighbours - had even recommended him to a few of them. He was just a friendly local labourer, doing his bit to help those who couldn't help themselves. The perfect cover.

As much as The Fox enjoyed the actual work of breaking into homes and stealing from the vulnerable, he got an equal thrill from the hunt. The planning, the watching, the waiting - it was all part of the game. His jobs gave him unparalleled access to people's lives. He saw how they lived, where they kept their valuables, and when they left their homes unattended. But he also paid attention to the little things: who had dogs, who had old locks, who left their windows unlocked at night.

His labour jobs often took him to affluent areas, where people were more trusting and less guarded. These were the perfect targets. Wealthy enough to have things worth stealing, but too comfortable in their surroundings to suspect that the man fixing their fence or trimming their hedges was silently plotting their downfall.

In Aylesbury, he worked for a middle-aged couple who ran a small antiques business out of their home. They had hired him to help clear out their garden, which had become overgrown and difficult to manage. As he worked, he couldn't help but notice the various pieces of valuable furniture and art they had stored in their home. The wife, a chatty woman named Sylvia, proudly gave him a tour of their collection, pointing out the more valuable items and telling him how much they were worth.

"We've been collecting for years," she said with a smile. "Some of these pieces are worth more than the house itself."

The Fox nodded, his mind already working. He knew he would be back for these items, but not yet. He'd wait until they trusted him completely. Maybe even take on a few more jobs for them. The longer he worked for someone, the less they questioned his presence around their home. People had a way of letting their guard down once they thought they knew you. That was their mistake, and The Fox was always ready to exploit it.

When the time finally came to commit a crime, The Fox was meticulous in his preparation. He'd never act on impulse; every burglary was carefully planned and executed with precision. His labour jobs were not just a cover - they were a way to gather all the information he needed to carry out the perfect crime.

In the weeks leading up to a job, The Fox would stake out the property, watching from a distance, and making a mental note of every detail. He'd observe the comings and goings of the household, learning their routines. He knew when the house would be empty, when the neighbours were most likely to be away, and how long it would take for someone to notice if something was amiss.

He had no remorse for his actions. To him, it was just another job. A means to an end. And as long as he maintained his cover, no one would ever suspect the quiet, hardworking labourer who lived in their midst. He was The Fox, and he would continue to hunt, always one step ahead of the law, always hidden in plain sight.

And so, The Fox lived his life between two worlds: by day, a simple labourer, fixing fences and painting walls, and by night, a nocturnal animal, stalking his prey, waiting for the perfect moment to strike. It was an ordinary life, but only on the surface. Beneath that thin veneer of normalcy, there lurked a dangerous and calculating criminal, always watching, always waiting for his next opportunity. And for the people of Hertfordshire, Bedfordshire, and Buckinghamshire, that danger was closer than they could ever imagine.

Part Two: The Hunt Intensifies

Chapter 12

The summer of 1984 was unbearably hot, but it wasn't just the oppressive heat making everyone sweat. It was anxiety. The Fox was still out there, flickering in and out of the night like a wavering lampshade. The news was everywhere - on TV, in the papers, on the lips of every person up and down the country. With every new headline, with every whispered story, fear turned into anger, and anger began to fester.

At first, it was a quiet rebellion. People started buying extra locks for their doors and windows, spending money they didn't have for a sense of security that felt increasingly like an illusion. Hardware stores couldn't keep up with the demand. In Berkhamsted, the owner of Smith's Security & Ironmongery stood behind his counter, wiping his forehead with a rag as he tried to calm the frantic customers.

"I'm telling you, Mrs Hopkins, this is the last set of window bars I've got," he said, his voice strained. "You're lucky to be getting them."

People nodded, grumbled, but mostly they understood. Demand had skyrocketed. No one felt safe anymore. They were sleeping with windows shut tight, despite the sweltering heat, or barring them altogether. And for those who lived in single-story homes or had bedrooms on the ground floor, every rasp, every groan of the old beams in their houses, sounded like a footstep.

"More locks won't stop him," muttered a tall man with a bushy moustache and a face weathered from years of working under the sun. "Not if he's already inside your sofa when you lock up."

A murmur of agreement spread through the shop. The story of The Fox hiding inside people's homes, creating his dens, was the kind of nightmare that kept the whole town awake. A woman near the back, clutching a pair of heavy-duty padlocks, crossed herself.

Gun shops too saw a steady stream of nervous customers. In Hemel Hempstead, Trent's Firearms & Outdoor Supplies had a line of people out the door and halfway down the street. The owner, Arthur Trent, a tired looking old man who'd been in the business since his army days, stared at the queue with a mix of disbelief and concern.

"Listen up, folks!" he shouted. "If you don't have a proper license, you're not leaving here with a firearm, you hear me?"

But it wasn't just guns they wanted. Knives, baseball bats, metal rods - anything that could be turned into a weapon was disappearing from the shelves faster than Trent could restock. People were desperate, and desperation had a way of clouding judgement.

News reports filled the airwaves with stories of residents forming vigilante groups, ordinary men and women turning into self-appointed defenders of their streets. The police were stretched thin, and the sense of vulnerability had become suffocating. In small towns like Leighton Buzzard and Linslade, whispers turned into meetings, and meetings turned into patrols.

"We'll take turns," said Allen James, a stout man with a strong jaw and a face lined with age. He was a landscape gardener by trade but had emerged as a leader among his neighbours. They'd gathered in his garage, a motley crew of men and women, some young and strong, others old but no less determined. "We watch out for each other. If we see anything - anyone who doesn't belong - we handle it."

"Handle it how?" asked Toni Rimm, a middle-aged woman with a determined glint in her eye. She was holding a flashlight in one hand, a kitchen knife in the other. "We're not the bloody police."

Allen set his jaw. "No, we're not. But we're not helpless, either. If we see him, we alert the authorities. But if it comes to it...we do what we have to do to protect our own."

There were nods, murmurs of agreement. Fear had forged a new kind of community here - a collective resolve born out of desperation. The police couldn't be everywhere, and The Fox had proven he could slip through their fingers. If The Fox was going to play his games, then they would play theirs.

Still, there were some who hesitated. "We can't take the law into our own hands, Allen," warned Paula Taylor, a retired estate agent who'd always been a voice of reason. "What if we get the wrong person? What if we hurt someone innocent?"

Allen's eyes darkened. "Better to make that mistake than to be another victim."

The room fell silent. No one wanted to say it, but they all knew the truth: the police were overwhelmed, and The Fox was getting bolder. There was no room for half-measures now.

In the small village of Aston Clinton, a group calling themselves 'The Night Watch' had already begun patrolling the streets. They were a mix of local farmers, shop owners, and factory workers, all united by a single purpose: keep their families safe from The Fox.

Jonny Reid, a former soldier with a scar running down his cheek, was their de facto leader. He stood in the middle of a dimly lit garage, surrounded by a dozen men and women. Each of them held some form of weapon - a bat, a crowbar, even an antique hunting rifle.

"You heard the copper on the telly," Reid said, his voice low but commanding. "He says don't take the law into our own hands. But what's he gonna do if The Fox comes knocking? By the time the coppers get here, it'll be too late."

There were nods of agreement, murmurs of approval. "We've got to protect ourselves," someone muttered.

Reid continued, "We stay off the beaten track. We don't go looking for trouble, but if trouble comes, we're ready. If anyone sees anything, we alert the group. We move fast, we move quiet. And if we catch him…" He paused, letting the weight of his words sink in. "We make sure he can't hurt anyone ever again."

The room was silent, the tension plain for all to see. They were ordinary people, turned into something else by an intruder. And if they caught The Fox, God help him - or them.

It wasn't long before things began to spiral. The reports came in daily - mistaken identities, false alarms, frightened neighbours turning on each other. A man in Hemel Hempstead was nearly beaten to death because he'd been walking home late at night and fitted the vague description of The Fox. In Tring, an elderly woman fired a shotgun through her front door at what turned out to be a stray cat.

Detective Chief Superintendent Mark Talbot felt the pressure mounting. His worst concerns were coming true. The community was on the brink of tearing itself apart, and still, The Fox remained elusive.

One night, as Talbot sat in his office, a call came through. It was his Press Officer, Katie McGee, her voice urgent.

"Mark, you need to see this," she said. "It's spreading."

"What is?" he asked, already dreading the answer.

"The vigilantes. There's talk of them organising into a proper militia. Some are even saying they want to march on the police station, demand more action."

Talbot ran a hand through his hair, feeling the weight of it all crushing down on him. "Damn it. We're losing control."

He slammed down the phone, rubbed his face in frustration and stared up at the ceiling. Instead of pursuing a single threat, they were facing a pack of threats - desperate, scared, and increasingly armed.

He picked up the phone and dialled the number for Detective Sergeant Sarah Kendrick. "We need more officers on the ground," he said as soon as the line clicked open. "And we need them now. We can't let the locals take matters into their own hands."

In the quiet village of Wingrave, a group of locals huddled in a small, dimly lit barn. The scent of hay and sweat overpowered their senses. They were scared, desperate. Glen Davies, now considered a leader of sorts, spoke to them with a steady voice.

"If we don't protect our own, who will?" he asked. "The police are too slow, too scattered. But we know our streets, our neighbours. We've got eyes everywhere."

Helena Coombes, still gripping her flashlight and kitchen knife, nodded in agreement. "We won't let him take another one of us."

From the back of the room, a younger man named Stevie Stathers stood up. "I say we set traps," he suggested. "Like they do for foxes in the countryside. If he's lurking around, he's bound to trip one sooner or later."

The idea sparked a murmur of approval. Fear had turned their hearts hard, their minds sharp with the thirst for justice - or revenge.

Davies nodded. "Alright, we start setting traps tomorrow. But remember, if you see him, you call for help. Don't try to be a hero."

The barn was filled with a dark, determined energy. They were ready. But as the nights stretched on and their patrols became more frequent, the danger only seemed to escalate. And all the while, The Fox watched through his binoculars in the Chiltern Hills, a twisted smile on his face. He knew they were hunting him, but he also knew they weren't smart enough to catch him.

And soon, the hunters would find themselves hunted, caught in a game they didn't fully understand - a game where the only rule was survival, and the price of failure was blood.

Detective Chief Superintendent Mark Talbot knew things were spiralling. Each day brought another report of a vigilante group forming, another case of someone taking the law into their own hands. It was only a matter of time before things got out of control. He sat at his desk, his face drawn and tired.

"Bloody hell," he muttered under his breath. His eyes were bloodshot, dark circles etched beneath them. He hadn't slept properly in weeks. Every day, he felt the pressure mounting - on him, on his team, on the entire community. And every day, the fear and anger seemed to deepen.

Katie McGee stepped into the room, her face taut with worry. "Mark, we've got to address this vigilante thing before it blows up in our faces. They're scared, and they're armed. We're looking at a potential disaster here."

Talbot nodded. "I know. I know. But they're scared for a reason, Katie. We've got a bloody madman out there, and we're no closer to catching him. People are losing faith."

"Then we need to restore it," she said firmly. "Get ahead of this before it turns into a bloodbath."

Talbot took a deep breath. "Alright. Set up a press conference. I want every local paper, every radio station, every TV crew we can get. They need to hear from me directly."

McGee nodded, already reaching for the phone. "I'll get on it."

Chapter 13

Detective Chief Superintendent Mark Talbot stood in the dimly lit hallway of the Dunstable police station, staring at his reflection in a grimy window. He looked like death warmed up, he felt it too. It had been weeks since he'd rested properly, and it showed. The Fox was running him ragged - running them all ragged.

Today, he would face the press.

He adjusted his tie in the window's faint reflection, feeling the weight of what was coming. The press conference had been called hastily, but it was necessary. The public's fear had reached a fever pitch, and if they didn't address it soon, the whole region could descend into chaos. He had to give them something - reassurance, hope, anything to cling to in this endless nightmare.

Katie McGee, his Press Officer, appeared beside him, her face just as tired and worn. She gave him a brief nod. "They're ready for you, Mark," she said, her voice low.

Talbot took a deep breath. "How bad is it out there?"

"Packed," McGee replied. "Journalists from every major outlet. Local and national. Even some international. They smell blood in the water."

Talbot exhaled slowly. "And they're expecting answers we don't have yet."

McGee nodded, her expression grim. "Just be honest. Let them know we're doing everything we can."

"Honest," Talbot muttered. "Not sure they want honesty, Katie. They want a monster in chains. And right now, we've got a monster on the run."

Talbot took a final deep breath, steadied himself, and moved toward the doors leading into the conference room. As he pushed them open, a wall of flashing cameras and murmuring voices hit him like a wave.

The room was packed - dozens of reporters, cameras, and microphones crowded together in a sea of faces.

He walked to the podium at the front, his every step echoing in the silence that fell over the room. As he stood behind the microphone, he could feel the eyes of every person in the room bearing down on him, waiting for him to say something – anything - that could make sense of the terror that had gripped their lives.

"Good afternoon," Talbot began, his voice steady despite the tightness in his chest. "Thank you all for being here today. I know there's a lot of fear and uncertainty in our community right now, and I want to address that directly."

The room was silent except for the clicking of cameras and the scribbling of pens on notepads. Talbot could feel the pressure, the anticipation evident in the way the reporters leaned forward, hanging on his every word.

"As many of you are aware, we are currently investigating a series of violent home invasions and assaults across Hertfordshire, Bedfordshire, and Buckinghamshire, committed by an individual we are referring to as 'The Fox.' Over the past several weeks, The Fox has targeted multiple homes, often breaking in and creating dens within the properties, where he waits until his victims are at their most vulnerable."

A murmur rippled through the crowd, a mix of shock and horror. Talbot continued, his eyes scanning the room, making contact with the faces before him. "These crimes have been methodical, calculated, and brutal. The victims have been left traumatised; their sense of safety shattered. We understand the fear that this has caused in our community, and we are doing everything in our power to bring this individual to justice."

A reporter in the front row raised her hand, not waiting to be called on. "Detective Chief Superintendent Mark Talbot, can you confirm whether The Fox has left any messages or clues at the crime scenes? Is he trying to communicate with the police or the public?"

Talbot took a moment to consider his response. "At this time, we cannot disclose specific details regarding evidence found at the scenes, as it is part of an ongoing investigation. However, we can say that The Fox's actions suggest a pattern of control and psychological manipulation. He is careful, precise, and seems to take pleasure in the fear he creates."

Another reporter jumped in; her voice tinged with impatience. "How close are you to catching him? Are there any suspects?" Talbot's expression hardened slightly. "I understand the urgency, believe me. But investigations of this nature are complex. We are pursuing every lead, examining every piece of evidence, and dedicating all necessary resources to this case. But this individual is highly elusive. He knows how to cover his tracks."

"Is it true that people are forming vigilante groups in response to the attacks?" another journalist asked, his voice rising above the others.

Talbot's jaw compressed. "Yes, we are aware of community groups organising patrols. While we understand the frustration that has led to this, we strongly advise against taking the law into your own hands. These actions, while well-intentioned, can complicate our investigation and potentially put more lives at risk. We ask the public to remain vigilant, but to trust the police to do our job."

The room erupted into more questions, voices overlapping as reporters tried to get their next inquiry in. "Detective Chief Superintendent Mark Talbot, how can you ask the public to trust you when The Fox is still out there?" one shouted.

Talbot held up a hand, his gaze steady. "Because trust is our most powerful tool right now. Trust between the police and the public, trust in our process. We understand the anger. We feel it too. But we need to work together to end this."

A reporter from a major network pushed forward, his voice loud and demanding. "Do you have any message for The Fox himself?"

The room fell deathly silent, every eye trained on Talbot, waiting for his response. He leaned slightly into the microphone, his eyes dark and unyielding.

"To The Fox, I say this: we will not rest until you are caught. You may think you're untouchable, hidden in amongst us, but your time is running out. This community is stronger than the fear you've created. And you will face justice."

The words lingered, charged with a tense energy. Talbot could see the headlines forming in the reporters' eyes, the way they scribbled furiously in their notepads, and the clicking of camera shutters intensified. He knew his words were bold, but they needed to be. The public needed to hear it, and The Fox needed to feel it.

Another reporter, one from a local paper, raised his voice with a more measured question. "DCS Talbot, you've been at the forefront of this investigation for several weeks. Can you give us an insight into what your team is feeling right now, working day and night to track down someone like The Fox?"

Talbot looked at him, and for a moment, the hardness in his eyes softened. "My team is exhausted, but they're also relentless. We've been working around the clock, following every lead, examining every detail. We're dealing with an adversary who thrives on chaos, and that weighs heavily on all of us. But I promise you, and I promise the public, we will not stop. We will not let him win."

The room fell silent again, a ponderous quiet that felt almost oppressive. Talbot could see the dread in the eyes of the journalists, the same worry that had gripped the community for weeks. He knew that nothing he could say would truly alleviate it until The Fox was caught, but he hoped he had at least given them some sense of direction, some belief that the darkness would not last forever.

As the press conference drew to a close, the questions continued to come, but Talbot's answers remained consistent - measured but firm. He would not give in to the hysteria. He would not allow The Fox to dictate the narrative.

"Thank you for your time," Talbot said finally, stepping away from the podium. "We will provide updates as they become available. In the meantime, please stay safe, stay cautious, and know that we are doing everything we can."

He turned and walked off the stage, the camera flashes bursting behind him like fireworks, the questions still flying. He could hear Katie McGee's voice behind him, trying to corral the press, but he needed a moment away from it all. He slipped through a side door into a quiet hallway, the noise of the conference room fading behind him.

He leaned against the wall, his head falling back as he closed his eyes. The weight of the last few weeks pressed down on him, and for a moment, he allowed himself to feel it - the exhaustion, the frustration, the distress. He knew the road ahead was going to be long, and he knew the press conference was only a small part of the battle. But it was a necessary one.

The door opened, and McGee slipped in beside him, her expression as tired as his own. "You did good out there, Mark," she said softly.

"Did I?" Talbot asked, his voice low. "It feels like shouting into the wind."

McGee nodded. "Maybe. But sometimes that's all we can do until the storm passes."

Talbot gave her a faint, tired smile. "Let's just hope we find this bastard before then."

McGee nodded, her expression hardening. "We will. We have to." Talbot took a deep breath, pushing himself off the wall. "Back to work, then. The clock's ticking."

As they walked back toward the operations room, the weight of the task ahead settled back onto his shoulders. The Fox was still out there, still lurking in the background. But so was he, and he wasn't going to let up. Not now. Not ever.

Chapter 14

The village of Slapton was simmering with a nervous hostility that had been building for weeks. Whispers of The Fox floated through the air like an invisible toxin, infecting every conversation, every cautious glance between neighbours. The local news was relentless, broadcasting reports of his assaults and burglaries across the area. The headlines were becoming more frequent, the crimes more brazen, and fear more widespread. No one felt safe. Even in broad daylight, windows were shut, doors double-locked. A sense of paranoia was taking root, twisting its way into every household.

For Claire Mathers, a single mother of a ten-year-old boy, life had already been full of unease. Her ex-partner, Ray, was unpredictable - sometimes sweet, sometimes volatile - and their split had only increased her anxiety. Living alone was not easy.

It was a warm Sunday afternoon when Claire returned home after lunch, her son Jake still with Ray for the weekend. She turned the corner onto her quiet cul-de-sac and pulled into the driveway. She sighed, grateful for a few hours of calm in the middle of the chaos that had become her life.

As she stepped out of her car, the late afternoon sun beamed down on the small, modest houses lining the street. She noticed nothing unusual - until she reached her back door. Her breath stalled in her chest. The door, which she distinctly remembered locking that morning, was slightly ajar. She froze, her heart hammering in her ribs. She knew she hadn't left it like that. She always checked. Twice. Her mind raced with images of the masked intruder known as The Fox, his cold eyes staring from beneath a balaclava, the shotgun gleaming in his hands. She had seen his masked face on the news a hundred times over.

She inched closer, peering through the kitchen window. Her eyes widened as she saw it - someone had made a makeshift den in her utility room. The towels and laundry piled up in a corner, an empty plate and glass on the floor, and the unmistakable indentation of someone having been there.

It was as if the oxygen had been sucked out of her lungs.

"Oh my God…" she whispered. Panic surged through her veins, but she knew better than to enter. She backed away. Slowly. Taking great care not to make a noise.

As she tiptoed away her mind was racing, which neighbour would be home. She needed to use their house phone.

"Mrs Hipwell, number twelve, she is always home," she quietly muttered to herself.

Once she was a safe distance away, Claire ran as fast as her legs could take her to number twelve. She knocked on the door. Once. Twice. A third time. "Come on, come on," she gasped. And as she was about to knock a fourth time, an elderly lady opened the door.

"Hi Mrs Hipwell," Claire gulped. "It's him. He's in my house. I need your phone".

"It's who dear?" replied Mrs Hipwell.

"The Fox. He's in my house". And without taking another breath, Claire burst into the house.

She dialled for the police, her fingers trembling, and brought the phone to her ear. It rang once, then again. She could hardly breathe.

"Emergency services. What service do you require?"

"Police," Claire stuttered. "It's… it's my house. Someone's been inside. I think it's him. I think it's The Fox."

The operator's tone changed instantly. "Stay calm, ma'am. Are you safe right now?"

"Yes, I'm at a neighbour's house> My house is number twelve, Emu Close in Slapton. Please, hurry."

"We're dispatching units to your location. Armed police are on their way. Stay where you are, do not enter the house. Officers will be with you shortly."

Claire hung up, her breath coming in shallow bursts. She sat down on a sofa. Her hands shuddered.

"Would you like a cup of tea, dear? You look like you've had an awful fright." Mrs Hipwell disappeared into her kitchen.

Claire, meanwhile, stood up again, walked to the living room window and stared across the street at her house. She scanned the windows, half-expecting to see a masked face peering back at her. She imagined the intruder inside, maybe watching her right now, deciding what to do next. She wished Ray was there, wished she wasn't alone. The minutes ticked by, feeling like hours.

Inside the operations room in Dunstable police station, Detective Chief Superintendent Mark Talbot was hunched over his desk, his team buzzing around him like a hive. A report had come in only a day earlier of another assault. Talbot was studying it with intent.

His radio crackled to life. "Control to DCS Talbot. We've got a call - possible sighting of The Fox in Slapton. A lady came home, found her back door open and there are signs someone is inside. Armed units are on route."

Talbot's head shot up, his eyes alight with urgency. "This could be it," he said, grabbing his jacket from the back of his chair. "Everyone, listen up! We have a possible sighting of The Fox in Slapton. Armed units are rolling out. This could be the break we've been waiting for."

The room erupted into a frenzy of activity. Officers grabbed gear, shouted orders, and relayed instructions. Talbot could feel the energy in the air; they'd been chasing The Fox for weeks, and now they finally had a chance to corner him. He turned to his right-hand, Detective Sergeant Sarah Kendrick, who was already strapping on her bulletproof vest.

"Sarah, you're with me," Talbot said. "Tell the team to expect resistance. This guy's dangerous, and we're not taking any chances."

Kendrick nodded, her face a mask of grim determination. "Got it, boss. We're ready."

The convoy of marked and unmarked police cars tore through the streets, sirens wailing, blue lights flashing against the blue sky. The armed response units followed close behind in tactical vehicles, officers checking their weapons and preparing for a confrontation. The atmosphere was electric with anticipation - this wasn't just another false alarm. It was a real possibility that they could end The Fox's reign of terror right here, right now.

When the first squad car screeched to a halt outside Claire's house, she nearly jumped out of her skin. Within moments, the street was filled with armed officers, their black uniforms stark against the calm suburban setting. Claire could only watch as they swarmed her property with military precision, weapons raised, ready to breach.

Talbot arrived on the scene moments later, stepping out of his car and surveying the area with a sharp eye. He saw Claire standing on the lawn of Mrs Hipwell's home, pale and visibly shaken.

"Are you Claire Mathers?" he asked, his tone firm but reassuring.

"Yes, that's me," she replied, her voice shaky. "Please, is it really him? Is he in there?"

"We're going to find out," Talbot said. He signalled to the armed units. "On my command. Prepare to breach."

The officers moved swiftly, taking up positions around the house, covering all exits. One of them held a battering ram, ready to break down the door. Talbot's heart thudded in his chest. This was it - the moment they'd all been waiting for.

"Breach!" Talbot commanded.

The door burst open with a deafening crash. Officers flooded into the house, shouting orders. "Armed police! Show yourself! Hands where we can see them!"

The strain was unmistakable, every second stretched taut like a wire about to snap.

Inside, the house was still. The officers moved room by room, clearing each one with quick, efficient movements. The kitchen was empty. The living room, empty. The bedrooms, empty. Then, they reached the utility room. There it was - a makeshift den, just as Claire had described. Officers surrounded it, guns trained, ready for anything.

"Police! Come out now!" an officer shouted. No response. Only silence.

Talbot pushed through the throng of officers, his eyes narrowing. Something felt off. He glanced at the den - at the hastily made bed of towels, the half-eaten plate of food. Then he spotted something that made his heart sink. A small backpack with a Spider-Man logo, a teddy bear and a colouring book.

"Stand down," he said softly, lowering his gun. "It's not him."

The officers exchanged confused glances. "Sir?"

"I said, stand down!" Talbot barked. "It's not The Fox."

Just then, the back door slid open, and a voice called out hesitantly, "Hello? Claire?"

Everyone turned, guns raised again, adrenaline still pumping. A man stepped into the kitchen, holding a young boy's hand.

"Who are you?" demanded Talbot.

"I'm - I'm Ray. Claire's ex-partner. What on earth is going on?" stuttered a very nervous Ray.

"There's been a mistake," replied a very disappointed Talbot.

Ray looked around at the swarm of armed police, his face a mixture of fear and bewilderment. "I - I brought Jake home early. He wasn't feeling well, so I let us in with my old key. Thought I'd wait until Claire got back. We were just in the garage looking for something."

Silence fell over the house, the dread dissipating in an instant. Talbot lowered his gun completely, a sigh escaping his lips as he shook his head. "You've got to be kidding me…"

As the armed police vacated the house, Claire called out to them "is it him, is he in there?"

"No," replied one of the officers. "But your ex-partner Ray is in there."

The colour from Claire's face drained once again. She ran to her house, entering via the smashed in front door. Her concerns had quickly turned to embarrassment. "I…I'm so sorry. I didn't know. I thought…I thought it was…"

"Never mind, ma'am," Talbot said, his voice calm but carrying an edge of frustration. "You did the right thing by calling us. It's better to be safe than sorry."

The remaining officers began to disperse, the worry draining away as the reality of the situation sank in. As the crowd thinned, Talbot turned to Kendrick, a wry smile tugging at his lips.

"Well, I guess that's one way to spend a Sunday afternoon," he said.

Kendrick chuckled, shaking her head. "Can't believe it. All that buildup…for nothing."

"Not for nothing," Talbot replied, his tone suddenly serious. "We're still on the hunt. The Fox is out there, and next time, it won't be a false alarm. We have to be ready."

As the police packed up their gear and prepared to leave, Claire stood by, holding Jake close. She could feel the stares of her neighbours from behind their curtains, could feel the weight of her mistake settling over her like a heavy cold. But more than anything, she felt a renewed sense of fear - because The Fox was still out there.

And with that thought, Claire's heart sank, knowing this was far from over.

Chapter 15

Detective Chief Superintendent Mark Talbot and his team were once again working into the night. Talbot leaned over the evidence spread out on desks in the operations room. The pieces of paper all connected in some way, forming a grotesque, spider-like web. It sprawled across the room, a chilling testament to The Fox's reign of terror. Talbot's brow was furrowed, his mind churning with half-formed thoughts and gut instincts. The chaotic web of paperwork was supposed to reveal something, but all it did was deepen the mystery.

"What's the latest with the names Metal Mickey has provided?" asked Detective Inspector Elaine Carter, stepping up beside Talbot. Carter was one of the sharpest on the team, a woman whose keen observational skills often pierced through the haze of complex cases. She held a stack of files close to her chest; her dark eyes fixed on the same piece of paper Talbot was studying.

Talbot sighed, pushing a hand through his short, greying hair. He straightened his back, casting a quick glance around the room where officers scribbled notes and sipped lukewarm coffee, their eyes tired but determined.

"We've cross-checked over one thousand names which Metal Mickey fed us," Talbot began, his voice a rumble of frustration. "Half of them were ghosts - aliases, identities that exist only on paper. The other half, well, they're either petty criminals with airtight alibis or people who vanished off the map years ago. It's like trying to grab smoke."

Carter's brows knitted in a mixture of disappointment and thoughtfulness. "And the contact we had in Aylesbury? Anything there?"

"Nothing," Talbot said, shaking his head. "The local force said the lead was stale before we even got to it. The name 'Robert Smith' is as common as it gets, and their records turned up nothing that matched our intel."

Carter glanced down at the spread of documents, eyes scanning names and numbers as if willing them to yield secrets. The harsh fluorescent lights cast deep shadows across her face. "Only another four thousand names to go."

"Not entirely," Talbot muttered, tapping a report that sat alone on a corner of the desk. "This one, Carter – Simon Petura. His name keeps showing up. Numerous calls on him, fits the description, bit of a weirdo. He's a small-time crook, but we need more intel on him."

Carter nodded, the fire of determination sparking in her eyes. "Then maybe it's time we rattle his cage."

Talbot's expression softened for a moment, admiration mixing with weariness. "That's the plan. Let's hope we can nail him before he strikes again."

The room fell into silence again, except for the faint rustling of papers and the ticking clock that marked the minutes toward midnight. Every second without a breakthrough felt like an eternity, but Talbot knew they couldn't stop. Not until The Fox was caught, and the web of terror was torn apart at last.

Meanwhile, in the quiet village of Markyate, the night was unnervingly still - a deceptive calm that belied the terror creeping through its streets. The Fox prowled through the darkness, moving with quiet, deliberate intent. He knew the layout of the bungalow ahead as if it were etched into his mind. The building was set back from the road, obscured by a deep row of overgrown hedges. Inside, an eighteen-year-old girl - Clare, her younger brother - Nigel, and her boyfriend - Stewart were nestled in a false sense of security, their lives hanging by a thread.

The Fox's balaclava was pulled snugly over his face, the fabric clinging to his breath. He gripped the shotgun tightly in his gloved hands, his movements accurate and prepared. As he rounded the back of the building, he addressed the flimsy lock on the kitchen door. It posed no challenge; within seconds, it was bypassed, and he slipped inside.

The bungalow was dimly lit, a single light casting a wan light in the hallway. The Fox soon saw to that. Treading on the floor lamp, he yanked the electrical cable until it became free. The Fox paused, letting the silence envelop him. The faint crackle of a vinyl record drifted through the air, a soft, tinny melody that contrasted starkly with the dark purpose of his visit. He crept forward, his sense heightened. In the living room, Nigel swayed to the music, his back turned, oblivious to the encroaching danger.

The Fox's steps were deliberate as he continued down the hallway toward the bedrooms. Clare was in the room at the end. He could hear the low, steady murmur of her sleep, a sound that quickened his pulse with twisted anticipation.

Suddenly, a door creaked open. The Fox spun around; shotgun raised. Stewart emerged from the bathroom; his eyes sprung wide with shock as they met the dark silhouette of The Fox. Stewart's mouth opened, but no words escaped.

"What the hell-" he began, his voice cracking with disbelief.

"Not another word," The Fox cut him off, his voice as cold as steel. "In the bedroom room. Now."

Stewart's face went pale. He raised his hands slowly, eyes darting nervously between The Fox and the living room, where the music still played. "Is that a real gun?" he asked, his voice a whisper of fear.

The Fox took a step closer, his finger brushing the trigger. "You want to find out?" he asked, his tone lethal.

Swallowing hard, Stewart turned into the bedroom, his movements rigid with terror. The Fox followed, the blackness swallowing them both. Clare, asleep, stirred as the door opened. She blinked; her eyes looked confused as they fell on the intruder.

"What's going on?" she asked, her voice groggy and laced with dread.

"Get up," The Fox ordered, jabbing the shotgun toward her.

Stewart moved immediately, but Clare hesitated, her eyes flickering between the gun and her boyfriend's anxious face. "Please, just do what he says," Stewart whispered urgently.

Clare's resolve crumbled. Trembling, she slid off the bed. The Fox marched them back into the hallway, where Nigel had finally emerged, drawn by the commotion. His eyes expanded in horror as he saw his sister and her boyfriend at gunpoint, the black-clad intruder behind them.

"What the-" he began, but The Fox silenced him with a piercing glare.

"All of you, back in the bedroom. Now!" The Fox's voice was unyielding, a command etched in menace. "Don't make a sound."

Fright and disbelief spread across their faces as they shuffled back into the bedroom. The Fox kept the gun trained on them as he pulled the lamp cable from his pocket, along with a silk tie.

"On the floor," he barked. "Face down. Hands behind your backs."

Stewart and Nigel exchanged a look of helpless dread before slowly complying. They lay flat on the carpet, their faces pressed against the rough fibres. The Fox moved with swift efficiency, tying their hands with rough, merciless jerks. The cable cut into Nigel's skin as he bound his wrists tightly, the pressure leaving red indentations.

Clare watched in horror, her breaths coming in rapid, shallow bursts. "Please...please, just take what you want and go," she pleaded, tears streaming down her face.
The Fox turned his gaze to her, his eyes narrowing behind the mask. "You don't get to make demands," he said, his voice devoid of empathy. "On the bed."

Clare hesitated, but the cold steel of the shotgun pressing against her shoulder forced her into compliance. She climbed onto the bed, her entire body trembling. The Fox grabbed a dressing gown cord hanging on the back of the door and bound her wrists to the headboard. He placed a pillow over her head, muffling her sobs.

The Fox, lifted up Clare's nightdress, ripped off her underwear, whilst sliding down his trousers and his underpants. All the while his eyes fixed on the two boys and his shotgun pointing at Clare. The room filled with the sound of Clare's distress and the muffled groans of the two boys, struggling against their restraints, as The Fox claimed yet another victim. His eyes darted around the room, surveying his handiwork. He pulled up his underwear and trousers. Then, without a word, he slipped out into the hallway, leaving the wreckage behind him.

The seconds dragged on like hours. The boys could hear The Fox's movements in the bungalow - opening cupboards, the squeak of the fridge door, boiling the kettle. Their hearts raced, each beat a drum of fear and desperation. They prayed he would simply take what he wanted and leave. Instead, he was refuelling with coffee and a sandwich.

Minutes later, they heard his footsteps returning. The door creaked open, and the room seemed to shrink with his presence. Clare couldn't see him through the pillow, but she could feel him there, looming over her.

She whimpered, her voice a faint, muffled plea. "Please...don't..."

The sexual assault that followed was ferocious and rapid, a ruthless display of power that left her shaking, broken and bleeding heavily. The boys could only listen, their own cries choked back by their restraints.

And then it was their turn.

The Fox walked over to Stewart, slipped his left hand into his pants and groped him. He licked his lips, and he watched the tears stream down Stewart's ashen face. With every stroke, there was a wince of pain. The Fox enjoying and savouring every moment. Stewart, frozen to the spot, praying his torture would soon end.

And then it was Nigel's turn. The same fate awaited him. The same pain was inflicted. And when it was over, The Fox stood up, breathing heavily, smiling to himself.

The three victims were hoping it was the end of their ordeal, but The Fox was already contemplating his next move. He untied Clare. "Get up, move over here." The Fox pushed her towards Nigel.

"Put your hands in his pants," ordered The Fox.

"But – but I can't." Clare sobbed.

"You can and you will." The Fox demanded. He was losing his temper.

"I can't, he's my, he's, my brother." sobbed Clare.

"Well just pretend he isn't then." The Fox snapped back. And without a moment's hesitation he grabbed Clare's hand and forced her to grope Nigel.

The Fox wasn't done. His final act was to force Nigel to reciprocate the horror on his own sister. Nigel froze to the spot, paralysed with shock. Stewart vomited onto the carpet, while Clare squeezed her eyes shut and turned away. The Fox watched, grinning with twisted satisfaction.

Finally, The Fox decided he had inflicted enough pain. He stood up, rifled through the room, grabbing a stack of videotapes from a shelf. He cast a final, lingering glance at his victims before sliding out into the night, leaving behind a trail of utter devastation. All three victims would be traumatised for the rest of their lives.

As the news of the latest attack began to filter through, Detective Constable Tom Hughes burst into the operations room in Dunstable police station, his face flushed and tie askew. "Guv, we've got another one. Just came in over the wire."

Detective Chief Superintendent Mark Talbot turned sharply, his eyes meeting Hughes's with a sharp, focused intensity. "Where?"

"Little village called Markyate," Hughes said, his voice taut with urgency. "About four miles out. Same MO - masked intruder, shotgun, no prints. Tied up a brother, a sister, her boyfriend, and sexually assaulted all three of them. Multiple times."

"Markyate?" Talbot snapped, his gaze fixing on the map on the wall. He located the village and marked it with a fresh pin. "Damn it. So much for our pattern."

"He's moving around," Carter interjected, her voice edged with anxiety. "He's impossible to trace."

Talbot's eyes located the new pin, the web of strings on the map converging toward a point he couldn't yet identify. "What's he doing, Elaine?" he murmured. "What's he after?"

"Control," she replied without hesitation. "He wants to control us, the towns, the villages, our thoughts. He's playing a game, and right now, we're just chasing our tails."

"Then we need to change the game," Talbot said, his voice hardening with resolve. He turned to Hughes. "Get more boots on the ground in these target areas. I want every road covered, every back alley watched. Get more plainclothes officers mingling with the locals. If he's working to some kind of twisted schedule, we need to be ready."

"Right away, Guv," Hughes nodded, already moving toward the door.

Carter stepped closer to Talbot, her voice dropping to a whisper. "Guv, we're running the team ragged. And The Fox…he's not just ahead of us; he's taunting us."

"I know," Talbot said, his face set in grim determination. "But there must be a pattern here, and if we find it, we find him."

She gave him a wary look. "And what if he's baiting us? Drawing us in like all the others?"

"Then we take the bait," Talbot replied. "But we'll be ready."

By midnight, every town and village within the reach of The Fox's terror was crawling with undercover officers. Cars were discreetly parked on the outskirts, and officers on foot patrolled the streets, their eyes scanning every alleyway, every potential hiding place.

Talbot arrived at the small bungalow, the scene of the latest crime, where three shaken occupants were being questioned. He moved quickly, asking for any details or descriptions they could provide.

Stewart, pointed to a floor lamp that had been knocked over. "He stood on this to rip out the electrical cord," Stewart explained.

Talbot examined the lamp before ordering forensics to analyse it for prints or any other trace evidence.

Nigel offered a description: "He was about five feet nine inches tall, wearing a blue and white stripey jumper, beige shoes, brown hair. He had a mask on, but I noticed he was left-handed - his wristwatch was on his right wrist."

Talbot nodded thoughtfully, thanking them for their help. He then instructed the forensic team to prioritise the analysis of the lamp, and the items used to tie the victims up.

On his way home, Talbot listened to his police radio crackling with intermittent updates, each silence stretching the nerves taut. "Any sign?" he barked into the radio.

"Nothing yet, Guv," came the reply from one of the units.

Talbot's grip tightened on the radio. He could almost sense The Fox lurking out there, hiding from them. The thought gnawed at him, an almost tangible presence that left him restless.

"Come on, you bastard," Talbot muttered under his breath, his eyes fixed on the road ahead. "Let's see how clever you really are."

The next day, the results came back from the Forensics team - confirming the footprint on the lamp was consistent with those found at other crime scenes, further linking the crime to The Fox.

Chapter 16

The late afternoon sun stretched across the quiet streets of Buckinghamshire, bathing the quaint homes in a golden hue. The village of Haddenham, known for its picturesque charm and serene atmosphere, seemed to be slumbering under the gentle warmth of the sunshine. Little did anyone know, a malevolent force was threading its way into their midst, drawn to the serenity like a hunter homing in on their target.

The Fox, dressed casually, moved silently through the leafy streets. His wiry figure slipping between the houses with an almost supernatural grace. He was methodical, his eyes constantly darting, scanning for the perfect opportunity to strike. Today, he had chosen a modest bungalow on Thistledown Road - a place that, from his observations, seemed to offer the perfect mix of vulnerability and isolation.

Emma Harcourt, the woman who lived there, had left her home an hour earlier, heading to the local shops for what was supposed to be a routine outing. Unbeknownst to her, her seemingly mundane errands were playing into The Fox's meticulously orchestrated plan. He had watched her leave her home from his vantage point in the Chiltern Hills. He knew she would be several hours, and he had time on his hands.

The Fox approached the bungalow, a nondescript building set back from the road behind a neat row of hedges. He crouched beside the back door, inspecting it with the keen eye of an expert. The lock was old and rusted, barely a challenge for someone with his skills. With a few deft movements, he popped it open and entered, leaving no trace of his entry.

Inside, the bungalow was calm, bathed in the soft afternoon light filtering through the lace curtains. It was an invitingly ordinary space - warm and homely. The Fox's eyes scanned the rooms, taking in the layout with care. The living room was decorated with cheerful floral prints, and family photos lined the mantelpiece. The master bedroom was neat and tidy, the smell of fresh flowers filled the air.

The Fox knew exactly what he wanted. He had a plan - one that required both patience and precision. He set to work, stripping the light bulbs from their sockets and locating belts from a cupboard. He located the phone lines and severed them, cutting off any chance of a call for help.

Next, he searched for materials to build his den - a place of concealment and control. The spare bedroom, filled with old furniture and dusty boxes, would serve his purpose well. He dragged an old wardrobe into the centre of the room, using it as a makeshift barrier. He then arranged the remaining furniture around it, creating a dark, claustrophobic nook where he could wait in silence.

The bungalow began to feel less like a home and more like a horror movie set for his grim performance.

Satisfied with his work, The Fox took a moment to ensure everything was in place. He stocked up on food and drink from the fridge and then positioned himself in the den, hidden from view, and waited.

Emma's day was turning out to be longer than expected. The shopping had taken more time, and she had bumped into an old school friend who offered to buy her a coffee. As she finally loaded her bags into the boot of her car several hours later than she had intended, she felt a sense of relief. But little did she know, her sanctuary had been violated, and a nightmare was unfolding within her own walls.

When she finally arrived home, the sun was dipping low on the horizon, casting an eerie twilight across the neighbourhood. Emma's footsteps were light as she approached her front door, her mind still preoccupied with mundane thoughts of groceries and dinner. As she unlocked the door and stepped inside, she felt an unsettling chill in the air. The usual hum of domesticity was conspicuously absent.

"Hello?" she called out, her voice echoing in the silence. The bungalow greeted her with a foreboding stillness. She stepped into the living room, the soft glow of twilight creeping through the lace curtains. "Hello? Is someone there?"

There was no response.

Emma's heart began to race, an instinctual alarm flaring up as she moved cautiously through the bungalow. The absence of light in the hallway was unnerving. She flicked the light switch. Nothing happened. A sense of dread washed over her as she reached the master bedroom. The door was slightly ajar, and she pushed it open with trembling fingers. The room was dark, the only light coming from the dying remnants of the day. Her eyes scanned the space, trying to make sense of everything.

She turned around, pushed open the door to the spare bedroom, and that's when she saw it – the wardrobe, its position unnatural. Emma hesitated, her mind racing with the possibility of an intruder. She turned on her heels and grabbed the phone, only to realise it was dead.

Panic surged through her as she fumbled around in the dark, her hands shaking uncontrollably. She turned to run, her instincts screaming at her to escape. But before she could make it to the front door, a noise from the hallway froze her in place - a deliberate, measured step.

The Fox emerged from out of nowhere, his balaclava concealing his face, his eyes cold and unfeeling. He was brandishing a shotgun, its metal gleaming ominously in the dim light.

"Emma Harcourt," he said, his voice muffled but menacing. "I've been waiting for you."

Emma's blood ran cold. She raised a hand instinctively, her voice trembling as she spoke. "Please...please, just take what you want and leave."

The Fox's eyes were emotionless as he took a step closer, the shotgun's barrel pointed directly at her. "It's not about what I want," he said calmly. "It's about what I'm going to do."

Emma's breath quickened, each inhale coming in short, panicked bursts. The room seemed to close in around her, the walls pressing in as she stumbled backward. The Fox moved with deliberate steps, his presence an overwhelming force.

"On the floor," he commanded, his voice cold and authoritative. "Face down."

Tears streamed down Emma's face as she sank to her knees, her body trembling wildly. She could barely see through the stream of tears as she complied, her heart pounding so loudly it felt like it might burst from her chest. The Fox moved swiftly, his movements exact as he grabbed belts from his pocket and bound her hands and feet.

Emma's mind was racing, trying to come up with a plan, a way to escape. But every attempt to think clearly was overshadowed by the overwhelming terror she felt and the reality of her situation. The sound of a car passing by her bungalow reached her, somebody inside could help her, but there was nothing she could do. She was utterly helpless.

The Fox didn't waste time. He dragged her toward the spare bedroom, his grip unyielding. The room had become a chamber of horror. Emma could barely make out the makeshift den within.

As The Fox positioned her in the centre of the room, he took a moment to savour the control he wielded. Emma's pleas fell on deaf ears, her sobs barely audible over the oppressive silence. The Fox's eyes were cold, his face obscured by the balaclava, but his presence was overwhelming. He moved with a calculated cruelty, placing her on the bed and securing her to the headboard with rough, tight knots.

Emma's terror was evident as she felt the pressure of the restraints cutting into her skin. The fear of what was to come was almost unbearable. She could hear his footsteps retreating, leaving her alone with her dread.

Moments stretched into eternity as she lay bound on the bed, the silence broken only by her ragged breaths. She could hear the faintest sounds - the creak of floorboards, the rustling of fabric. Each noise heightened her anxiety, a cruel reminder that The Fox was still in control.

The Fox returned, his footsteps purposeful and slow. He was carrying an assortment of items - a glass of water, a flashlight, and a few other objects that he set down with deliberate care. Emma's heart pounded as she heard the distinct click of the flashlight being turned on, the beam slicing through the darkness and illuminating The Fox's mask.

His eyes met hers, cold and impassive. "You see, Emma," he said, his voice smooth and devoid of empathy, "this is just the beginning."

Emma's pleas became more frantic as she struggled against her restraints, her body shaking uncontrollably. The Fox's calm demeanour contrasted starkly with her escalating terror. He methodically prepared himself, his actions precise and deliberate, a stark contrast to the chaos unfolding in Emma's mind.

The Fox took his time, savouring the fear he had instilled. He seemed to relish in the control he held, a sadistic pleasure evident in the way he moved. Emma's sobs filled the room, a haunting accompaniment to the tense silence.

As The Fox approached, Emma's pleas became more desperate. "Please...please, just let me go..."

The Fox's response was cold and unyielding. "You're not in a position to make demands," he said. And with that, he ripped at her clothes until she was naked from the waist down. An evil smile formed under his mask. He was in control, not her.

The onslaught that followed was cruel and cold blooded. The Fox showed no mercy. His actions a chilling display of dominance. Emma's screams were muffled, her body wracked with violent shudders as she endured the violation. The Fox's presence was a dark, unrelenting force, leaving her broken and shattered.

When the ordeal was finally over, The Fox stood over her, breathing heavily. He stood up, pulled his clothes up around his waist, and with a final, cold look at Emma, he turned and casually walked out the room and the bungalow.

The Fox had left his mark once again, another life had been ruined.

Chapter 17

It was a warm, quiet evening in Edlesborough. The small village nestled within the rolling hills of Buckinghamshire had seen very little crime over the years, its peaceful streets lined with modest homes and well-kept gardens. But on this night, an unseen destroyer stalked the streets, planning his next move. The Fox - Britain's most notorious and elusive criminal - had already left a trail of panic and turmoil in his wake. And now, he had his eyes set on number forty Meadow Lane.

The house stood at the end of a quiet cul-de-sac; its occupants blissfully unaware of the threat creeping ever closer. Inside, a couple slept soundly in their bedroom upstairs, tired from the day's activities and the seasonably warm night. Downstairs, The Fox broke in via the back door thanks to his trusty screwdriver making light work of the lock. Once inside, he moved carefully, trying his best not to disturb the peacefulness of the home as he searched for anything of value.

He rifled through drawers in the living room and kitchen. His hands moved with the confidence of someone who had done this countless times before, pulling out papers and small items without making a sound. After several minutes of searching, he found some cash tucked away in an envelope inside a drawer in the living room.

He picked up the envelope, his heart racing with the thrill of the theft. But as he bent down to retrieve his shotgun, which he had placed against a side table for easy access, disaster struck. The gun slipped from its precarious position and crashed to the floor with a loud, metallic thud.

The noise shattered the stillness of the house.

Upstairs, the muffled sound of voices reached his ears. The Fox froze, every muscle in his body tensing as he listened. The couple had been woken by the noise, and it didn't take long for them to realise that something wasn't right. Panicked, they reached for the phone and called the police.

The Fox cursed under his breath. He had been too careless, too rushed. But it wasn't in his nature to panic. He grabbed the cash, hoisted the shotgun over his shoulder, and headed for the back door. Years of practice had taught him that the key to escaping was speed and precision. Within seconds, he was out of the house and into the warm night air, disappearing across back gardens before anyone could see him.

He knew the police would arrive soon, but he also knew the area well. He had scouted it for weeks, noting every pathway, every alley, and every possible hiding spot. The police must have been in the area as he could hear sirens fast approaching. He needed a place to lie low, just for a few hours, until the heat died down.

The police, led by Detective Chief Superintendent Mark Talbot, arrived at Meadow Lane within minutes of the call. Sirens blared as officers poured out of their cars and surrounded the area. The couple, Marco and Sasha Hazell, still shaken, met them at the door and explained what had happened: a loud noise downstairs, followed by the discovery that drawers had been rifled through and some cash was missing.

Officers immediately began to search the area. The Fox had left signs of forced entry on the back door, his usual calling card, so they knew it was highly likely to be him. They swept the street, knocking on doors and questioning neighbours. One by one, the occupants of Meadow Lane opened their doors and provided what little information they had. Most had heard nothing; it was too late, and the night had been its usual calm self.

When the officers knocked on the door of number twenty-two, just a few houses down from the scene of the crime, there was no answer. They shone their torches through the windows, peering inside. The house looked empty - no lights, no movement, nothing to suggest anyone was home.

A quick conversation with one of the neighbours confirmed it: the family who lived at number twenty-two was on holiday. They had been gone for nearly a week, and no one expected them back for several more days.

Satisfied, the officers moved on, never suspecting that the man they were searching for was already inside.

The Fox watched from behind a sofa as the police officers swept past the house. His heart pounded in his chest, but he remained still, hidden in the darkness. The irony wasn't lost on him - the very people hunting him were just a few feet away, completely unaware that their quarry had already taken refuge inside the house they had dismissed as empty.

He had slipped into number twenty-two not long after fleeing from number forty. The house had been an easy target; he knew the occupants would be on holiday having fixed a back garden panel for them a week earlier. It provided the perfect place to lay low for a few hours. Once inside, he had quickly set to work creating a makeshift den in the living room, using blankets and cushions he found around the house. He draped one of the blankets over himself and the television to prevent any light from being seen outside.

The Fox knew he needed to be cautious. The police would be searching the area, and if they thought he was still nearby, they would lock down the village. But he had time. They wouldn't suspect that he had chosen to hide so close to the scene of the crime.

As he settled into his makeshift hideout, he began to rifle through the homeowners' belongings. In a cabinet by the television, he found a small collection of VHS tapes. One title caught his eye: *Gregory's Girl*, a British comedy about a teenager navigating the awkwardness of adolescence and love.

Smirking to himself, The Fox loaded the tape into the VCR player and pressed play. He had never seen the film before, and despite the absurdity of the situation - him, a wanted man, hiding from the police and watching a light-hearted comedy - he couldn't help but be drawn in. For a while, he forgot about the chase, the police, and the danger. He let himself disappear into the world of the film, the soft glow of the television illuminating his face as he sat beneath his blanket fort.

Outside, the police were growing increasingly frustrated. They had combed the neighbourhood, searched the surrounding streets, and even called in a helicopter to scan the area from above. But there was no sign of The Fox. It was as if he had vanished into thin air.

Detective Chief Superintendent Mark Talbot walked up and down the street, his face set in a bleak expression. The Fox had slipped through their fingers once again, and Talbot knew the media would be all over the story by morning. His superiors would want answers, and the public would be demanding to know how a single man could continue to evade capture so effectively.

"Anything?" Talbot asked one of the officers as he walked by. "Nothing, sir," the officer replied, shaking his head. "We've checked the area, knocked on all the doors. No one's seen or heard anything out of the ordinary."

Talbot cursed under his breath. "What about number twenty-two? I heard the families on holiday."

"We checked sir. Looks empty. No signs of anyone inside."

"Double-check," Talbot ordered. "I don't want any mistakes. If he's holed up in there, we need to know."

The officers did as they were told, shining their torches through the windows once again. But the house remained dark and silent, just as it had before. Talbot, now pacing the street, glanced up at the helicopter circling overhead. They were running out of options. The Fox was out there, somewhere, but the more time passed, the colder the trail would grow.

Inside number twenty-two, The Fox waited. He had turned off the television and now sat in the dark, listening to the faint buzzing of the helicopter above. It wouldn't be long before they gave up the search, he knew. They couldn't stay out there all night, and eventually, they would move on.

He glanced at his watch. It was nearly midnight. The village would soon fall back into its usual quiet tempo, and when it did, he would make his escape. He had no intention of staying in Edlesborough any longer than necessary. The cash he had taken from number forty was stuffed into his pocket, and his shotgun was slung over his shoulder. All he needed was an opportunity.

Another hour passed, before the helicopter eventually moved on, and the number of police officers in the area began to dwindle. The Fox, ever patient, waited until he was sure the coast was clear. When he finally moved, it was with the same precision and caution that had kept him one step ahead of the law for so long.

He slipped out the back door of number twenty-two, moving like a stray cat through the garden and over the back fence. The village was quiet now, with only the occasional distant sound of a car passing on the main road. He knew the area well, and within minutes, he had disappeared into the surrounding countryside, vanishing once again.

The next morning, the residents of Edlesborough awoke to the news that The Fox had struck again. Meadow Lane had been cordoned off, and police officers were once again combing the area for any clues that might lead them to the elusive criminal. But there was nothing. No prints, no witnesses, no sign of where he had gone.

Detective Chief Superintendent Mark Talbot stood outside number forty, his frustration evident in the look on his face. He had underestimated The Fox, and now the village was on edge, knowing that the man responsible for a string of burglaries and violent attacks had been right under their noses.

As Talbot made his way back to his car, he couldn't help but glance toward number twenty-two. It was still quiet, still empty, but something about it gnawed at him. He shook his head, trying to dismiss the thought. They had checked it twice, after all.

But little did Talbot know, The Fox had been there all along, hiding in plain sight.

Chapter 18

"Nine-nine-nine, what's your emergency."

"Yes, hello, police. I think I just saw The Fox," the man said, his voice urgent and breathless.

"Sir, can you provide your exact location and explain why you believe it was The Fox?" the operator asked, her tone steady and precise.

"He was wearing a balaclava, dressed head-to-toe in black, and moving quickly across the fields toward the woods in Little Gaddesden," the man replied, panic edging his words.

"Understood, sir. A police unit is being dispatched immediately." The woods in Little Gaddesden were a labyrinth of shadows and whispers. As twilight surrendered to the darkness of the late summer evening, Detective Chief Superintendent Mark Talbot led his team through the dense underbrush, the eerie quiet punctuated only by the occasional snap of a twig underfoot. The sky was filled with the earthy scent of damp soil and decaying leaves, a lingering reminder of recent rain.

The team were responding to yet another sighting. This time, they had picked up a trail.

"Stay sharp," Talbot commanded, his voice cutting through the oppressive silence of the woods. "The Fox might still be here, and he will know these woods better than we do. He's turned this into his own private hunting ground."

Detective Inspector Elaine Carter, her face illuminated by the beam of her flashlight, checked her watch. "It's nearly eleven p.m.," she said, sweat trickling down the sides of her face. "He's had time to set up traps or hideouts. This could turn into a wild goose chase if we're not careful."

Detective Sergeant Jake Miller, his face streaked with grime and sweat, glanced up from a map laid out on a makeshift table. "According to this, there's an old hunting cabin around here. It's not far from where we picked up his trail. It's worth checking out."

Talbot's eyes narrowed as he considered the suggestion. "Agreed. If he's trying to stay hidden, that cabin could be his base of operations. Let's move."

The team pressed deeper into the woods, their boots squelching in the muddy undergrowth. The canopy overhead was a dense tapestry of leaves, allowing only slivers of moonlight to seep through, casting an eerie glow on the floor. Every rustle of leaves, every snap of a twig seemed magnified in the stillness, heightening the sense of unease that clung to the night.

"Keep your eyes peeled," Talbot instructed. "And be mindful of the terrain. It's rough, and The Fox is counting on that."

As they traversed through the tangled thicket, Carter's flashlight beam fell upon an old, gnarled tree, its bark twisted and cracked. "Guv, look at this," she said, her voice low. "Fresh footprints. They're not ours."

Talbot crouched beside the muddy prints, his heart quickening. The footprints were distinct - shoes with a tread pattern that suggested someone wearing outdoor boots. "He's close," Talbot said, his voice excited. "Let's keep moving."

The warmth in the air intensified as they approached the suspected location of the cabin. Miller, his breath increasing with every step, scanned the area. "Nothing visible yet," he reported, peering into the distance. "But the cabin isn't far. If he's still inside, he's not trying to stay low."

Talbot signalled the team to spread out, their movements calculated and deliberate. The sense of anticipation was unmistakable, each officer focused and prepared for what might lie ahead. "Let's surround the cabin. Remember, he'll be prepared for us. Watch your step and be ready for anything."

The cabin emerged from the darkness like a forgotten relic of the past, its weathered wooden walls and broken windows blending seamlessly with the surrounding forest. Carter and Miller approached the door, their weapons drawn, each step cautious and measured. Talbot covered their backs, his eyes scanning the perimeter for any sign of movement.

Carter nudged the door open, the hinges clanking loudly in the stillness. The room beyond was dim, illuminated only by the flickering glow of a small fire in the hearth. The shadows danced across the walls, casting an eerie light that made the room feel more like a stage set for a sinister play.

A figure stood facing the fire, momentarily illuminated by the flames. The man's silhouette was unmistakable, a stark contrast to the darkness that enveloped the room.

"Freeze!" Talbot's command sliced through the silence.

The man, clad in dark clothing and a hooded coat, turned slowly, his face obscured by his balaclava. "Don't shoot," he said, his voice trembling with nervousness.

Talbot's heart pounded in his chest. This was not the moment they had hoped for. "Come out where we can see you," he ordered, his voice taut with urgency. "It's over for you Mr Fox."

The man stepped forward into the light, his ungloved hands raised in a gesture of surrender. Talbot's heart sank as he took in the man's features. He was mixed race, a stark contrast to The Fox's known description of having pale white skin. Disappointment and frustration surged through Talbot.

"Guns down everybody, it's not him," sighed a disappointed Talbot.

"What are you doing out here by yourself?" Talbot barked, trying to keep his voice steady despite the letdown.

The man slid off his balaclava, his gaze wary. "I'm in the military, sir. I'm on leave and like camping out at night. I didn't think I was doing anything wrong, sir."

Talbot's expression softened slightly, but the nervousness remained. "Well, be careful. There's a serial criminal in the area. He doesn't care who he attacks."

The man nodded, his eyes wide with concern. "I'll head back to town. I didn't mean to cause any trouble."

As the man gathered his belongings and left the cabin, Talbot and his team exchanged irritated glances.

"Let's keep searching, just in case," barked Talbot. "Don't let this deter us."

The search continued late into the early hours of the next morning, each moment stretching longer as they navigated the wood's maze. The sense of urgency was intense, with every crackling branch and rustling leaf seeming to hold secrets, and every dark corner potentially concealing The Fox.

But The Fox was nowhere nearby. It was another false alarm, unbeknown to Talbot and his team. The hours ticked by the team moved with grim determination; their every step fraught with strain.

"Spread out and search the perimeter," Talbot instructed, his voice firm. "If The Fox is still in the area, he'll be trying to cover his tracks."

The team fanned out, their flashlights cutting through the darkness as they combed the woods for any sign of The Fox. Talbot's mind raced with possibilities, each scenario more disheartening than the last. The sense of failure gnawed at him, a relentless threat that refused to be ignored.

As Talbot moved through the woods, he couldn't shake the feeling that they were being toyed with. The Fox had always been elusive, his actions calculated and precise. The false lead, the discarded footprints - it was all part of a twisted game.

"This isn't just about evading capture," Talbot muttered to himself. "He's enjoying this. He's playing us."

Carter, looking determined, moved alongside Talbot. "Guv, we need to rethink our strategy. He's outsmarted us again."

Talbot nodded, his mind racing as he considered their options. "We need to get ahead of him. If he's moving from place to place, we need to predict his next move. He's leaving a trail, even if it's not immediately visible."

At dawn, the first light of morning began to filter through the trees, casting a pale glow over the ground. Talbot and his team gathered at the base of a large oak tree, their faces drawn and tired. The search had yielded no results, and the weight of their failure hung heavy.

"We've got to regroup," Talbot said, his voice hoarse from hours of shouting over the radio. "We need to reassess our strategy and figure out our next move."

Carter nodded, her face etched with worry. "We need to re-analyse his patterns, find out where he's likely to strike next."

Talbot gathered his team, "Go home, get some rest, and come back re-energised. Thanks for your hard work tonight, I know it's not easy chasing dead ends."

As the team collected their gear and prepared to leave the woods, Talbot's thoughts were consumed by the realisation that The Fox was always one step ahead. The hunt was far from over, and he was no closer to capturing him.

Chapter 19

The scorching weather continued to rage over the 'Triangle of Terror' like a fever, oppressive and inescapable. Heat waves shimmered off the asphalt, baking the streets, but the real fire burning in the hearts of the people was a different kind - fear, raw and unrelenting. The Fox had seen to that. His reign of terror had held a long stranglehold over the area, turning the ordinary lives of residents into a waking nightmare.

Detective Chief Superintendent Mark Talbot felt the weight of it everywhere he went. It was in the faces of the people on the street, their eyes darting suspiciously from one person to the next. It was in the hushed tones of conversations overheard at the corner shops, in the way children were pulled closer by anxious parents, their steps quickening as they passed darkened alleys.

Talbot stood outside a small, nondescript hardware store in Leighton Buzzard, watching as an elderly woman exited with a new set of locks clutched tightly to her chest. She glanced around nervously, her hands trembling, before hurrying away. Inside the shop, a line of customers waited, every single one of them there to buy some form of protection - locks, bolts, chains. Anything to keep The Fox at bay.

"Extra deadbolts, door chains, window bars," muttered Talbot under his breath, shaking his head. "People turning their homes into prisons."

Beside him, Detective Sergeant Sarah Kendrick took a long drag from her cigarette, blowing the smoke out into the hot, sticky air. "Can you blame them? They're terrified, Guv. And it's not just locks they're buying." She nodded toward a gun shop further down the street, where a small crowd had gathered. The owner, a heavyset man with a grim face, was talking to a customer, gesturing to a rack of shotguns behind him.

"Gun sales are up three hundred percent," Kendrick continued. "People who've never even held a gun before are stocking up like it's the apocalypse. And those who can't get their hands on a firearm? They're keeping kitchen knives under their pillows. Some are even making their own weapons."

Talbot rubbed his eyes, feeling the fatigue seeping into his bones. "It's a tinderbox," he muttered. "One spark and this whole place could go up in flames."

They'd already had several close calls - frightened residents firing shots at anything that moved, mistaking stray cats for intruders. One man had nearly put a bullet through his own son, coming home late after a night out. And then there were the vigilantes - groups of people, some armed, patrolling the streets after dark, ready to take the law into their own hands.

"They're scared, Guv," Kendrick said quietly. "And scared people do stupid things."

Talbot nodded, "That's what I'm afraid of."

They had tried to calm the rising panic, holding press conferences, distributing flyers, warning people to stay vigilant but not to take matters into their own hands. But the fear was too deep-rooted now, and every new victim The Fox left behind only fed the flames.

The sun was setting as the officers arrived at the local community centre, where a meeting had been called for residents. The hall was packed, a sea of anxious faces. Talbot could feel it, a live wire humming just beneath the surface. As he made his way to the front, he could hear snippets of conversation, voices raised in anger and fear.

"We can't just sit around waiting for the police to do something!"

"How do we even know if we can trust them?"

"They keep telling us to lock our doors, but what good is that when he breaks in easily?"

Talbot took a deep breath, stepping up to the makeshift podium. The chatter died down, all eyes turning toward him. He could see the distrust in their faces, the frustration. They wanted answers, and they wanted them now.

"Ladies and gentlemen," he began, his voice steady but firm, "I understand your fear. I understand your anger. We're doing everything we can to catch this man, but we need your help. Stay vigilant, yes, but don't take the law into your own hands. We're dealing with a dangerous individual here."

A man in the crowd stood up, his face flushed with fury. "And what happens when he comes for one of us, eh? Are we supposed to just sit around and wait for you lot to show up after he's already done his work?"

Murmurs of agreement rippled through the crowd. Talbot could feel the heat rising, along with his blood pressure.

"I understand your frustration, sir," Talbot said, trying to keep his voice calm. "But going out there with guns and knives, forming vigilante groups - that's not the answer. You could get yourselves hurt, or worse."

"Or we could stop him!" the man shot back. "I've got two kids at home. I'm not going to sit around and let some psycho come for them. If the police won't protect us, we'll protect ourselves."

Talbot's eyes swept over the crowd. There were others nodding, muttering in agreement. He knew he was losing them, the fear too deep to reason with. "We're doing everything we can."

"Not enough!" someone else shouted. "We're the ones living in fear every damn day!"

Kendrick stepped up beside him, her voice sharper, more commanding. "We understand that, believe me. But the best thing you can do right now is follow our advice. Lock your doors, yes, but also report anything suspicious. Don't engage. Let us handle it."

A woman's voice cut through the clamour, trembling with emotion. "Handle it? Like you handled it with Emma Harcourt? She was found bound, gagged, beaten and raped in her own bloody home!"

That one stung. Talbot felt the sting of it deep in his chest. Emma Harcourt was another victim of The Fox. And they had nothing - no solid leads, no standout suspects, just an area gripped by fear and a violent criminal who seemed to vanish into thin air after every attack.

"We're close," Talbot insisted, but the words felt hollow, even to him. "We've got leads, we're following up every line of enquiry. It just takes time."

"You're not close enough," the man spat. "And until you are, we're going to do what we have to do."

Talbot knew when he was beaten. The resentment - it was too much. He looked at Kendrick, who gave him a slight nod, her face grim. They were fighting a war on two fronts now - against The Fox, and against the fear he'd unleashed.

"Just be careful," Talbot said finally, his voice tired, almost pleading. "We don't need more blood on the streets."

Back at the station, the atmosphere was no less tense. Officers moved with a hurried purpose, phones ringing off the hook, radios crackling with constant updates. The fear wasn't just out there - it had seeped into the station itself.

Talbot slumped into his chair, rubbing his face with his hands. He hadn't properly slept in days, his mind a tangle of dead ends and false leads. Every time they thought they were close, The Fox slipped away, leaving another victim in his wake.

Kendrick dropped a file onto his desk, snapping him out of his thoughts. "You need to see this."

He opened the file, his eyes narrowing as he scanned the contents. "What am I looking at?"

"A report from one of the vigilante groups," Kendrick explained. "They've been using codewords to identify each other - so they know if it's one of their own coming to the door or someone else."

"Codewords?" Talbot raised an eyebrow. "Like some sort of secret society?"

"Exactly," she replied. "They're getting organised, Guv. They're serious. And if they get their hands on him first…"

Talbot leaned back, the weight of it all pressing down on him like an oversized stone. "We're losing control, Sarah. We're supposed to be protecting these people, and now they're taking matters into their own hands."

"And can you blame them?" Kendrick shot back. "The Fox is still out there, and every day we don't catch him is another day people are living in fear."

Talbot looked at her, his eyes tired but resolute. "We have to find him, Sarah. Before they do. Because if they catch him first, this whole area is going to explode."

The night was hot and stifling, the kind that pressed down on you, making it hard to breathe. Talbot sat in his car, parked on a quiet secluded street, the engine off. He was waiting, watching, his eyes scanning the darkened houses. He had followed one of the main suspects, Anos Kempster, from his house in Leighton Buzzard to the Stewkley area.

He wasn't alone. Kendrick sat beside him, her eyes fixed on the same row of houses. "You think he'll strike here?" she asked, her voice barely a whisper.

Talbot nodded. "Metal Mickey alerted us to Anos. He's a serial burglar and spent five years inside for aggravated assault. He matches the description of The Fox too."

"Why's he in this area late at night?" Kendrick asked.

They waited in silence, the minutes stretching into hours, the tension thickening like a rope tightening around their throats. And then they saw it - a flicker of movement. A figure, moving low and fast, darting between houses.

"There," Kendrick hissed, pointing.

Talbot's heart pounded in his chest as he reached for his radio. "All units, we've got movement on Finchley Avenue, suspect may be on-site. Move in quietly, do not engage until we have confirmation."

Talbot and Kendrick slipped out of their car, moving swiftly and quietly. The figure was moving toward a house at the end of the street, an elderly lady lived there alone, she was the perfect target.

Talbot's eyes caught the glint of metal in the figure's hand. His pulse thundered in his ears, each breath shallow and quick. "Steady," he hissed to Kendrick. "We need to catch him in the act."

A shout shattered the tense silence - a man stormed out of his front door, a baseball bat raised high. "Oi! You there!"

The figure spun around, and in that instant, Talbot's gut tightened. Everything was about to go sideways. "Stop!" Talbot roared, surging forward.

The resident charged, bat brandished, as the figure bolted around the side of the house. Talbot and Kendrick were in hot pursuit, feet pounding against the ground.

"Stop, police!" Talbot commanded, but the resident was deaf to his warning, disappearing after the figure. Talbot reached the corner, breath ragged. "Round the back, now!" he shouted, adrenaline spiking.

They rounded the house to find the resident pressing the figure against the wall, the bat wedged against their throat.

"Drop it!" Kendrick yelled, her voice slicing through the chaos.

The bat clattered to the ground. Kendrick lunged forward, shoved past the resident, and locked her grip on the figure. She twisted his arm behind his back and slapped on the cuffs.

"Spread your legs. Don't move," Kendrick ordered.

"Careful, Sarah, he's got a knife," Talbot warned, whilst trying to catch his breath.

Kendrick's fingers moved delicately, patting down the suspect before dipping into his hoodie pockets. Out came a set of keys and a cheese grater.

"What the?" Kendrick's brow furrowed. "Where's the knife?"

The suspect, barely more than a boy, stammered, "What knife?"

Kendrick's eyes widened as she pulled back the hood, revealing a teenage face, no older than sixteen.

"My nan lives here. She called my mum and said she needed a cheese grater. I was just bringing it over," he said, voice trembling.

"Christ," Kendrick breathed. "Guv, it's not him."

Talbot's gaze fell, his stomach twisting into knots. Just a kid. Not The Fox. The taste of defeat was bitter on his tongue. Excitement morphed into fury as he realised the truth: they'd failed. Again.

Meanwhile Anos Kempster, a main suspect, was on the front doorstep three houses down, meeting up with a female companion he had become familiar with. Talbot and Kendrick past them on their way back to their car.

Talbot clocked Anos acting amicably. "Oh great, another dead-end," he blurted out. "This is getting worse."

Chapter 20

The next morning, Detective Chief Sergeant Mark Talbot sat at his kitchen table, staring into the black void of his coffee. It was early, too early, and the world outside was shrouded in the dim, grey light of a dreary morning. He'd been awake since four a.m., tossing and turning, his mind running through the endless details of a case that had come to dominate his life. The Fox - the elusive, cunning serial burglar and rapist had been terrorising the local towns and villages for weeks, slipping through the fingers of law enforcement like water. Every step forward was followed by two steps back, and the pressure to catch him weighed on Talbot like a lead cloak.

It didn't help that his superiors at headquarters were breathing down his neck. The media had latched onto The Fox case with fervour, and Talbot, the man in charge, was their favourite scapegoat. Every failure was his failure, every delay his incompetence, at least in the eyes of the public and his bosses. The stress was unrelenting, and even the little things, the simple routines of life, seemed to slip out of his control.

He glanced at the clock. Six thirty a.m. He poured himself a fresh coffee. The milk should be on the doorstep by now.

Talbot got up slowly, his body stiff from sleeplessness, stress and chasing teenagers down the road. He shuffled to the front door and opened it, expecting to see the usual glass bottle of fresh milk waiting for him. Instead, he found nothing but an empty milk bottle lying on its side, rolling gently in the morning breeze. Frowning, he bent down to pick it up, and it was then that he saw it - a small slip of paper tucked inside the bottle.

Pulling out the note, Talbot squinted at the hastily scrawled message:

"YOU'VE BEEN MILKED BY THE MILK BANDITS!"

For a moment, he simply stared at the note, unable to process it. He read it again, slower this time, but the words didn't change. "Milked" by the Milk Bandits? Was this some kind of sick joke? Or was it The Fox leaving him a message? His hand tightened around the bottle, and a surge of anger swelled in his chest.

Talbot closed the door behind him with more force than he intended, the slam reverberating through the house. As he walked back into the kitchen, his mind raced. He could feel the frustration building in him, the way it had been building for weeks. This wasn't just about the milk. This was about everything - his job, the pressure, the sleepless nights, the feeling that he was losing control.

He sat back down, the note crumpled in his fist. The absurdity of it only made him angrier. Detective Chief Sergeant Mark Talbot, head of a major police investigation, reduced to dealing with a milk thief.

His coffee had gone cold. He couldn't drink it anyway.

By lunchtime, Talbot had regained some measure of composure, though the incident still simmered beneath the surface of his thoughts. He'd decided not to mention it to his colleagues at the station. The last thing he needed was for his team to see him rattled by something as trivial as stolen milk. Besides, he had bigger problems to worry about - like finding The Fox before the man struck again.

But word travelled fast in a small town.

By two p.m., Claire Milford, the local journalist who worked for the Leighton Buzzard Observer, had somehow heard about the incident. Claire was relentless when she sensed a story, and Talbot knew that if she was on the case, it would be plastered all over the front page of the local paper by morning.

Sure enough, just as Talbot was wrapping up a meeting with his team, his phone rang. It was Claire.

"DCS Talbot, I've heard some rather...curious news," she began, her voice laced with barely contained amusement. "Something about a milk theft at your house this morning?"

Talbot closed his eyes, a wave of irritation passing through him. He should have known the town's grapevine would get hold of this. He hadn't planned on giving it any attention, but with Claire sniffing around, he knew he couldn't avoid it.

"Claire," he said, his voice clipped. "This isn't a story. It's a childish prank. There are far more important things going on right now."

"Oh, I'm sure there are," she replied, "but the public loves a good laugh, and right now, the town could use something to take their minds off The Fox. Don't you agree?"

Talbot could hear the smile in her voice. She wasn't going to let this go. He rubbed his temple, feeling a headache coming on. Fine. He'd give her what she wanted - just enough to get her off his back.

"Alright," he sighed. "Yes, someone stole my milk this morning. Left a stupid note about being 'milked by the Milk Bandits.' But that's it, Claire. There's no story here."

"Well, it sounds like the local kids are getting creative," Claire said lightly. "Mind if I pop by for a quick interview? I promise I won't take up much of your time."

Talbot could hardly refuse without it looking like he had something to hide, so he reluctantly agreed. Thirty minutes later, Claire Milford was sitting in his office, her notepad ready and a sly smile playing on her lips.

"So, DCS Talbot," she began, "how did it feel to wake up this morning and find yourself the victim of the notorious 'Milk Bandits?'"

Talbot stared at her, unamused. "I don't find this funny, Claire. Someone trespassed on my property, stole from me, and left behind a note mocking me. It's not exactly the highlight of my day."

Claire raised an eyebrow. "You don't think it was just a harmless prank?"

"A prank, sure," Talbot said, his frustration barely contained. "But it's also a reminder of how little respect some people have for the law. If they think stealing and taunting is funny, they're part of the problem."

He leaned forward, fixing her with a sharp look. "Let me be clear, Claire. This kind of behaviour might seem small to you, but it represents a larger issue. If people can't respect the basics - other people's property, their privacy - then it's no wonder we have criminals like The Fox out there."

Claire scribbled in her notepad, nodding along but clearly relishing the drama of it all. "So, you're taking this seriously?"

"I'm a police officer, Claire. I take all crimes seriously," Talbot replied, his tone making it clear that the interview was over.

Claire stood, gathering her things, her smile never faltering. "Thank you for your time, DCS Talbot. I'll let you get back to the real work of catching The Fox. But you know, I think the town will get a kick out of this story."

Talbot saw her out, his mood soured even further. This wasn't what he needed - a public spectacle over a stolen bottle of milk. He had a real case to focus on. The Fox was still out there, and Talbot was no closer to finding him than he had been weeks ago.

The next few days passed in a blur of meetings, paperwork, and dead-end leads. Talbot tried to put the Milk Bandits out of his mind, but every time he stopped by the corner shop to buy something, he saw bottles of milk and was reminded of the prank. Worse, the local newspaper had run Claire Milford's story on the front page, complete with a photo of an empty milk bottle. The headline read:

'MILKED BY THE MILK BANDITS: EVEN THE POLICE AREN'T SAFE!'

It was meant to be light-hearted, but to Talbot, it felt like another jab at his authority. He was supposed to be the one protecting the town, and now he was the punchline to a joke.

A week after the incident, despite Talbot not pursuing it, the case of the Milk Bandits took an unexpected turn.

Liam Knowles, a local teenager who worked part-time at the bakery in Tesco, had been overheard bragging to a friend about the prank. He was laughing about how he and his mates Adrian Petrie, Martin Lynes, and Max Macleod - had been out drinking that night and decided it would be hilarious to take some milk on their way home and leave the note. What they didn't know at the time was that they had chosen the home of the town's top police officer.

A shopper overheard the conversation and, recognising Talbot's name, immediately reported the boys to the police.

Within hours, Liam Knowles was sitting in Dunstable police station, pale-faced and sweating as he confessed to the crime. The prank had seemed funny at the time, but now that the police were involved, it didn't seem so funny anymore. He gave up the names of the others quickly, and soon Adrian, Martin, and Max were brought in for questioning as well.

Talbot was informed of the arrests, and though he was still angry about the situation, he took little satisfaction in it. The boys were young, foolish, and had been drinking. It wasn't a calculated crime, just a stupid prank that had spiralled out of control.

In the end, all four boys were issued cautions. They had learned their lesson, and Talbot didn't see the need to drag them through the court system for something so minor. Still, he made it clear that any further incidents would result in more severe consequences.

With the Milk Bandits dealt with, Talbot turned his attention back to the real issue at hand: The Fox. The elusive criminal had struck again, this time burgling a house in Wolverton.

Talbot knew that catching the Fox would require all his focus and energy. The media circus surrounding the Milk Bandits had been an unwelcome distraction, but now it was over. He could put that nonsense behind him and get back to the work that really mattered.

As he sat at his desk that evening, reviewing the latest reports on The Fox case, Talbot felt a renewed sense of purpose. The prank had rattled him, but it had also reminded him why he did this job. There were real criminals out there - dangerous ones - and it was his job to stop them.

The milk could wait. The Fox, on the other hand, would not slip through his fingers. Not again.

Talbot leaned back in his chair, the fatigue of the past few weeks catching up to him. The road ahead was long and uncertain, but he was ready for it. He had to be. Everybody was depending on him.

Chapter 21

The warm summer rain came down in a relentless sheet, blurring the edges of the town of Dunstable under a shroud of bleak grey. The streets were slick with it, the gutters overflowing, and the distant wail of a siren cut through the damp air like a hot knife through butter. Detective Chief Superintendent Mark Talbot stood by the large windows of his office, staring out at the town he'd sworn to protect. His eyes were heavy, dark circles etched beneath them, testament to the endless hours he'd spent chasing dead ends.

The Fox continued to prowl the underbelly of the area, striking without warning, leaving a trail of destruction in his wake. A cold-blooded criminal, calculating and precise, he took great delight in playing games with the police. The entire force was on edge, frayed nerves barely holding together under the mounting pressure.

"Three hundred calls an hour, sir," muttered Detective Sergeant Sarah Kendrick, leaning against the doorway of his office, her face as pale as the fluorescent light overhead. Her voice trembled just slightly, betraying the fear that was seeping into the bones of every officer on the case. "Every damn hour. It's like the world's gone mad."

Talbot turned to face her, his face a mask of exhaustion and resolve. "And every single one of them needs to be followed up, Sarah," he said, his voice a low, gravelly rumble. "Every lead, no matter how small or absurd. We can't afford to miss anything. And it all gets fed into Metal Mickey."

The office was bursting with the smell of stale coffee and the sour tang of sweat. Files and paperwork were piled high on every surface, overflowing from their folders, each one a different thread in the tangled web they were trying to unravel. Talbot rubbed his temples, feeling the pressure coiled tight in his neck and shoulders.

"We're hunting a master of deception," Kendrick muttered, shaking her head. "The bastard's always two steps ahead of us."

"A fox is clever, but he's still an animal," Talbot replied, his eyes narrowing. "Animals make mistakes. We just need to wait for him to slip up."

He moved back to his desk, a scarred thick oak thing that had seen better days and sat down heavily.

"Observation and protection of the public," he murmured, almost to himself, repeating the mantra that had become his lifeline. "Alongside the detective work. That's our job. We can't afford to lose focus."

Kendrick nodded, her face grim. She had been with him from the start, her sharp mind and unyielding determination making her one of his best. But even she was beginning to show signs of wear.

"Speaking of observation," she said, "we've got the surveillance teams doubling up on the red zones. More eyes, more ears. If he so much as breathes out of line, we'll know."

"Good," Talbot replied, though his voice lacked the confidence he wished he could muster. "And what about the profiler's report?"

Kendrick handed him a thick dossier. "Fresh off the press. According to Dr Hardwick, he's not just in it for the assaults. He's in it for the thrill of outsmarting us. He wants us to know he's observing, ready and waiting. It's a game to him."

"A game," Talbot repeated softly, flipping through the pages. His eyes skimmed over words like 'narcissistic tendencies' and 'compulsive behaviour', but his mind was elsewhere. "Every game has an end. And when we find him…"

The phone on his desk rang. Talbot snatched it up, his voice terse. "Talbot."

"Chief, it's Harris from Dispatch," came the hurried voice on the other end. "We've got another one. Same MO - north side of the triangle, house near an old railway bridge. Patrol's on-site, but it's not looking good."

Talbot's eyes met Kendrick's, and she could see the storm brewing behind them. "Get the car ready," he said, slamming the phone down. "Let's move."

The drive to the crime scene in Bushey was tense and silent, the only sound the rhythmic thud of the windshield wipers fighting against the relentless downpour. Talbot stared straight ahead, his mind racing. Next to him, Kendrick sat rigid, her fingers tapping a nervous rhythm against her thigh.

When they arrived, the area was already crawling with officers, the blue and red lights of the patrol cars casting a surreal glow over the scene. The old railway bridge loomed overhead, a rusting giant against the darkened sky. Yellow police tape flapped in the wind, cordoning off the area.

"Jesus," Kendrick muttered as they approached. Sprawled on an ambulance stretcher, a woman, her face pale, bruised, battered and pouring with blood.

"Same as the others," muttered Detective Sergeant Jake Miller, one of the first responders, his face drawn and white. "No witnesses, no prints, nothing."

Talbot crouched beside the woman, his eyes scanning every inch, every detail. He could feel the weight of the scene pressing down on him, the cold, creeping realisation that they were once again too late. "He's not perfect," he said quietly. "He's just good at hiding."

For a moment, there was silence, broken only by the distant rumble of thunder. Kendrick stood beside him, her arms crossed tightly over her chest. "How the hell does he keep doing this? Right under our noses."

"He's good at what he does," Talbot replied, his voice hardening. "And he wants us to know he's still out there. That we can't catch him."

Miller stepped forward, his voice tinged with frustration. "We're running ourselves ragged, Chief. People are terrified. If we don't get a break soon."

"We will," Talbot cut in sharply, his eyes never leaving the woman. "We don't stop until we do."

The forensic team moved in, their white suits ghostly in the rain. Talbot, his back aching from being overworked, turned to Kendrick. "Get back to the station. I want every detail of this cross-checked with the other scenes. There must be something, we're just not seeing it yet. And get the team to follow up on our top suspects. Where were they when it happened and where are they now. Check their alibis twice if you must."

Kendrick nodded, "Ok Guv. And what about you?"

"I'm staying," Talbot said. "I want to take another look around."

As she walked away, Talbot's gaze lingered on the gloominess beneath the bridge, the dark places where the light didn't reach. He could feel The Fox was relishing in yet another easy escape.

Hours passed, and the rain began to let up, tapering off into a light drizzle. Talbot stood beneath the bridge, his clothes soaked through, but he didn't care. His eyes were fixed on the distance, scanning the deserted streets and fields for any sign of movement.

He pulled out a cigarette, lighting it with shaking hands. The first drag filled his lungs with a rough, bitter warmth, and he closed his eyes for a moment, letting the smoke curl out into the night. "Where are you, you bastard?" he muttered under his breath.

Talbot's eyelids drooped, the weight of exhaustion pulling them down like lead. The rain hissed around him, relentless, drumming a rhythm that seeped into his bones. He swayed, catching himself with a jolt as a sudden, soft rustle split through the downpour. His eyes snapped open, darting to the edge of the light cast by his torch. There, near the field, a figure shifted, half-concealed in shadow.

"Who's there?" Talbot's voice cracked, then steadied, echoing with forced authority.

The figure stood motionless. Talbot's vision blurred, and he blinked rapidly, trying to refocus. The edges of the world shimmered, morphed. His pulse thundered as the silhouette twisted, reshaping until the head of a masked man sat unnaturally atop a fox's sleek body, eyes glittering with cunning.

"Back again, are you?" Talbot's voice trembled, addressing the impossible creature as though it was an old adversary. The masked fox tilted its head, a sneer playing at its lips. Its mouth moved as though speaking, but only silence came forth. Talbot's breath quickened, panic licking at his mind.

"Why now?" he demanded, taking an unsteady step forward, gun wavering. "I told you... I told you to stay away."

The fox-thing blinked slowly, the rest of its body perfectly still, statuesque. A sense of dread seeped into Talbot's chest. He rubbed his eyes, but the image remained, mockingly solid.

A sudden, guttural laugh - his own - escaped his lips, jarring him. The absurdity struck him like ice water. Talbot staggered back, eyes wide, and in that instant, the vision dissolved into the night.

He blinked, breath ragged, and found himself staring at a patch of empty grass, rain soaking into his collar. His torchlight caught the gentle leap of a baby deer bounding away into the distance.

He sagged, lowering his gun with a shuddering sigh. "Get a grip, Talbot, you're losing the plot," he muttered, shaking his head. His fingers flexed around the cold metal of the gun before he holstered it and turned away. His mind was playing tricks on him. He shook his head and called it a night.

Chapter 22

Phoenix Close in Leighton Buzzard was as quiet as ever, bathed in the soft glow of a fading summer sunset. The houses, neatly lined with their manicured lawns and potted plants, stood in peaceful silence. The only sounds breaking the calm were the distant drone of passing cars and the occasional bark of a dog. Yet, for all its suburban serenity, there was something unsettling in the air that evening. Something that would make Phoenix Close the centre of conversation for weeks to come.

At number eleven, Pat McBride sat in her upstairs bedroom, sipping on her usual cup of chamomile tea. The day had been uneventful, much like most days since she'd retired from her post at the local school. She had developed a routine of watching the world from her bedroom window in the evenings - observing the faint movements of her neighbours' lives as they went about their nightly rituals. It wasn't voyeurism, not in her mind at least; it was just a way to stay connected in a world that was rapidly becoming more isolated since her retirement.

Her view stretched across the street and into the back gardens of the homes that lined Phoenix Close. From her window, she could see almost everything, though not with any invasive detail - just enough to feel a sense of community. Tonight, her eyes wandered absentmindedly across the usual scene of closed curtains, dim porch lights, and the occasional glow from a television set.

But something was different tonight. A shadow, swift and deliberate, darted into her view.

Pat blinked and leaned closer to the window, pressing her forehead against the cool glass. At first, she thought it might be a stray cat or perhaps a fox, common visitors to the suburban gardens. But this shadow was too large, too quick, and much too deliberate. Her heart skipped a beat.

The figure moved stealthily along the pathway that ran along the back gardens of numerous homes. For a moment, it seemed to vanish behind a lamp post that stood on the edge of her neighbour's property at number thirteen. Diane Fletcher, a divorcee in her late twenties, lived with her two young sons, aged three and five. She was known for her immaculate gardens - filled with roses, hydrangeas, and a thriving strawberry patch.

Suddenly, the figure reappeared, clearer this time. It wasn't an animal at all. It was a man.

He was tall and lean, dressed in dark clothing that blended seamlessly into the dark of the evening. He appeared to be wearing a mask which obscured his face. He crouched low, as if trying to avoid being seen, and made his way along the fence. Then, with a swift and practiced movement, he vaulted over Diane's back fence, disappearing into her garden.

Pat's heart raced, her fingers trembling as she set her mug down on the bedside table. She hadn't seen anything like this before. Phoenix Close, wasn't the sort of place where crime happened. The most excitement they'd had in recent months was a lost dog that had wandered into a neighbour's shed. But this…this was different.

For a split second, Pat hesitated. Maybe she should alert Diane first. But what if he attacked her too. Without another thought, she reached for her phone and called the police.

"Emergency services, what's your emergency please?"

Pat's voice was shaky as she spoke. "I - I think there's a man in my neighbour's garden. He just jumped the fence. It's at number thirteen, Phoenix Close in Leighton Buzzard."

The operator's voice was calm, reassuring. "Stay on the line, ma'am, while I despatch a police unit. Can you describe the man for me?"

Pat glanced out of the window again, but the man was no longer in sight. Her eyes scanned the garden, but there was no sign of movement. "He was wearing dark clothes, a mask... I couldn't see his face. He jumped over the fence into my neighbour's garden, Diane is her name. I - I don't know where he is now."

The operator asked her to stay at home until the police arrived. Pat's eyes remained glued to the window, her mind racing. Who was this man? Was it The Fox? Was Mrs Fletcher home? She rarely went out in the evenings, but Pat hadn't seen her today. Had something already happened?

The minutes stretched on, each one feeling longer than the last. Pat could hear her own heartbeat in her ears, the tension mounting with every passing second. For her own safety, she decided to lock herself in her bathroom.

Then, as the sound of police sirens could be heard in the distance, the man reappeared in Mrs Fletcher's back garden. He moved quickly, leaping back over the fence with the same ease he'd entered. He paused for a brief moment, scanning the area as if checking to see if anyone had noticed him. Then, just as swiftly as he'd arrived, he disappeared into the darkness, slipping away into the nearby fields.

Moments later, the flashing blue lights of a police car illuminated Phoenix Close. Pat emerged from her bathroom and quickly moved to her front bedroom window. She watched as two officers emerged, quickly making their way to Mrs Fletcher's front door. One officer knocked while the other circled around to the back garden, where the man had been moments earlier. Pat could do nothing but watch, her heart pounding in her chest.

Inside number thirteen, Diane Fletcher, sat huddled with her two sons in her bedroom. The curtains were drawn, but the sound of a police helicopter now circling above, combined with the sight of flashing blue lights reflecting off the walls, made the situation impossible to ignore. Her boys, clung to her, eyes wide with fear. She had tried to keep them calm, telling them it was all a precaution, that everything was fine, but the truth was, she was just as terrified.

They had all heard the stories. The Fox had been terrorising the area for months, breaking into homes, and sometimes much worse. His methods were brutal, his evasion of the authorities a source of constant dread. Tonight, that terror felt closer than ever.

The loud knock on the front door jolted her out of her thoughts. She froze, her heart throbbing in her ribs. For a moment, all she could hear was the steady hum of the helicopter and the muffled sound of her own breathing. Her sons looked up at her, their small faces pale and expectant.

"Who is it, Mum?" the youngest boy asked, his voice trembling.

"I don't know," she whispered, trying to keep her own fear at bay. She stood up slowly, walking down the stairs toward the front door. The knock came again, more insistent this time. Her hand hovered over the door handle, unsure if she should open it.

Taking a deep breath, she moved to the living room, pulled back the edge of the curtain and peeked through the window. A police officer was stood on the front porch, their face illuminated by the harsh glow of the helicopter's searchlight.

Her anxiety eased momentarily. She opened the front door. The police officer held up a small sign, and though it was difficult to read in the glare, she could just make out the words: NOD IF YOU ARE BEING HELD CAPTIVE. BLINK IF YOU ARE OKAY.

Diane's heart leapt into her throat. It was a precaution she had heard of before, used in cases of home invasions or kidnappings, a silent way to ensure everything was safe inside without tipping off a potential intruder. She quickly blinked several times, then stepped back from the door, her breath coming in short, panicked gasps. The officer didn't move for a moment, but after receiving her signal, lowered the sign.

Diane sagged against the wall, relief and fear colliding inside her. She wasn't sure how much more of this she could take. Even though the police inspected her home and assured her she was safe, the presence of The Fox lurking so close was more than unsettling - it was suffocating.

Detective Chief Sergeant Mark Talbot had arrived on scene and was stood listening as officers relayed updates over their radios as they searched the area. Phoenix Close backed onto a series of fields, one that led to a brook running alongside two nearby schools. The dense trees made it an ideal escape route, a tangle of blind spots and cover that The Fox could easily navigate, especially in the dead of night. He had used this kind of terrain before - always vanishing into the undergrowth just as the police closed in.

The police presence remained substantial throughout the night. Officers canvassed the area, knocking on doors, asking questions, combing through back gardens with flashlights. But no results. The Fox had evaded capture once again.

By the next morning, Phoenix Close was buzzing with nervous energy. The Fox was still at large, but the residents had a new layer of fear to contend with. At every front door and garden gate, neighbours gathered, exchanging hurried words about the events of the previous night. Gossip spread like wildfire.

"I heard he was hiding in somebody's shed in Hydrus Drive," one man muttered as he stood by his gate, talking to his next-door neighbour.

"They had dogs out all night," the woman responded. "Nothing. Not a single trace of him. It's like he just vanished."

"He's done it before," another neighbour chimed in. "That brook runs all the way down past the school. If he's clever enough - and he is - he could've slipped through the fields and been gone long before the helicopter showed up."

Detective Chief Sergeant Mark Talbot was sat at his desk, piecing together the information gathered during the hunt. The neighbour's sighting had been credible, but as always, The Fox had vanished before they could get close. They had tracked his trail to the edge of the playing fields, but from there, the scent had gone cold.

This was his MO - always sliding away just as they were closing in. Talbot knew the pattern well, and it was maddening. The Fox seemed to be everywhere and nowhere all at once, sneakily moving through the suburban streets and woodlands, impossible to catch.

The rumour mill churned furiously throughout the day. Some said he was long gone, having fled the area, while others believed he was still hiding nearby, waiting for another chance to strike. Parents kept their children close, refusing to let them play outside, even in broad daylight. The police continued to patrol, but a sense of unease hung over Phoenix Close.

By dusk, the adrenaline from the previous night had started to fade, but the fear remained. The Fox had slipped through their fingers again, and no one knew when - or where - he might strike next.

In the small community of Phoenix Close, one thing was certain: The Fox had come too close for comfort, and until he was caught, no one would truly feel safe again.

Part Three: Closing In

Chapter 23

The village of Eggington, nestled in the English countryside near Leighton Buzzard, was the kind of place where secrets didn't stay buried for long. With its thatched cottages and narrow, winding lanes, it was a tight-knit community where everyone knew everyone else's business.

On most evenings, the village was quiet - an idyllic picture of rural life - but tonight, the hot summer air bared down on the cottages like an invisible force.

Helen Thompson's cottage, with its ivy-covered walls and neatly trimmed garden, was one of the older homes in the village. A single woman in her thirties, Helen lived alone, but she liked it that way. She kept to herself, a private person by nature, and most of her neighbours respected that.

Two of her neighbours, Alan Briggs and his wife, Susan, were out walking their Labrador, Max. They strolled along the narrow lane, the dog trotting contentedly beside them. They were a good-humoured couple, retired and settled into a life of routines. Walking the dog was part of that routine. As they passed Helen's cottage, they heard something that stopped them in their tracks.

"Alan, did you hear that?" Susan whispered, her brow furrowing as she tugged on Max's leash.

Alan paused, tilting his head towards the sound. It was faint but unmistakable - a woman's muffled cries. He turned to Susan, his face creased with concern. "Sounds like it's coming from Helen's place," he said quietly.

They moved closer, straining to see through the semidarkness. The late evening summer haze seemed to creep closer, wrapping itself around the small stone cottage. Susan's eyes widened as she spotted something up ahead. "Look, the bedroom window…it's open," she said, pointing to the second floor.

Alan's breath hitched. The window was indeed open, the lace curtains fluttering slightly in the breeze. But that wasn't what drew their attention. In the dim glow of the bedroom light, a male silhouette could be seen moving behind the sheer fabric. A sense of dread gripped them both.

"Do you think it's him?" Susan whispered, clutching Alan's arm.

"Who?' Alan replied.

"The Fox" Susan whispered.

"I don't see a car out front," Alan replied, his voice tense. "And Helen wouldn't have a guest over without a car parked outside. I don't like this, Sue."

The muffled sounds of whimpering continued, more pronounced now - a desperate, muted sound. Susan's heart pounded in her chest. "We need to call the police, Alan. This doesn't feel right."

Alan didn't hesitate. He raced home and dialled for the police, his voice steady but urgent. "Yes, I'd like to report a possible sighting of The Fox. We can see a man in a neighbour's house, and it sounds like a woman is in distress. Please, hurry."

The operator responded quickly, and within minutes, the peacefulness of the village was shattered by the sudden approach of police sirens. Blue lights flashed across the stone walls of the cottages.

An armed response unit arrived first, skidding to a halt outside Helen's gate, their doors flying open. Officers in tactical gear spilled out, weapons drawn, they took up positions around the property.

Alan and Susan stood across the street, clutching Max's leash tightly. Their eyes were wide with the gravity of the situation they had inadvertently set into motion. They hadn't expected such a dramatic response.

"Bloody hell," Alan muttered. "I didn't think they'd send in the cavalry."

Susan swallowed, her eyes never leaving the cottage. "What if it is The Fox? You heard what's been happening. It's been all over the news."

The officers moved quickly, some taking cover behind cars while others positioned themselves at the front and back doors.

The lead officer, Detective Chief Superintendent Mark Talbot, signalled his team to move in. His face was set in a grim expression; they couldn't afford to take any chances. The sound of a woman's muffled groans, paired with a strange rustling noise, drifted from the open window above.

"Back entrance, now," Talbot ordered, his voice commanding. "We're going in quiet but be ready for anything."

Two officers, flanked by Talbot, moved to the rear of the cottage, their footsteps soft on the well-trimmed lawn. There were no signs of a forced entry, so with a swift motion, one of them used a pry bar to pop open the back door.

They entered silently, their boots making only the slightest sound on the wooden floor. The house was dark, save for the sliver of light from the partially open bedroom door upstairs.

Talbot nodded to his team. "Everyone in position. On my count." The three officers crept up the stairs, each step slow and deliberate, their breathing controlled, weapons at the ready. As they ascended, the sounds became clearer - heavy breathing, a man's low, urgent whispers, and the distinct, muffled grunts of a woman. The hairs on the back of Talbot's neck stood up. He'd been in enough high-pressure situations to recognise when things were about to go sideways.

"Three, two, one - go!" he barked.

They burst through the bedroom door, guns raised, laser sights cutting through the dim light like sharp blades. "Armed police! Hands where we can see them!" Talbot shouted.

The scene that unfolded before them was not what they expected. Not by a long shot.

A man and a woman lay tangled in the sheets, their faces flushed with surprise and…embarrassment. The man, startled and clearly naked under the covers, threw his hands up instinctively. Beside him, Helen Thompson's eyes were wide, her cheeks a deep shade of crimson. She was not tied up. She was not crying for help. She was very much there of her own free will.

"What the - what's going on?" the man blurted out, his voice half-strangled with confusion.

Helen pulled the sheets up to cover herself, her mortification plain as day. "Oh my God, I - this isn't - there's been a mistake!"

The room fell into an awkward, stunned silence as the officers slowly realised what was happening. Talbot lowered his gun, his shoulders sagging slightly as he turned to his team. "Stand down, everyone. False alarm."

The younger of the two officers couldn't help but stifle a laugh, which quickly earned him a glare from Talbot. "Quiet, Roberts."

Helen, still clutching the sheets, could barely meet anyone's gaze. "I'm…I'm so sorry," she stammered. "I didn't realise my window was open, and we must have made some noise…I can't believe this is happening."

The man beside her, who looked just as mortified, nodded. "I'm Jack. Uh…I'm sorry too. I didn't think our night would end like this."

From outside, Alan and Susan stood rooted to the spot, watching the officers file out of the cottage with sheepish expressions. When they saw Talbot approach them, they knew they were in for it.

"Are you the ones who made the call?" Talbot asked in a stern voice, though he already knew the answer.

"Yes, that was us," Alan admitted.

"It was a false alarm, it appears your neighbour has a 'friend' staying with her," replied Talbot.

Alan, his face flushed with embarrassment. "We thought…we thought she was in trouble."

"We didn't mean to cause a fuss," Susan added quickly. "It just sounded so strange, and with all the news about The Fox…"

Talbot sighed, the strain of the night finally easing from his frame. "Look, I appreciate you being vigilant, but next time, maybe knock on the door or call your neighbour first. No harm done tonight, but let's try to avoid getting the whole armed response unit involved in people's private affairs, yeah?"

Alan nodded sheepishly. "Right. Got it. Sorry about that."

A few minutes later, Helen stood on her front step, wrapped in a blanket and looking utterly mortified as her neighbours passed by, offering awkward waves and apologies. The last of the police vehicles were pulling away, the street slowly returning to its quiet, rural stillness.

Jack stood beside her, still half-dressed but trying to lighten the mood. "Well, that's definitely a first for me," he said with a chuckle.

Helen managed a small smile, though her cheeks were still burning. "I don't think I'll ever live this down."

"Hey," Jack said softly, nudging her with his elbow. "If nothing else, you've got one hell of a story for your next dinner party."
"I suppose you're right," Helen chuckled.

As the last police car disappeared down the lane, Helen took a deep breath, she'd deal with the embarrassment in the morning, but for now, she was just grateful it was over. She looked up at the stars that were starting to peek through the clouds, thinking to herself how life in a quiet village could suddenly turn chaotic in the blink of an eye.

But in Eggington, a quiet life didn't necessarily mean a boring one. And tonight, had been anything but boring.

Chapter 24

The Fox sat in his brother's small, cluttered living room in Leighton Buzzard. To the world outside, he was just another labourer, another man making his way through life with little trace. But to the police, he was an elusive criminal who had terrorised communities across Herts, Beds and Bucks for months, leaving only sporadic clues in his wake.

His brother, a quiet man named Steven, had no idea who he really was. To Steven, he was simply his brother, someone who had always been a little rough around the edges, prone to disappearing for long stretches of time, but family, nonetheless.

Steven had never been one to ask too many questions. His brother would be around some evenings, they'd have a few drinks, reminisce about old times, and other evenings he would disappear again, as he always did. The brothers were close, in a way, though there was a certain distance between them, an unspoken understanding that some things were better left unsaid.

Steven was a builder by trade, a hardworking man who lived a quiet life in his modest home on the outskirts of town. He had lived there for years, his days a steady routine of early mornings and long shifts. His home, though small and unassuming, had become something of a sanctuary for his brother in recent weeks. It was the perfect place to lay low while the police dragged their feet in the pursuit of the faceless criminal haunting their nightmares.

The newspapers were full of reports about The Fox - the clever, calculating criminal who always seemed to be one step ahead of the authorities. The Fox had always taken a certain pleasure in hearing about himself, seeing how the media and the police spun their theories, all the while completely oblivious to the fact that he was sitting quietly in the comfort of his brother's home, right under their noses.

But The Fox couldn't read. He had never learned, and the irony of it wasn't lost on him. The newspapers printed daily updates about his exploits, but he had to rely on his brother, oblivious to his true identity, to read them aloud.

Steven sat across from his brother, his reading glasses perched on the end of his nose, flipping through the pages of that day's newspaper. The headline caught his eye: POLICE CLOSE IN ON ELUSIVE 'FOX' - DOOR-TO-DOOR BLOOD TESTS TO BEGIN'.

"They're really coming for him now," Steven said, his voice a mixture of fascination and apprehension as he scanned the article. "They reckon they'll get him soon."

His brothers face remained impassive, though inside, his mind raced. He leaned back in the worn armchair, feigning nonchalance.

"Is that so?" he said casually, running his hand through his hair. He had learned long ago that showing emotion was dangerous - it gave people a glimpse into the chaos within.

"Yeah," Steven continued, his eyes glued to the paper. "They're gonna start going door to door, taking blood samples from every man in the area. They think he's local, you see. They reckon he's hiding somewhere, maybe even around here."

The Fox felt a chill run through him. Blood tests? This was new, and it was dangerous. It was one thing to stay a step ahead of the police, but if they were taking blood samples, it meant his days of running were numbered. His hands tensed slightly, but he kept his expression neutral.

"They really think that'll work?" he asked, keeping his tone light.

"Dunno," Steven said with a shrug. "But it's a hell of an operation they've got going. Must've roped in half the bloody country to help. They're bringing in experts, too. Some newfangled science stuff. They'll match it to the crime scenes."

The Fox had heard whispers about it, but he hadn't considered it would be used against him so soon. The police were smarter than he had given them credit for, it seemed. He knew that if they came to Steven's door, they would demand his blood too - and that would be the end of him. No clever disguise or hastily forged identity could save him from the truth written in his own blood.

Steven, oblivious to his brother's inner turmoil, continued reading. He occasionally chuckled at the sheer scope of the police efforts, shaking his head at the idea of the infamous Fox living in some unsuspecting village. "I mean, can you imagine it?" Steven said with a grin. "The bloke could be right under our noses, just sitting there while everyone's looking for him."

The Fox forced a smile. If only his brother knew.

As the afternoon wore on, Steven suggested working on some odd jobs around the house. His windows were old and needed reinforcing. He was planning to nail them shut to try and prevent The Fox from gaining entry. His brother, eager to maintain appearances and appear helpful, followed him around the house.

Steven hammered away at the windows with an absent-minded determination, chatting about the case as he worked. "You know, they say he's been seen all over the place – Leighton Buzzard, Luton, even Tring. But no one ever seems to get a good look at him."

The Fox said nothing, watching the nails go in one by one, the windows sealing shut with each strike of the hammer. His brother was effectively locking him in, oblivious to the fact that he was the very criminal the world was hunting for. The irony wasn't lost on The Fox. In a strange way, it felt comforting. Safe. But he knew it wouldn't last.

When the windows were secured, the brothers settled back into their routine, sharing beers and watching TV. But the mention of the blood tests had unsettled The Fox, and he knew he couldn't stay much longer. He needed to get out of Leighton Buzzard before the police started knocking on doors.

That night, The Fox lay awake in his bedroom, staring at the ceiling. He couldn't stop thinking about the police, about their relentless pursuit, about the blood tests that would eventually lead them to him. He needed to act fast, to disappear again before they could pin him down.

Somewhere far enough away like Milton Keynes would be the logical next step. It was far enough from his brother's home to give him breathing room, but close enough that he could slip back into anonymity if necessary. And there were plenty of new opportunities there - new marks, new crimes. The temptation was already pulling at him.

But first, he needed to visit his wife and kids.

The Fox's family lived up north, in a small town in Durham that had remained largely untouched by his crimes. The drive from Leighton Buzzard was long and cumbersome, he set off early evening, once he had finished a local gardening job for a repeat customer.

Several hours passed before he reached the M18, an area he knew well, having driven through it so many times. It cut through the South Yorkshire countryside like a scar, a dark ribbon stretching toward an unknown end. The Fox drove along it with a sense of detached purpose, the summer heat swirling around, wrapping the vehicle in a stifling cloak of mystery. The night was still, the kind of oppressive calm that made every sound seem louder and every shadow more foreboding.

It was ten o'clock, and the warm air seemed to seep into the car, settling deep into The Fox's bones. A feverish heat of anticipation coursed through him, mingling with an anxious undertone - a nagging worry that tonight might be the one where his meticulous plans unravelled. Yet, the thrill of his predatory control over his victims was intoxicating, and the buzz of it drove him forward.

Brampton-en-le-Morthen, the village he had chosen for tonight's encounter, was a quaint, almost dreamlike place, its streets lined with sleepy cottages and narrow lanes that meandered through the landscape. The soft glow of streetlamps created a sense of eerie calm that perfectly suited his intentions. The Fox navigated the winding roads, his eyes scanning for the perfect spot to park his car. He eventually found a secluded wooded area, hidden from view by a dense thicket of trees.

As he parked and turned off the engine, the silence was punctuated only by the distant call of an owl. The Fox emerged from his vehicle. He looked around, scanning the area for reasons not to proceed. The coast was clear, so he reached for his bag and set off across a field.

He eventually approached his target, a secluded cottage at the end of a lane, its single porch light beaming over the neatly kept garden. The window of the downstairs toilet was slightly ajar - an oversight he intended to exploit.

With deft movements, he slipped through the gap in the window, the action smooth and soundless. Inside, the cottage was static. The Fox paused to listen, his breath slow and measured.

He located the phone in the living room and pulled out the cable ensuring the occupants would be unable to call for help. Carrying the cable with him, The Fox made his way to the bedroom, slowly and methodically. In the dim light, he could make out the silhouettes of the occupants, their recurring breathing a signal of their deep slumber.

The bedroom door creaked softly as he nudged it open. The couple lay in peaceful repose, their faces relaxed in sleep. The Fox's heart quickened, not from fear but from a twisted excitement that had become his driving force. The balaclava he wore clung tightly to his face, hiding his identity but not the intensity of his dark pleasure. He raised the shotgun, the weight of it familiar and comforting.

"Wake up," he said, his voice a cold whisper that cut through the stillness like a sharp blade.

The couple, Michael and Abigail Jones's eyes snapped open, their peaceful expressions transforming into ones of horror as they took in the sight of the masked intruder and the gleaming shotgun. The husband's eyes extended in dread, he stumbled out of bed, his voice cracking with a mix of fear and confusion.

"What do you want?" he asked, his voice barely more than a whisper.

The Fox's response was sharp and unyielding. "Quiet. Get up. Both of you."

The couple's panic was deep, their movements shaky. Abigail clung to her husband's arm, tears streaming down her face. Their eyes darting around the room, trying to grasp the gravity of their situation.

The Fox pushed them back down on the bed. He swiftly secured Michael's wrists with the phone cable. His attempts to maintain some semblances of courage were overshadowed by his visible dread. Abigail, trembling and sobbing, was ordered to bind her own feet. Her movements were frantic, her fingers fumbling with the cable The Fox had handed her.

"Face down," The Fox commanded, his voice accepting no argument. "And stay quiet."

As the couple complied, their breaths coming in short, terrified gasps, The Fox's gaze swept the room with cold detachment. He tied Abigails hands behind her back, lifted her night dress, and pulled down her underwear.
"Please, no," cried Michael.

The Fox slammed the butt of the shotgun into Michael's mouth, knocking out his two front teeth. Michael's head snapped back, blood squirted from his mouth onto the bed. The Fox slammed the shotgun into his nose, just to make sure he understood who was in control.

His actions were orderly, driven by a routine that had become disturbingly familiar.

Michael lay semi-conscious, while the Fox assaulted Abigail with swift and aggressive attacks. She was frozen to the spot. Unable to defend herself.

Once the ordeal was over, The Fox, content with his night's work, dressed himself with an evil smirk appearing through his mask. As he turned to leave, he noticed his semen on the bedsheet. A rare mistake. He retrieved a knife from his coat pocket and sliced through the sheet ensuring the evidence was removed. The portion of the sheet he targeted was a dark reminder of his recent act. This was his signature - a taunting memento of his dominance.

With the stained fabric in hand, The Fox worked quickly, stuffing it into his coat pocket along with his gloves and balaclava. The act was performed with clinical efficiency, every movement calculated and unemotional. He cast a final, disdainful glance at the restrained couple before slipping out of the cottage.

Outside, a thick fog had formed, the world around him reduced to a swirling mist. He trudged across the open field back to where his car was parked. A million thoughts were racing through his mind, the break-in, the assault, the semen spill. Oh no, the semen spill - he needed to make sure that vital clue would never be found.

He approached his car, and ever cautious but growing more careless with each passing crime, discarded key items near the spot where it was parked. The balaclava he had used to conceal his face, leather gloves, and the semen-stained piece of bedsheet, were hastily buried in a shallow grave nearby. These items, seemingly insignificant in the vastness of the landscape, held the potential to unravel his carefully constructed anonymity.

The Fox got into his car, the engine roaring to life and accidentally shifted it into reverse. The crunch of gravel and the scrape of the rear bumper against overgrown bushes filled the night air.

"Damn it," he muttered, his voice tinged with irritation. He quickly shifted the car into drive and sped away, his mind racing as he left the scene behind.

Inside the cottage, the couple lay bound and paralysed with fear as the night stretched endlessly before them. After what felt like an eternity, they mustered the courage to free each other and sat huddled on the bed, clinging to one another, sobbing. It was hours later before they finally called the police.

Chapter 25

Later that morning, Detective Chief Superintendent Mark Talbot and his team were alerted by South Yorkshire Police. Responding to a distress call from The Fox's latest victims, the local officers had swiftly connected the dots - it bore all the hallmarks of another chilling crime committed by The Fox. It all felt very familiar, despite it being a long way away from The Fox's usual crime area. A Forensics team also descended on the scene, their movements careful as they began their investigation.

In a nearby field, Farmer John Wilkins guided his tractor across the wide expanse. He had lived on this land for over four decades, and the rhythm of the seasons had become second nature to him. Due to the extended heatwave, the soil was tough to plough, but thanks to a recent downpour it was just damp enough to turn easily under the weight of his tractor. As the engine rumbled along, the large plough blades sliced through the earth, carving neat rows that stretched from one end of the field to the other.

It was a monotonous task, one that allowed his mind to wander as he worked. He'd been thinking about his livestock, which needed to be moved to a different pasture soon, when something caught his eye - a small object against the dull green of the hedgerow that bordered his field. Squinting into the near distance, the farmer noticed something unusual. There, tangled in the thorns and branches, was a glove.

He slowed the tractor to a stop, curiosity getting the better of him. Stepping down from the cab, the farmer approached the hedge, wiping his hands on his overalls. The glove was odd - out of place, it didn't belong in his field, as there was no public footpath nearby. It wasn't the sort of thing you found around here, where the only litter was usually a stray plastic bag blown in from the motorway.

Reaching out, he tugged the glove free from the hedge. It was leather, stiff from exposure, and looked like it had been there overnight. What was strange, though, was that he knew this glove hadn't been there when he'd been in the same field a day earlier. It seemed new, dropped or discarded recently. He turned it over in his hands, frowning. A chill ran up his spine, and without knowing why, the farmer felt the hairs on the back of his neck prickle with unease. This wasn't right.

His thoughts were interrupted by the sight of police cars in the distance. The farmer saw them parked at the cottage of Michael and Abigail Jones. The glove still in his hand, he climbed back into his tractor, tossed the glove into the cab, and drove toward the Jones' house. Whatever was happening over there, he figured the police might want to know about this strange discovery in his field. As he arrived, the officers outside the house took notice, and the farmer waved them over.

"Morning, officers," he said as he climbed down from the tractor. "I found something in my field that I think you'll want to see."

Detective Sergeant Jake Miller stepped forward. "What have you got?"

"This." The farmer held out the glove. "Found it caught in the hedge. Wasn't there yesterday."

Miller took the glove, examining it with interest. "Where exactly did you find this?"

"Just over that rise, down by the far side of my field."

Miller turned to the others, his face gloomy. "Let's get a team out there, now."

Inside the Jones' cottage, Talbot sat interviewing the couple, going over events from the previous night. His thoughts were interrupted by the sound of hurried footsteps in the hallway. Miller entered the room, his expression tense.

"Sir, there's been a development. A farmer found a glove in the hedge near to here. Looks like it could be connected."

Talbot straightened, his pulse quickening. "Where?"

"On the far side of the field. We've got a team heading out to search the area now."

Talbot didn't hesitate. "Let's go."

The scene by the M18 was eerily quiet. The search team had cordoned off the area near the hedgerow where the glove had been found, and forensic officers were already combing through the site with painstaking care.

Talbot stood at the edge of the field, watching as the team worked. His gut told him that this was it - the break they had been waiting for. The glove could be the key to unlocking the mystery of The Fox's movements. But they couldn't take any chances. They needed to act fast, especially if The Fox realised that he had left something behind.

"Jake," Talbot said, turning to Miller, "we need to expand the search. If he left something as obvious as a glove, there could be more. Check all of the fields and any area he may have walked to or parked in."

"Forensics, continue to sweep the area, I want every last detail he has left behind. Miller, I've got a plan. Come with me."

Within an hour, the nearby section of the M18 was awash with flashing lights of emergency vehicles. Talbot had decided to stage a seemingly routine traffic accident involving a bus, hoping to divert any suspicion. Officers, dressed as paramedics and emergency workers, moved swiftly, blending seamlessly into the scene.

"We need to search the area, now," Talbot ordered, his voice resolute. "We can't risk him coming back before we've gathered everything. If he realises we're onto him, he'll disappear."

The forensic team worked methodically, inch by inch, scanning the area for any other signs of disturbance. It was slow painstaking work.

There was nothing else of interest in and around the Jones' cottage or the field where the farmer had discovered the glove. So, the search moved to a secluded wooded area, not far from the field. And it wasn't long before one of the forensic team called out.

"Sir! Over here!"

Talbot and Miller hurried over to where the forensic officer was kneeling by tyre marks in the earth and a patch of recently disturbed earth. The forensics officer carefully brushed away some of the loose soil, revealing the edge of something metallic.

"Keep digging!" barked Talbot.

The forensic officer dug further, revealing a shotgun, buried just below the surface. The discovery sent a jolt of adrenaline through Talbot. This was no ordinary piece of evidence. The shotgun was exactly the kind of weapon they had suspected The Fox of using in most of his attacks. But finding it here, not far from the Jones' cottage, confirmed their suspicions: The Fox had been in the area.

"Get that bagged and tagged," Talbot ordered. "And keep digging. There's more here, I can feel it."

The forensic officer continued to dig. More vital pieces of evidence were revealed.

"Sir, look, a piece of cloth and a glove."

Talbot and Miller's eyes lit up. "That has to be the other glove to what the farmer just found," said Miller, excited.

"Get them bagged, tagged and sent to the lab for examination, The Fox has slipped up big time. We are finally onto him," said an almost joyous Talbot.

The forensic team, buoyed by their discoveries, continued to sweep the area.

Moments later, they uncovered the most crucial piece of evidence the investigation had seen.
"Sir, over here."

"What is it?" demanded Talbot.

"A tiny speck of paint on a broken twig. It is barely visible to the naked eye, but could this be from a vehicle?" replied the forensic officer.

"Get it bagged and tagged. It's worth investigating." A very happy Talbot responded.

The forensic officer collected it carefully, sealing it in a bag for further analysis. And then studied the bushes more closely. She focused on the height of the branch which had the speck of paint.

"Sir, it measures forty-five inches from the ground. That's the typical height of a hatchback car model."

"Excellent work officer. Get this all sent to the lab. I want to know every car make and model with this paint type and colour," replied Talbot. And with that, Talbot afforded himself a rare smile. Was this the breakthrough he had been waiting for.

"Keep searching the area, I want this place turned upside down," demanded Talbot. But no further evidence was uncovered.
It was a major breakthrough; one Talbot had been praying for.

The next day at the Crime lab in Huntingdon, Cambridgeshire, the paint sample was analysed under high-powered microscopes. Talbot stood in the observation room, watching as the technicians worked. They had sent the gloves, the shotgun, and the sheet for testing, but it was the paint that intrigued him the most. A tiny, nearly microscopic fleck of paint was often all it took to link a suspect to a crime scene. Talbot was hoping that in some way, it would help him to finally nail The Fox.

After several hours of analysis, the results were in.

"DCS Talbot?" The forensic technician called out. "We've got something."

Talbot stepped inside the lab, his heart pounding. The technician held up a report.

"We began by physically examining the paint sample, which matched the questioned sample in the first stage of our analysis. Next, we conducted a chemical analysis using Fourier-transform infrared spectroscopy, which identified the binders, pigments, solvents, and additives unique to the paint formula. Using our colour charts, we matched it to sample seven-nine-one-nine Harvest Yellow. The key detail? This specific type of paint was exclusively used on Austin Allegro models produced in the last two years."

Talbot's mind raced. The Fox drove a yellow Austin Allegro. They had already linked the car to several of the crime scenes, but they hadn't been able to track down the exact make or model. This paint sample narrowed the search considerably. They now knew the car driven by The Fox, and with the forensic evidence linking the gloves and shotgun to The Fox, they had taken a huge step forward in capturing him.

"Excellent work," screeched an almost euphoric Talbot.

In the days that followed, the investigation intensified. Talbot and his team focused on tracking down every yellow Austin Allegro that matched the paint profile. They combed through vehicle registration databases, and discovered there were fifteen-hundred owners of this type of vehicle.

The discovery of the glove had been the turning point. It had led them to the shotgun and sheet, which had, in turn, led them to the paint. Every piece of evidence was falling into place, and for the first time in months, Talbot felt that they were closing in on their elusive target.

Talbot stood tall in the operations room, his chest puffed out. "Everybody, listen up," he called out.

"We finally have a major breakthrough in our search for The Fox. We now know he drives a yellow Austin Allegro. Miller, Hughes, I want you to review each and every owner of a yellow Austin Allegro against the five-thousand names Metal Mickey has given us. Any matches, you let me know straight away," barked Talbot.

"Yes sir," Miller and Hughes responded simultaneously.

"And if there are no matches, find every person on that list of fifteen hundred car owners, visit them, rule them in or out of this investigation," demanded Talbot.

"Crikey, this is going to take us ages, Guv," retorted Hughes.

"Well, you had bloody well start now then, son," countered Talbot.

And with that, both Hughes and Miller, grabbed the list of car owners, and set about what could prove to be the most important task in the hunt for The Fox.

In the quiet village of Brampton-en-le-Morthen, the search for justice had begun in earnest. The relentless pursuit of The Fox was no longer a matter of chance but of time, as the investigation unfolded with increasing urgency. The fog of anonymity that had once shielded him was beginning to lift.

But The Fox was still out there, still watching, still waiting for his chance to strike again. Talbot knew that time was running out. They needed to find him before he disappeared for good - or worse, before he claimed another victim.

Chapter 26

The morning after his assault on the Jones', The Fox had arrived home in Durham. His wife, Sarah, was a practical woman who had learned long ago not to ask too many questions about her husband's comings and goings. Their relationship had always been one of convenience rather than passion, but it worked for them. Sarah ran the household, raising their two children with a quiet resilience, while The Fox drifted in and out of their lives, always returning just long enough to remind them he was still around.

This time, he had planned something special. His birthday was coming up, and he had promised to take the family on holiday to the Scottish Highlands - a rare treat, something to make up for his frequent absences.

When he arrived at their home, Sarah greeted him with a mixture of surprise and suspicion, as she always did. But the promise of a holiday softened her. She smiled when he mentioned the Highlands, and the children were thrilled at the idea of a road trip.

For a few days, The Fox allowed himself to slip into the role of a family man. He played with the kids, helped Sarah around the house, and even managed to push the thoughts of the police and the blood tests to the back of his mind. But the itch was still there - the pull toward the hunt, the need for control. He could feel it gnawing at him, growing stronger the longer he stayed in one place.

The Fox, an attacker cloaked in anonymity, manoeuvred his vehicle through the narrow streets of Peterlee like he'd never been away. He drove around like any other normal person going about his business. Inside his car, the temperature was cool, the vibration of the engine a soothing backdrop to the dark thoughts that churned in his mind.

He'd been successful so far, eluding capture and spreading fear wherever he went. Tonight, Peterlee would be his stage, the town's calmness shattered by the violence he had planned. He had chosen his targets carefully, selecting two homes on the outskirts of town, isolated enough to ensure that his presence would go unnoticed until it was too late.

The first house was a modest, two-story structure, its garden overgrown with weeds and unkempt hedges. It was the kind of house that blended into the background, easily forgotten in the hustle of daily life. He parked a short distance away, and he watched, and he waited, making sure the house was still and silent.

Inside, the family was unaware of the impending danger. A young couple, David and Laura McGinn, were asleep in their bed, dreaming of an untroubled life. Their bedroom was a cosy haven, filled with the warm glow of bedside lamps and the soft whizz of an old fan.

The Fox approached silently, slipping through the garden gate and down the side of the house. He moved quickly, his footsteps muffled by the thick grass that clung to the ground. He made his way to the back door, which he knew from his prior reconnaissance would be poorly secured. A quick flick of his screwdriver and the turn of the handle, and the door was open, creaking softly as he snuck inside.

The interior was eerily quiet, the only sound the soft murmur of the fan. The Fox lingered at the threshold of the bedroom, his breath sturdy and relaxed. He had done this many times before, but the thrill of the hunt never faded. He stepped inside, his movements deliberate and controlled.

David and Laura stirred slightly as he approached, but their slumber was deep. The Fox's presence was a dark cloud in their dreams, an invisible threat that they could not perceive. He moved closer, his heart pounding with a mix of anticipation and cold determination.

Laura woke first, her eyes fluttering open as she sensed something amiss. She saw the shadowy figure standing beside the bed and let out a soft gasp, her face a mask of confusion and fear. David stirred, his eyes slowly focusing on the intruder. The Fox acted swiftly, his gloved hand clamping over Laura's mouth as he brandished a knife glinting menacingly in the dim light.

"Stay quiet," he whispered, his voice a chilling growl. "No one needs to get hurt if you cooperate."

David's eyes widened in terror as he tried to grasp the horror unfolding before him. He struggled to stand, but The Fox overpowered him effortlessly. The fight, though brief, was vicious - filled with desperate gasps and muffled cries. Within moments, a sickening silence fell over the room. The Fox's attack left David with two broken ribs, a shattered nose, a detached testicle, and several missing teeth. Blood streamed from his face onto the bed as he gasped for breath.

Laura's ordeal was even worse. The Fox headbutted and elbowed her into submission, leaving her battered and bruised, her face a mess of injuries as she had no option but to comply with his violent demands. The bottom of her nightie was soaked in blood from the brutal sexual assault she endured.

The aftermath of The Fox's brutality would leave David and Laura scarred for life.

After the grim assault was complete, The Fox exited the house, leaving behind a scene of horror that would soon shake the small town to its core. He moved back to his car, the summer heat adding to the sweat already dripping from his forehead. He drove away with the same calculated calmness he had arrived with.

The following night he was back on the prowl. The second house was a similar picture of suburban normalcy, a single-story home with neatly trimmed hedges and a small garden. This time, the occupants were an elderly couple, Harold and Margo Lynch. They were nestled in their sofa in the living room, the soft glow of the television flickering across their faces.

The Fox was hiding under the sofa, having slipped into the house through a side window earlier in the day. The house was quiet, the kind of silence that spoke of an ordinary, untroubled life, albeit apart from the sound of Harold and Margo's favourite TV show blasting out. They both sat, blissfully unaware of the danger.

The Fox continued to observe them, his expression hidden behind the mask of his balaclava. He relished the moment, savouring the contrast between the peaceful domestic scene and the horror he was about to unleash. He slowly moved out from under the sofa, so he was positioned at the back, out of eyesight.

And then he pounced.

Margo was the first to spot him, her eyes widening as the shadow approached. Her scream was cut short as The Fox lunged, clamping his gloved hand over her mouth and wielding his knife with deadly precision. Harold rushed to intervene but was met with brutal force - The Fox swung the handle of the knife with chilling accuracy, smashing it repeatedly into Harold's face. Blow after blow shattered his eye sockets and nose, leaving him unconscious on the floor.

Margo sat frozen in horror. Moving quickly, The Fox bound her hands and feet with electrical cord he pulled from his jacket. Helpless, she was forced to watch as he returned to Harold, stripping off his trousers and underwear. He flipped Harold onto his stomach, pressing his face into the carpet.

"Don't move, or I'll slit his throat," he barked at Margo.

The Fox slid down his trousers and underwear and climbed onto the back of Harold. With each violent thrust, each guttural grunt, Margo flinched and let out soft, broken sobs.

The scene was a grotesque tableau of violence and terror. The peaceful family time broken by the harsh reality of The Fox's actions.

The assault lasted a few minutes. When he was done, The Fox stood up, pulled his clothes up and then smashed the handle of the knife into Margo's face repeatedly until she was unconscious. Her face was unrecognisable.

When he finally left, the house was a picture of horror, the aftermath of The Fox's brutality a stark contrast to the ordinary life that had existed moments before. Another two victims. Another two lives ruined forever.

The next morning, The Fox woke up with his family, and acted like he always did, as if nothing had happened the night before. They set off for Scotland, the car packed with suitcases and snacks, the children bouncing in the backseat. The Fox kept his eyes on the road, his mind already drifting to the possibilities that lay ahead. The Highlands were remote, sparsely populated. It would be the perfect place to lie low for a while, to escape the growing pressure from the authorities. But even as he thought about the safety of isolation, the darkness in him stirred.

The journey north was long, and by the time they reached the halfway point, The Fox's patience was wearing thin. They stopped at a service station for a break, and as Sarah took the children inside to use the restroom, The Fox found himself scanning the parking lot with the same predatory instinct he always had. His eyes locked on a young woman standing by her car, fumbling with her keys.

He knew he shouldn't. He had promised himself he wouldn't. But the urge was too strong. He opened the boot of his car, located the hidden compartment containing his balaclava and gloves, and snuck them on.

The Fox moved quickly, approaching the woman from behind. In a flash, the predator inside him took over. It was over in seconds. Quick, brutal, efficient. The woman's bloodied body slumped against the side of her car, her keys still dangling from her hand. The Fox glanced around to make sure no one had seen him. The parking lot was quiet, the sun just beginning to set over the horizon.

He hurried back to his car, his heart pounding, the thrill of the assault coursing through his veins. Sarah and the children were still inside the service station, oblivious to the horror that had just unfolded in the parking lot. The Fox forced himself to breathe, to calm the adrenaline surging through him. He needed to keep his composure.

When Sarah and the kids returned, they found him leaning against the car, smiling as if nothing had happened.

"Ready to go?" he asked, his voice steady, betraying none of the chaos swirling inside him.

They continued their journey north, unaware that The Fox had just added another victim to his tally.

The Scottish Highlands were everything The Fox had hoped they would be - vast, remote, and wild. It was the perfect place to disappear, to leave behind the growing anxiety in England. For a while, he allowed himself to enjoy the peace and solitude of the landscape, spending time with his family, hiking through the hills and exploring the rugged terrain.

But the respite was short-lived. The newspapers were still full of stories about The Fox, and even in the remote villages of the Highlands, people were talking about the case. Every pub, every small shop, seemed to have someone discussing the elusive criminal who had managed to evade capture for so long.

The Fox listened to these conversations with a mixture of pride and paranoia. He had always enjoyed the notoriety, the idea that he had outsmarted the police at every turn. But now, with the blood tests looming, he feared his time was running out.

One evening, as they sat by the fire in their rented cottage, Sarah mentioned the case, her voice laced with concern.

"They're saying they're getting closer to catching him," she said, her eyes flickering with a hint of worry. "This 'Fox' fellow. They're doing blood tests now. Going door to door."

The Fox tensed, but he forced a laugh, dismissing her fears.

"They've been saying that for weeks," he said, waving a hand. "They'll never catch him."

But even as he said the words, he could feel the walls closing in.

The holiday ended, and they returned home, the drive back to England long and quiet. The Fox could feel the pressure building, the need to move, to act, to stay ahead of the police. The darkness inside him stirred once more, and he knew it wouldn't be long before he had to strike again.

He had escaped the net for now, but the hunt was far from over. The Fox was still on the run, but the hunters were closing in, and he knew that his next move would have to be his most calculated yet.

As they pulled into the driveway of their home, The Fox glanced at his wife and children, their faces tired but content. He smiled, knowing that the façade of the family man was still intact.
For now.

The following day, on the way back to Leighton Buzzard, The Fox felt the familiar pull, that dark urge that had become his constant companion. The holiday in the Highlands had offered him a temporary escape, but it had done little to quench the growing hunger inside him. As he drove south with the memory of his last victim still fresh in his mind, he began thinking about his next move. He couldn't resist the need for another thrill. This time, he was looking for something more personal, more brutal, something that would assert his dominance in a way he hadn't done in a while.

The drive was long, and as the miles blurred past, The Fox's thoughts turned to a small house just off the motorway - Yvonne Chamberlain's house. He had seen it before, having studied its movements in the past. It was isolated, set back slightly from the others, and backed onto an alleyway that would allow him to disappear quickly if needed. He didn't know much about Yvonne personally, just that she lived alone and kept to herself, the kind of victim he preferred.

As the car approached the familiar turn-off, The Fox's heart rate quickened. He pulled off the main road and parked a few streets away from Yvonne's house. The sky had darkened, and the neighbourhood was quiet, just how he liked it.

He moved quickly, slipping through the night as he approached the house. The back door was locked, of course, but that wasn't a problem for him. He had a knack for breaking and entering, something he had honed over recent months. Within seconds, he was inside, his footsteps silent on the wooden floors. The house was dark, but he could hear the faint sound of a television playing in one of the rooms.

For a moment, The Fox stood in the hallway, letting the tension build, savouring the power he held. He could hear Yvonne in the living room, oblivious to the danger lurking just feet away. He tightened his grip on the knife he had taken from his car, a tool he now used since he discarded of the shotgun.

He entered the living room quietly. Yvonne was sitting on the couch, her back to him, completely unaware of his presence. The TV was so loud, The Fox could barely hear himself think. He slowly crept towards her, step by step. And then bang, he attacked her from behind. She didn't notice him until it was too late. But before she could scream, he was on her, his gloved hand clamping over her mouth.

But Yvonne was different. She didn't take prisoners. She fought back harder than The Fox had expected. She bit down on his gloved hand, breaking through the material, her teeth sinking into his flesh with a ferocity that surprised him. The pain was sharp, searing, but it only fuelled his rage. Snarling in anger, The Fox brought the knife handle down on her face, the sound of the impact echoing through the small room. Yvonne cried out, her nose breaking under the force of the blow. Blood sprayed across the couch, splattering against the walls as she crumpled to the floor.

But she wasn't done fighting. Even with her face bloodied and her vision blurred from the damage to her face, Yvonne lashed out, kicking at him with a strength born from sheer survival instinct. The Fox, momentarily thrown off by her resilience, hit her again, this time across the side of her head. Her body went limp, collapsing into a heap on the floor.

Breathing heavily, his hand throbbing from the bite, The Fox took off his glove to inspect his injury. His wound was bleeding badly, unknown to the Fox, his blood dropped onto the carpet. It was another mistake, which could prove costly.

He put his glove back on and stood over Yvonne, watching as she gasped for breath, her face a mess of blood and bruises. He hadn't expected her to put up such a fight, and now, with his blood mixing with hers in her mouth and on the floor, he knew he had to leave. This was messier than he had planned. The adrenaline was still pumping through him, but something in the back of his mind was screaming for him to get out before it was too late.

Without another word, he turned and bolted, leaving Yvonne lying unconscious on the floor. He ran through the alley behind the house, his injured hand throbbing as he made his way back to the car. His pulse was racing, his thoughts scrambled. This attack had been too close, too sloppy. He hadn't expected her to fight back like that, and now he had left behind evidence - his blood.

As he drove away from Yvonne's house, the full weight of what he had done began to sink in. This was no longer just a game. The police were already closing in on him, and now he had left behind more evidence than ever before. They would find Yvonne, they would take samples from the blood he had spilled, and they would use it to track him down.

The Fox gripped the steering wheel tightly, his mind racing as he sped down the darkened roads. He couldn't afford to make any more mistakes. Leighton Buzzard was no longer safe. If he stayed, they would find him. He had to keep moving, to stay ahead of the hunt, to disappear once again.

But even as the fear of capture gnawed at him, the thrill of the attack still coursed through his veins. The Fox knew he would strike again. It was only a matter of time.

Yvonne's house, now a crime scene, would soon be swarming with police. By the time Yvonne regained consciousness and called for help, the damage had been done. Her face was swollen and bruised beyond recognition, her broken nose making it difficult for her to breathe, and her left eye so damaged that she could barely see. But Yvonne was tough. Despite the immense pain, she managed to describe the attack to the paramedics and later to the police - though her details were vague, it was enough to give the authorities something to work with and to link the crime to The Fox.

Forensic teams arrived soon after, combing through the scene for anything that might give them a clue. Blood was everywhere: Yvonne's from the brutal blows to her face and The Fox's from where she had bitten his hand through a thin glove. The team carefully collected samples from both Yvonne and her house, hoping that something in the forensic analysis would help them narrow down their suspect pool.

The next day, back at the lab, the forensic team worked quickly to process the blood samples, and soon, they had something significant: The Fox's blood type. He was blood group O, a common group but still one more piece of the puzzle that they hadn't had before. While it wasn't enough to pinpoint his exact identity, it allowed the police to refine their list of suspects further.

But the clues didn't stop there. Through their meticulous analysis of past crime scenes and witness reports, the police had a profile of their elusive suspect. They knew he was approximately five feet nine inches to five feet ten inches tall. Yvonne's description, despite her injuries, confirmed that the man who had attacked her was of similar height. Her description of his hair - brown and curly - was also corroborated by past witness accounts, though many had only caught fleeting glimpses of him. Forensics were even able to determine that the man had been wearing gloves, as there were no fingerprints left behind. But his bite mark, recorded by Yvonne's desperate struggle, would help identify a man with a recent hand injury.

Each new piece of information brought the police closer to visualising their suspect, even if his identity remained hidden. They knew his height, his blood group, his hair colour and texture, his preference for gloves, and his left-handedness. This, combined with the make and model of his car gave them a better chance of identifying him.

The Fox had always relied on his ability to disappear into the cracks of society, to evade detection by blending into the background. But now, it seemed his time was running out. With each mistake, he was giving the police more to work with.

And there was another crucial factor: his modus operandi. The Fox had always used specific tools to break into homes. His methods were precise - doors picked, windows jimmied open with a flathead screwdriver, always something that allowed him to enter quietly and quickly. He was methodical, but with Yvonne, his impatience had led him to slip up. His usual care in leaving no trace was compromised by the sheer aggression of the attack.

As the details started to come together, Detective Chief Superintendent Mark Talbot stood in the operations room in Dunstable police station, surrounded by maps, photos, and piles of paperwork. He was hunched over the table, reviewing the profile they had built on The Fox. The pressure to catch this man was immense. The Fox was getting sloppy. Talbot knew that it was only a matter of time before they caught him.

"His blood group is O," Detective Sergeant Jake Miller, said, entering the room with the latest forensic report.

Talbot nodded. "Good. Another piece of the puzzle. Make sure you cross reference that with the list of names from Metal Mickey. Strike off anyone whose blood group isn't O."

Miller spread the papers across the table. "We've got his height, hair colour, hair type, blood type, he's left-handed and we know the car he drives.

Talbot looked up, narrowing his eyes as he scanned the papers. "He's left-handed. That narrows things even further, they're a rare breed."

"It does," Miller replied. "And we know the kind of tool he uses – flat head screwdrivers. He's got experience, maybe even spent time inside. We'll need to check records, see if anyone with a similar profile has been released recently."

Detective Constable Tom Hughes, chimed in. "It's just a matter of time, sir. A yellow Austin Allegro isn't exactly subtle. It's just a question of when we find him, not if."

Talbot sighed, rubbing his temples. "We can't afford to waste time. He's growing more erratic by the day. Yvonne Chamberlain's lucky to be alive, but we won't always be so lucky."

Talbot felt another glimmer of hope. The Fox had been untouchable for so long, but now they almost had him cornered.

But even as the investigation gained momentum, Talbot knew that The Fox wasn't going to stop on his own. He was like a bully backed into a corner, and that made him more dangerous than ever. They had to catch him, and soon, before he struck again.

The Fox, though unaware of the full extent of the police's progress, could feel the noose tightening. As he returned to Leighton Buzzard, he couldn't shake the feeling that time was running out. His instincts screamed at him to move again, to disappear, but a part of him - darker and more primal - wasn't ready to stop.

And so, as he lay low at his brother's house once more, the thought of running faded, replaced by the familiar itch to strike. He would move to a new area, yes, but he would not run. Not yet.

There was still unfinished business to attend to.

Chapter 27

The room was suffocating, bathed in darkness save for a single flickering bulb that swung slowly overhead, casting warped shadows across the walls. This was his sanctuary, a hidden nest deep within a decaying building on the outskirts of town. Here, amidst the peeling wallpaper and the smell of mildew, he could let the mask slip. Here, he could be himself.

He sat on a rickety chair, the kind that groaned under the slightest weight, and stared into the cracked mirror on the opposite wall. The man who stared back at him was not the man the world knew. No, this was a different face - a face that wore a twisted smile, eyes burning with a manic, predatory glint. He tilted his head slightly, examining his reflection like a scientist would study a specimen, trying to understand what lay beneath the surface. But he knew the answer. He always had.

He was The Fox, and he thrived in the spaces between fear and chaos.

His real name didn't matter anymore. He had left that behind like a snake shedding its skin. Out there, he was an urban legend, a phantom who stalked the night. People whispered his name in hushed tones, as if speaking too loudly might summon him. And he liked it that way. He relished the power it gave him, the way it made them feel small and helpless. It was intoxicating.

He stood up, his movements deliberate and measured. He took slow, even breaths, feeling the oxygen fill his lungs and feed the cold fire that burned within him. Each breath was a reminder of his existence, of his control over his own fate. Control was everything. Without it, he was just another man; with it, he was something else entirely.

He walked to the window and pulled back the tattered curtain, peering out into the night. The town lay before him like a carcass waiting to be picked clean. The streets were empty, but he knew they were watching. Watching for him. He could almost feel their eyes, hidden behind curtains, peering through the darkened glass, waiting for a glimpse of the monster they feared. And it filled him with a dark, euphoric pleasure.

What did they think he was? A lunatic? A common criminal? They had no idea. They couldn't see the intricate web he was weaving, couldn't comprehend the depth of his mind. He wasn't just breaking into homes or brandishing weapons for the thrill of it. No, each action was a calculated move in a game only he understood. A game that required skill, patience, and an understanding of fear.

Fear. That was his weapon. More potent than any gun or knife. Fear seeped into a person's bones, crawled beneath their skin, and took root in their soul. It paralysed them, made them weak, and he had learned to wield it like a craftsman with a finely honed blade. He could smell it, taste it, feel it radiating from his prey. And once he had it, once he had them in that perfect moment of terror, he could do anything.

He remembered their faces - those he had chosen to visit in the dead of night. Their eyes, wide with terror, their breath catching in their throats. The way their muscles tensed, the way their hands shook as they clutched at anything that could offer them some semblance of protection. It was like music to him, a symphony of vulnerability.

He smiled, running a hand through his hair, feeling the sweat and grime clinging to his skin. His mind drifted to that couple in Leighton Buzzard. He could still hear the sharp crack of the shotgun, see the flash of muzzle fire illuminating their pale, horrified faces. That instant when the gun went off - was it intentional? Even he wasn't sure anymore. He had felt his finger tighten around the trigger, almost as if guided by some primal instinct. The result was magnificent chaos.

The man had lunged at him, wild with a mix of fury and survival instinct, and The Fox had felt a thrill unlike any other. It was rare to see such fight in them. Usually, they cowered, pleaded, or froze. But this one...he had something different. And that's what had made it so exhilarating. The unexpected was always more delicious.

He turned away from the window, his smile fading into a thin, contemplative line. He walked over to a small table cluttered with newspapers; each one emblazoned with photo fits of his supposed look and of headlines that screamed of his exploits.

'THE FOX STRIKES AGAIN!', 'MASKED INTRUDER TERRORISES VILLAGE!', 'POLICE FRUSTRATED AS FOX ELUDES CAPTURE!'.

He ran his fingers over the photo fits, feeling the rough texture of the cheap print. The papers thought they understood him, thought they could reduce him to a caricature of madness and malice. They didn't understand a thing.

They spoke of him like he was a beast, a deranged animal with no sense or strategy. Fools. They couldn't see the layers, the strategy, the game unfolding before them. They thought they were hunting him, but they were just pawns on his board. Every move they made was a reaction to his. Every time they thought they had him cornered, he slipped through their fingers, leaving behind only the stench of fear and the echoes of his laughter.

He relished the feeling of being in control, of pulling strings that no one else could see. He knew the country was on edge, that people were locking their doors and peeking out their windows. Parents were keeping their children close, and men who once scoffed at the idea of a bogeyman now slept with weapons by their bedsides. And it was all because of him. He had transformed the mundane into a theatre of terror, turned their quiet lives into a never-ending nightmare.

But the game was not without its challenges. Detective Chief Superintendent Mark Talbot. That name kept coming up, etched into his mind like a stubborn stain. Talbot was different from the others, less predictable. A thinker. Someone who could see past the surface and into the deeper patterns of his work. The Fox had watched him from a distance, seen him pacing in his office, pouring over maps and reports. He could almost smell the desperation on the man. It excited him.

Talbot was a problem that needed solving. The detective was beginning to understand his methods, starting to connect the dots in a way that no one else had. It wouldn't be long before he got too close. The Fox knew it was time to turn the tables, to let Talbot know that the hunt could go both ways.

His lips curled into a smile at the thought of it. The thrill of the chase - he could feel it building inside him, a friction that needed release. But how? How to up the stakes without losing the upper hand? He wanted to draw Talbot deeper into the game, to pull him into his world where the rules were different, where fear was the currency and chaos the reward.

The Fox walked to a corner of the room where a small, battered chest sat on the floor. He opened it carefully, revealing a collection of items - souvenirs from his various exploits. A man's belt, photos from an album, a flashy tie. Each one told a story, each one was a reminder of a night well-spent. His fingers brushed over them, feeling the cold metal of the belt buckle, the soft fabric of the tie. They were pieces of lives he had touched, changed forever.

A thought struck him then, a sudden, dark inspiration that sent a shiver of excitement down his spine. Talbot. He would make the detective his next subject, his next project. Not in the way he had done with the others, no - this one needed to be different, special. He would get inside Talbot's head, make him see the world as he saw it. He would make him understand.

The thrill of it sent a jolt through him, and he laughed - a low, guttural sound that echoed off the walls of his lair. He had never felt so alive, so powerful. The world outside this room was his to mould, and the people within it, his to manipulate. They were all playing parts in a script he had written, actors in a drama of his own design.

The Fox's eyes burned with a feverish light. He could hear the rain starting to tap against the broken window, a soft, steady rhythm that filled the room. The night was calling to him, whispering in his ear, urging him to step out into the darkness and continue his work.

He grabbed his coat and slung it over his shoulders, pulling the hood up over his head. He took one last look at his reflection in the cracked mirror. The smile was gone, replaced by something colder, something more determined. This was his moment. The next act in his grand play was about to begin, and he was ready.

Tonight, he would rewrite the rules. Tonight, he would take the game to a new level. And when it was all over, they would know. They would all know what it meant to truly fear The Fox.

And so, with the night as his cloak and Milton Keynes as his canvas, he disappeared into the darkness, his mind alight with visions of terror yet to come. The hunt was on, and he was ready to paint the town red with it.

Inside their modest home in Oldbrook, Milton Keynes, Wesley and Haylee Adams were settling in for the night. Outside, the rain had consumed the skies, the summer sun having recently disappeared. Somewhere, not far from where they sat, The Fox was watching. He could almost hear their breaths, feel their anxiety.

The Fox was ready to go. He moved like a raider in his element, his senses sharpened by the thrill of the hunt. Milton Keynes was his new playground, its streets and alleys etched into his mind like an intimate map. He knew every corner, every hiding spot, every path that led in and out of this area. And tonight, he felt the pull of those streets, like an old addiction resurfacing. The failure of his last assault lingered, and he was eager to redeem himself.

The Fox's mouth slowly arched into a smile beneath the dark mask that covered his face. He could feel the fear that gripped this area like a vice. It was electric. And he was the spark that could ignite it.

He crouched low, moving with a cat-like grace along the side of the house. He could hear a TV show - laughter, a cheerful jingle. A sitcom, perhaps. How quaint, he thought. How ordinary. He paused by a window, peeking through the tiny crack in the curtains. Inside, Wesley and Haylee sat on a brand-new leather sofa, eyes fixed on the screen. They looked tired, weary, but there was a certain comfort in their togetherness. The Fox watched them for a moment, feeling a strange mix of amusement and contempt. They were so blissfully unaware, so wrapped up in their little bubble. It would be so easy to shatter it.

He could feel his pulse quickening, his senses sharpening. This was the moment he lived for - the anticipation, the buildup to that perfect, terrifying crescendo. He had planned it carefully, mapped out every detail in his mind. This time, there would be no mistakes.

The Fox moved closer to the backdoor, his footsteps silent on the long grass. He knew the layout, knew exactly where he needed to be. He had chosen his entry point carefully - it would take only a moment to slip inside.

With the precision of a seasoned hunter, his gloved hands gently forced open the door. The sound was barely audible, drowned out by the loud television. He crept through the opening, and he waited, listening to every sound. He could hear their voices in the living room, discussing the program they were engrossed in.

Carefully, he edged toward the doorway, his eyes adjusting to the dim light. Wesley and Haylee were blissfully oblivious of the intruder who stood so close to them. He remained out of sight, watching them, feeling the rush of power that came from being so close, from being unseen. It was intoxicating.

Wesley's eyes flicked toward the doorway, and for a moment, The Fox thought he had been seen. But Wesley turned away. The Fox smiled to himself. They were still so vulnerable. He could push them further, break them completely. But he needed to do it right.

He moved back into the darkness, deeper into the kitchen, his mind racing with possibilities. He could wait for them to go to bed, slip into their room as they slept. Or he could make a noise, draw them out, let them feel the terror of knowing he was inside, so close they could almost touch him. The thought sent a shiver of excitement down his spine.

But he decided on something simpler, he would be more direct.

He took a breath, clutched his knife tightly in his left hand, and burst into the living room. Haylee and Wesley startled; their eyes wide with fear as The Fox seized the moment. He wasted no time in letting them feel his presence. He smashed the handle of his knife into Wesley's face, breaking his nose with a sickening crunch. Wesley slumped forward, hands instinctively covering his blood-soaked face.

Before Haylee could react, The Fox turned, silencing her with a swift blow to the jaw that left her gasping in pain. Her scream barely escaped before his hand clamped over her mouth, muffling it to a whimper.

Wesley, hunched over and shaking, looked up through blood-streaked eyes. "Please, don't hurt her," he pleaded, voice cracking. The Fox's expression remained impassive as he struck again and again, until Haylee crumpled to the floor. He stepped toward Wesley, delivering a brutal kick to his jaw that sent him sprawling, unconscious.

Moving quickly, The Fox bound their hands behind their backs.

He then prowled the house, eyes flicking over every detail, his twisted mind piecing together a message for Talbot that would echo long after he left.

Minutes passed before he returned, eyes gleaming with dark intent. His search had yielded items that would etch the memory of this night into Talbot's mind - a toilet brush and a marrow from the fridge.

The Fox ripped at Wesley and Haylee's clothes like a dog ripped at a chew toy. He was sending a message loud and clear to Talbot. He was in control and there was nothing he could do about it.

What followed was vile and vicious. Relentless violence at its worst. The toilet brush snapped in half; such was the force used on Wesley. The marrow was reduced to mush. Both items were soaked in blood.

Once The Fox had finished his tirade of abuse, he calmly stood up, fixed his clothes and walked out of the house.

Wesley and Haylee remained bound, broken and unconscious. Their simple quiet lives would never be the same again.

Outside, the dark night sky swallowed The Fox as he ran for his life. His mind was racing, but there was a grin on his face. This was what he lived for - the thrill of being so close to the edge. Tonight, had been a warning to Talbot, a taste of what was to come.

He eventually slowed to a walk, his grin fading into a cold, calculating smile. His mission was complete.

Minutes later both Haylee and Wesley stirred from their unconscious states and called the police.

Detective Chief Superintendent Mark Talbot received the news with a heavy heart. It was another grim reminder that The Fox was growing increasingly erratic and vicious.

"Milton Keynes?" Talbot repeated, his voice taut with barely concealed anger. "He's back in the area then."

At the scene, the devastation was immediate and horrifying. Officers stood in stunned silence, their faces pale and drawn as they gathered inside the house now marked by the violence of The Fox.

As the team worked to comfort Wesley and Haylee and to gather evidence, Talbot's office phone buzzed with updates. Each new piece of information only deepened the sense of urgency. The Fox's latest act of aggression wasn't just an attack; it was a deliberate provocation, a challenge to the task force.

"I want all available officers to increase patrols in the Milton Keynes area. The Fox is back, and if we don't catch him now, he's going to tear the place apart," Talbot ordered, his voice steely. The pressure on Talbot's shoulders was immense.

The next day, the media frenzy was immense, and public fear was at an all-time high. The headlines screamed about the attack, each one more sensational than the last.

"THE FOX STRIKES AGAIN: POLICE FAIL TO PROTECT!" read one banner.

The police task force convened for an emergency meeting, the room buzzing with urgent voices. Talbot addressed his team with a steely determination.

"Listen up. The Fox is back. He's more dangerous than ever. Last night's attack was the worst so far. He's taking things to an unprecedented level. We have more boots on the ground in the Milton Keynes area, our focus switches there."

"He's a sick man. Who thinks to assault somebody with a toilet brush?" replied a distraught Detective Sergeant Sarah Kendrick.

"A twisted individual that's who. Hughes, Miller, where are we with the list of car owners, we must be getting close?"

"We've got through eleven hundred and fifty-nine of them, guv. Nothing but dead ends so far. Only another three hundred and forty-one to go," confirmed Detective Constable Tom Hughes.

"Keep going, I want an update every morning and every afternoon," barked Talbot.

The team discussed The Fox's return and his likely motives for moving to a new area. The meeting ended with Talbot sighing a huge sigh of frustration. The time for hesitation was over. He needed to put an end to The Fox's reign of terror once and for all.

Part Four: The Trap Is Set

Chapter 28

Since his return, The Fox had emptied his brother's bedroom of any evidence linking him to the crimes – the photographs, the ties. He was wary of a knock on the door from police asking for a blood test, so he decided against staying at his brother's place again. Unknown to all but himself, for the past few years, he also rented a secret residence, a quiet hideout in North London. He parked his car at the house to keep up appearances, and mostly used his work van for day-to-day operations.

Inside his house, he was rarely idle.

Now, he was ready to strike again, this time with a torrent of violence that would shatter the uneasy calm of Milton Keynes. Eleven houses. Eleven lives. Eleven brutal, calculated attacks.

The Fox was ready.

Milton Keynes wore the early hours like a shroud, a sprawling, soulless expanse of roundabouts and concrete cows under a blanket of darkness. The weight of a summer storm was waiting to break. The town felt tense, almost sentient, as if it knew what was coming - an onslaught of madness and horror that would leave its mark in blood and terror.

His mind was a dark place, a labyrinth of twisted thoughts and perverse desires. He fed off the fear, the chaos, the control. Every house he broke into, every terrified face he saw, was another piece of his puzzle, another stroke in his masterpiece of insanity. He had been haunting the dreams of his victims, but tonight, he would be something more. He would be their worst nightmare.

The first house in Shenley was a modest bungalow at the end of a quiet cul-de-sac, its windows dark as the occupant, Clara Compton was leaving to run an errand. The Fox, sharp and calculating, observed from a distance, waiting for his moment. When the coast was clear, he slipped into action, his gloved hands picking the back door lock with practiced precision. His heartbeat steady, almost calm. The door swung open with a soft click, and he slipped inside. The bungalow was silent except for the chirp of a canary, oblivious to the dangers The Fox presented.

After a quick scan of the surroundings, he wasted no time. He made himself at home, setting up a makeshift den with blankets as though it was his own. He brewed a cup of tea, rummaged through the kitchen, and helped himself to quiche Lorraine and a cheese and pickle sandwich. Then, he waited.

Hours later, Clara returned, unsuspecting. As soon as she stepped inside, The Fox emerged from his hiding spot, knife in hand. His eyes locked on her, cold and calculating. Without hesitation, he threatened her, waving the blade to assert control.

"Make a sound, and you die," he hissed, his voice a low, menacing growl.

The Fox felt a cold smile spread across his face beneath his mask. He reached into his pocket, pulling out a length of cord he had prepared earlier.

He moved quickly, efficiently, looping it around Clara's neck. She was about to scream. But The Fox was ready. He clamped a hand over her mouth, leaning close to whisper in her ear.

"Keep quiet, or you won't see tomorrow."

Clara froze, her eyes filled with tears, her body trembling beneath his grip. She gasped for breath, her hands clawing at the cord around her throat. The Fox tightened his grip, feeling the rush of power surge through him. This was control, pure and unfiltered. This was his art.

Fear flooded her face. Without warning, The Fox struck her with his fist, sending her crashing to the floor. And with another swift movement he kicked her in the stomach. The assault continued, blow after blow rained down on her. By the time he had finished, The Fox had inflicted serious injuries to Clara. Injuries both physical and mental. Injuries that would never heal.

As she lay on their floor, bruised, battered, covered in blood, The Fox collected his thoughts, regained his composure, and slipped out the back door. He didn't need to linger any longer. The damage was done.

The next day, The Fox was back on the prowl. The house was a semi-detached in Bradwell Common, its narrow front facing a row of identical homes. He knew this one well - a young professional, Sabrina Townsend. He approached from the back, scaling the garden fence with ease. He moved quickly, finding the rear door and creeping inside.

Sabrina slept soundly upstairs, oblivious to the intruder crawling through her home. The Fox moved with quiet accuracy, exploring the ground floor until he found an old, worn duvet in a closet. With a quick glance around the living room, he dragged some chairs together, fashioning a makeshift den. Satisfied with his hidden nook, he settled in, sipping milk he'd taken from the fridge and munching on a packet of biscuits he'd found in a cupboard.

For hours, he watched videos on the tv, the stillness of the house around him, biding his time. When the moment felt right, he rose silently, leaving behind the comfort of his temporary nest, and made his move up the stairs toward the slumbering occupant.

His footsteps were slow and deliberate as he ascended the stairs, each creak muffled beneath his weight. The house quiet, broken only by the rhythmic breathing of Sabrina sleeping soundly in her bedroom. He reached the door and pushed it open, the hinges barely whispering as he slipped inside.

The room was dimly lit by moonlight streaming through the curtains. The Fox approached the bed, looming over her for a moment before prodding Sabrina awake with the cold blade of his knife. She jolted, eyes wide with confusion, as The Fox brought a finger to her lips in a gesture for silence.

"Not a sound," The Fox hissed, his voice low and intimidating. "Do exactly as I say, or things will get ugly." The threat hung over her like a thunderstorm, as she lay frozen in the grip of terror.

Her eyes locked on him, her body trembling with fear. The Fox felt a dark satisfaction wash over him. He could see the helplessness in her eyes, could feel the power he held over her. He moved closer, his knife trained on her. He wanted her to know how close she was to death, how easily he could end it all.

He didn't though. That wasn't his style. He had other plans. He ordered her out of her bed and to drop to her knees. Without a moment's hesitation he slammed his fist into her face, sending her crashing to the ground. The onslaught that followed was beyond evil.

While she lay on the carpet, dazed, confused, bloodied, The Fox went hunting. He found a purse on a bedside table, emptied the cash into his pocket and when he had taken what he wanted, he left her there, broken and terrified, her life forever changed by his abuse.

Day after day, house after house, he moved through Milton Keynes like a dark tide, his presence felt but never truly seen. Talbot and his team were scrambling, their radios crackling with frantic orders and garbled communications. They were always two steps behind, chasing their tails. The Fox revelled in it. He could feel Talbot's desperation.

By the time he reached the seventh house, he was intoxicated with his own power. This one was different - a small, single-story dwelling on the outskirts of Stony Stratford. An elderly woman lived there, alone since her husband passed away. She had been easy to track, easy to follow. The Fox slipped in through a back window. He found her in the living room, asleep in a recliner, the television casting a dim, flickering light across the room.

He watched her for a moment, his breath shallow and steady. She was frail, vulnerable. She would break easily. He moved closer, his shadow falling over her like a death shroud. She stirred, her eyes fluttering open, and she gasped when she saw him. He moved quickly, one hand over her mouth, the other pressing the blade of his knife against her temple.

"Shh," he whispered. "No one's coming to save you."

Tears streamed down her face, her body shaking with silent sobs. The Fox felt nothing. No pity, no remorse. This was the game. This was what he lived for. He took his time with her, drawing out the fear, the helplessness. He wanted to see her spirit crumble, to watch the light fade from her eyes. When he was done sexually and physically assaulting her, he left her there, broken and alone.

The Fox continued his rampage through the area, each house a new chapter in his twisted narrative. He was writing his story in blood and fear, each scene meticulously crafted, each victim chosen with care. He was an artist, and this town was his canvas.

But even artists grow tired. By the time he reached the eleventh house, he could feel the fatigue setting in, the weight of his work pressing down on him. This one was a detached home on the edge of a wooded area in Blakelands, secluded, isolated. It was perfect.

He approached cautiously; his instincts honed to a razor's edge. He could see movement inside - a male figure passing by a window, a glimmer of light. He waited, watching, letting the tension build. He could feel the storm brewing, both inside and out. The wind was picking up, rattling the branches of the nearby trees, sending litter skittering across the ground like whispers of the dead.

He moved to the back of the house, finding a side door. It was locked, but that wasn't a problem. He pulled out his tool, the lock clicked open, and he snuck inside. He could hear him now - his voice, hushed and urgent, coming from a room down the hall. He moved towards him, his heart pounding in his chest, his senses alive with anticipation.

The door to the room was slightly ajar, and he pushed it open slowly, peering inside. A middle-aged man, Jonathan Meakin, sat on his sofa, eating crisps, watching tv, minding his own business.

The Fox moved fast. Without hesitation he stormed towards Meakin. The Fox felt a dark, cold smile spread across his face. This was it - the final act. He raised his knife, taking a step forward. Meakin finally saw him coming and foolishly lunged at him, a desperate, futile attempt to protect himself. The Fox sidestepped him easily, slamming the handle of the knife into the back of his head. Meakin crumpled to the floor.

The Fox stood over the semi-conscious Meakin, his chest heaving, adrenaline coursing through his veins.

The Fox took a step toward him, his presence looming over him like a black cloud. He watched him for a moment, savouring the sight of his terror. This was what he had come for - the pure, unadulterated fear, the raw power it gave him.

He slowly lowered the knife and reached out with his free hand, taking a handful of his hair and yanking him forward. He whimpered, his hands clawing at his gloved fingers. He pulled him close, his breath hot against his ear.

"Remember this feeling," he whispered. "Remember it every time you close your eyes. I want you to wake up every night, drenched in sweat, afraid that I'm still here, watching, waiting."

The physical assault that followed was bone breaking and relentless. Blow after blow rained down on Meakin's body until it was limp. The Fox wanted more. He stripped Meakin naked and violently assaulted him, leaving scars that would be felt for the rest of his life.

The Fox took a deep breath, surveyed the scene, and smiled to himself. He slipped out through the back door, the summer heat blasting against his skin like a furnace, humid and relentless. It was suffocating. Sweat trickled down his neck, clinging to his clothes as if the heat itself had wrapped around him.

As he made his way through the back streets, his mind was a whirlpool of dark thoughts and twisted satisfaction. The police would be converging on the scene soon, late again. He could almost hear their frantic voices, see their frustrated faces as they realised just how thoroughly they'd been outplayed.

He ducked into a narrow alley, his senses still on high alert, his eyes darting back and forth. He could feel the town around him, its heartbeat pounding in time with his own. He had become a part of it, a phantom etched into its very bones. His presence would be felt in every corner, every alleyway, every darkened room.

The Fox knew he needed to get to his car which he had stashed nearby, make his exit clean and quiet. But even in the chaos, his mind was already racing ahead, plotting the next move, the next act in his ever-escalating game.

He reached the car and slipped inside. The engine turned over with a low growl, and he pulled away from the curb, merging into the sparse late-night traffic. His face was impassive, his eyes scanning the road ahead, but inside, a fire burned. Eleven houses in Milton Keynes. Eleven lives shattered. But it wasn't enough. Not yet.

As he drove, he could feel the adrenaline beginning to fade, leaving behind a hollow emptiness that gnawed at him. The thrill, the power - he needed more of it, needed it to fill the void that seemed to grow larger with every passing day. His mind raced, thinking of the next town, the next unlucky souls who would cross his path. There was always another place, always another game to play.

The headlights of a passing car swept over his face, and for a moment, his eyes seemed to glow in the darkness. He grinned, a cold, thin smile that held no warmth, no humanity. He was The Fox, and he was far from finished.

Later that evening, Detective Chief Superintendent Mark Talbot stood still, his eyes locked on the house in front of him, the front door swinging open in the wind. Inside, he could see the paramedics moving frantically, their faces grim and gaunt in the dim light. He had seen this scene too many times before, and each time, it gnawed at him a little more.

"Eleven in this area now," he muttered. "He's relentless."

Beside him, Detective Sergeant Sarah Kendrick nodded, her face drawn with exhaustion. "He's back with a vengeance. How many more is he going to clock up."

Talbot nodded, his eyes never leaving the house. The detective felt the weight of eleven assaults pressing down on him. The Fox was still out there, somewhere, and he needed a breakthrough to help catch him.

On the night of ninth of September 1984, The Fox, a man whose criminal exploits had spread fear throughout the region, was preparing for yet another assault. His pattern of breaking into homes, building dens and assaulting the occupants, had earned him a chilling reputation. For months, he had successfully preyed on unsuspecting families, couples, and individuals, sneaking into their homes, instilling terror before slipping back into the night. His attacks were calculated, his movements precise. He had evaded the law and remained a faceless enigma. But that night, he would encounter an unexpected force: a woman who would refuse to be another victim in his long line of conquests.

It was a sweltering night. The summer heat was suffocating, and the suburban streets were empty, save for the occasional distant drone of a passing car or the chirp of crickets hidden in the grass. The Fox moved through the darkness with the same fluid, predatory grace that had served him so well. His target was a house on the edge of Wolverton, its lights long extinguished, the sole occupant asleep inside. From his observations over the past few days, he had learned that the woman who lived there was alone, no children, no partner. It was perfect, he thought. Easy, like all the others.

He approached the house with confidence. The back door was his usual entry point, and as he had done countless times before, he knelt and began to work the lock with his gloved hands. His heartbeat steady, his breathing controlled. There was a thrill in these moments - the anticipation, the power of knowing that he was in control. Within seconds, the door clicked open, and The Fox glided inside, as silent as a whisper in the night.

The house was still, the faint ticking of a clock the only sound that greeted him as he moved through the kitchen and into the hallway. He paused, listening for any sign that the woman might have stirred. Nothing. The house felt almost lifeless, as if it was holding its breath, waiting. The Fox advanced, his movements careful and deliberate. He had done this many times before. His victims rarely woke up until it was too late. He imagined it would be the same tonight. He would subdue her quickly, instil fear, maybe take a few valuables as a memento of his visit. Then, like always, he would vanish before dawn.

But as he made his way up the staircase, something shifted in the air. A faint creak of wood beneath his foot, perhaps a bit louder than intended, caused him to stop abruptly. He stood still, his muscles tensing as he listened. From the room at the end of the hall came the faintest rustle, the sound of someone stirring. The Fox continued forward, more cautious now, his steps as light as a feather.

The bedroom door was ajar, and through the sliver of space, he could see the outline of the bed, the figure beneath the sheets. The woman was still asleep, or so he thought. He pushed the door open slowly, his hand hovering near the knife tucked into his pocket - his insurance. He had learned that the fear of violence was often enough to render people compliant. But tonight, something would be different.

As The Fox stepped into the room, the woman's eyes snapped open, her body reacting instinctively to the presence of danger. She had been in a light sleep, the oppressive heat making it difficult to rest, and some sixth sense had alerted her to the intrusion. Before The Fox could fully comprehend what was happening, she sprang up, her eyes wide with shock and adrenaline.

The Fox moved to grab her, but she was faster than he had anticipated. In one fluid motion, she lunged toward him, her hands pushing against his chest with a force that caught him off guard. He stumbled back, momentarily losing his balance. She screamed, a sound that ripped through the stillness of the house, piercing the night.

The Fox, now panicked, raised his knife, but the woman was relentless. Fuelled by terror and the instinct to survive, she fought with everything she had. She clawed at his face, her nails scraping against the skin of his neck, her legs kicking with furious strength as she struggled to push him away. She was not going to be another victim, not tonight.

The Fox, used to quick and quiet control, was overwhelmed by the unexpected resistance. He had never faced someone who fought back with such intensity. The woman's screams echoed through the house, and in his mind, he knew it was only a matter of time before someone nearby heard the commotion. Panic set in, overriding the calculated precision that had defined him for so long.

He swung his arm wildly, trying to strike her, but she ducked, managing to evade his knife. Her knee came up, colliding with his midsection, and for the first time that night, The Fox felt real pain - a sharp, blinding shock that knocked the wind out of him. The woman seized the moment, shoving him back with all her strength. He crashed into a nearby bedside table, knocking over a lamp in the process.

The Fox staggered to his feet, his mind racing. This was not how it was supposed to go. He could feel his control slipping away, and in that moment, he made the decision to flee. Without another thought, he turned and bolted out of the bedroom, the woman's voice chasing him down the hall as she screamed for help. He nearly tripped down the stairs in his rush to escape, but managed to catch himself, sprinting through the house and out the back door where he had come in.

The hot night air hit him like a sledgehammer, the sweat drenched his body. He ran blindly through the darkened streets, his pulse thundering in his ears, heart pounding from a combination of exertion and disbelief. He had failed. The Fox had been humiliated.

The woman he left behind stood trembling in her bedroom, her breath coming in ragged gasps as the reality of what had just happened sank in. She had fought him off. She had survived. And though the terror still clung to her, she knew that she had done something that no one else had managed before - she had stopped The Fox.

Chapter 29

The date eleventh of September 1984 would go down in criminal history.

Detective Chief Superintendent Mark Talbot had faced many challenges in his career. He had led investigations into some of the most high-profile cases the country had ever seen, but none compared to the pursuit of the predator the media had dubbed "The Fox". For nearly six months, The Fox had terrorised the region, leaving a trail of destruction and taunting the police with flawless execution. Talbot's reputation was on the line, and he knew that if this case wasn't cracked, it would stain his otherwise exemplary career.

But today was different.

The small flick of yellow paint had been a breakthrough - though at the time, it was unknown how significant it would be. It was just a tiny shard, barely noticeable to the naked eye, scraped from a branch. Forensic teams had poured over the scene, hoping for something, anything, that would offer a clue. And there it was, a trace of yellow paint. Ordinary. Unremarkable. Yet, to the trained eye, it could mean everything. After hours of analysis, they had identified it: the paint belonged to a specific make of car, an Austin Allegro.

The discovery was a long shot, but when the forensic team had narrowed it down further - the yellow paint was used only on a particular model of the Allegro, and only fifteen hundred of those had ever been registered in the UK - it felt like the needle in a haystack had just grown a little larger. But it was still a needle.

Detective Sergeant Jake Miller and Detective Constable Tom Hughes, the police officers working on the case knew the gravity of what they were dealing with. They had been chasing The Fox for months. He had slipped through their fingers at every turn, leaving a trail of terrified victims.

Now, they had something. Something tangible. A list. A frustratingly long list of fifteen hundred registered Austin Allegro's, scattered across the UK. Their first task had been to review the list against the names Metal Mickey had provided as potential suspects. It bore no fruit. None of the key suspects were registered keepers of an Austin Allegro. So, that meant, five thousand suspects could be written off, all thanks to a single piece of evidence.

The next task was to sift through the list, cross-referencing names and addresses, methodically checking each lead. It was the sort of painstaking police work that didn't make the headlines - boring, monotonous, gruelling. But it was necessary. Many of those cars had been sold, resold, scrapped, or shipped off to unknown destinations. And with every change of ownership came a new challenge - tracking down the current owners, finding addresses, and hoping one of these cars would lead them to The Fox.

The late summer days of 1984 had blended into a blur. Detective Sergeant Jake Miller and Detective Constable Tom Hughes worked sixteen-hour shifts, barely stopping to catch their breath. Dunstable police station had become a second home, the scattered files and overflowing coffee cups evidence of their dedication. Every day felt the same: reviewing names, calling former owners, tracking down scraps of information, and more often than not, hitting dead ends.

Miller had grown used to the grind. His wife, Emma, understood - mostly. She had grown tired of hearing, "Just one more case, love. It'll be done soon," knowing full well it wouldn't be. His children, two boys aged seven and nine, were starting to get used to him not being around at dinnertime. It gnawed at him, the time lost, but Miller was a man driven by duty. He had been in the police force for nearly ten years and had never encountered someone like The Fox. His elusive nature, his ability to disappear without a trace - it had turned the case into an obsession.

Hughes, on the other hand, was younger and still new enough to believe in the system, in the idea that if they just worked hard enough, long enough, justice would prevail. But even he was starting to crack under the weight of the investigation. His girlfriend had left him three months ago, tired of the late nights and missed dates. Now, he had nothing but the case, and it seemed every time they thought they were getting closer, The Fox would slip away again.

There were moments - long stretches - when both men questioned whether The Fox was even catchable. Maybe he was too clever, too careful. Maybe he was just lucky. But then, on the morning of eleventh of September, they got a hit that would change everything.

It had been a routine start to the day, the list of names still as long and daunting as ever. That morning, the two detectives found themselves sifting through more files. Miller was on the phone, tracing another dead end. Hughes was reviewing the list of owners when a new name stood out: Malcolm Fairley.

"He's listed as having moved to this address in Kentish Town a couple of years ago," Hughes said, rubbing his tired eyes.

Miller looked up from his notes. "That's not far."

Hughes nodded. "Worth checking out, don't you think?"

It was more a formality than anything. They had followed leads like this before. But it was one of the few that hadn't required hours of searching for a forwarding address, and they needed a break from the office. Within an hour, they were on the road, driving toward North London.

The atmosphere in Kentish Town was grim and oppressive. The heavy scent of impending rain filled the environment, while dark, bruised clouds loomed low over the terraced houses like a suffocating blanket. It was the calm before the storm - a storm that echoed the nervousness gripping the nation, as if the streets themselves sensed that the abuser who had haunted them for so long was nearing his end.

The address was unassuming. Sixty-Five Oseney Crescent, Kentish Town - a row of Victorian terraces with narrow gardens, all squeezed together in a crooked line. There was nothing remarkable about it, nothing that screamed of a man capable of such acts of brutality. Evil never wore a uniform; it blended in, wore the same faces, spoke the same words, lived the same lives.

Miller and Hughes pulled up to the curb outside the house. Miller glanced at the house. Nothing special. "Think this could be it?"

Hughes didn't answer right away. He stared out the window at the figure on the pavement - a man bent over with tools laid out by the side of a yellow Austin Allegro. The car looked as tired as its owner, but the scratches on its rear told a different story. His pulse quickened. "Maybe," he said finally. "Let's find out."

The two officers stepped out into the cold air. The man didn't look up as they approached, too focused on his task, his tool moving in slow, deliberate circles on the car's wheel. Up close, he looked ordinary – average height, brown curly hair and a face that could fade into any crowd.

"Morning," Miller called, his voice cutting through the stillness.

The man finally looked up. His eyes were dark, like two dirty marbles. He blinked, wiping his forehead with the back of his hand, smearing water and sweat across his skin. "Morning, what can I do for you?" he replied, in a soft Geordie accent.
Miller's senses sharpened. "We are looking for a Malcolm Fairley, is that you sir?"

"That'll be me. How can I help?" replied Fairley.

Miller gave him a smile that didn't quite reach his eyes. "Nice car you've got there. Austin Allegro, isn't it? 'Harvest yellow' they call it?"

Fairley's lips twitched in what might have been a smile. "That's right. She's a bit old, but she gets the job done."

Miller nodded, glancing at the scratches again. "Had some trouble with it, though, by the looks of it. Those scratches… any idea how they got there?"

Fairley's eyes flicked to the back of the car, a flash of something dark and sharp crossing his face before he masked it. "Oh, that? Just some kids mucking about. You know how it is."

Hughes stepped closer, his eyes narrowing. "Kids, huh?"

Fairley shrugged, his gaze sliding away, back to the car. "Yeah, well, you know how they can be."

Hughes meanwhile noticed a screwdriver which matched the description of what had been used to break into homes. And in the back seat of the car, two pairs of green overalls, one of which had a missing leg.

Miller watched Fairley closely. There was a stiffness in his movements now, a difficulty that hadn't been there a moment ago. He was hiding something. He decided to push a little harder.

"Mind if we ask you a few questions?" Miller asked, his tone casual. "Just routine."

Fairley hesitated, his hand tightening around the tool in his hand. "Sure. What about?"

"Do you know Bedfordshire at all?" Miller replied.

"Erm, yeah, my brother lives in Leighton Buzzard." Fairley looking more uneasy on his feet.

"Oh right, you must've visited him there then?" quizzed Hughes.

"Yeah, I've been a few times," replied Fairley.

Miller noticed a watch on the front seat of the car, and thinking on his feet, made a final shot at piecing all the evidence together.

"Ok, well I tell you what, let's pop inside your house and have a chat away from your neighbours. Maybe put your watch on, you don't want to leave that out here, in case those kids steal it. You know how they can be eh," Miller afforded himself a slight chuckle.

Fairley opened the passenger side door to his car, and with his left-hand picked up the wristwatch, placing it on his right wrist. And with that, Miller and Hughes looked at one another. They both felt a chill run down their spines. Victims had described The Fox as left-handed - something only someone trying to disguise their true nature would be aware of. And here was Fairley, putting on his watch on his right wrist.

Miller caught Hughes' eye, a silent understanding passing between them. They were close, so damn close. Miller kept his voice steady, calm, as if he were talking about the weather. "Shouldn't take but a minute."

Hughes opened a car door, reached in, grabbed the overhauls. He then bent over and picked up several screwdrivers and tools from the toolbox on the ground. "I think we might need to talk about these too," as he placed them into a clear plastic evidence bag.

Fairley's eyes darted from Miller and Hughes and back again. His shoulders tensed, and for a moment, Miller thought he might bolt. But then he sighed, a long, weary sound, and nodded. "Fine. Let's go."

All three men walked towards the entrance of Sixty-Five Oseney Crescent. Hughes and Miller's eyes not once leaving Fairley. As they reached the front door, Hughes noticed scratches on Fairley's neck, consistent with those reported by the last victim of The Fox. And he noticed teeth-shaped scar on his right hand. The pieces of the jigsaw were all falling into place.

Once inside, Hughes held up the evidence bag containing the overalls. The fabric was rough and faded, but there was no mistaking the fact that the leg had been cut clean off from one pair. His heart began to pound, a cold sweat breaking out on the back of his neck. "What happened to these?" he asked, keeping his voice level.

Fairley shrugged again, but there was a tremor in his voice now. "Work clothes. They get torn up sometimes."

Hughes moved in closer, holding up an evidence bag containing screwdrivers. "These look pretty worn, too. You use these a lot?" Fairley swallowed, his Adam's apple bobbing. "Yeah. I do a bit of repair work, here and there."

But Hughes wasn't listening anymore. His mind was racing, pieces falling into place like the final moves in a deadly game of chess. The overalls, the missing leg - perfect material for a mask, crude but effective. The screwdrivers - tools that had been matched to the marks left at several break-in scenes. And the scratches on the car – the same height the forensics team said they'd be. Fairley matched the height the victims all said he was, he had brown curly hair, a Geordie accent, scratches on his neck and above all, he was left-handed.

Miller looked up, locking eyes with Fairley. "Malcolm Fairley, I think you'd better come with us, you're under arrest."

Malcolm Fairley's face went pale, his eyes wide with a sudden, naked fear. For a second, Miller thought he might fight, might try to make a run for it. But then his shoulders sagged, and he nodded, defeated. "All right," he muttered. "All right. Just…let me get my coat."

Miller stepped forward, his hand moving to his belt. "No sudden moves, Malcolm."

Malcolm Fairley nodded again, his movements slow and deliberate as he turned around and placed his hands behind his back.

Miller snapped the cuffs around Malcolm Fairley's wrists with a practiced efficiency. Hughes watched, his heart still hammering in his chest, as the reality of what they'd just accomplished began to sink in. The Fox had been caught.

As they led Malcolm Fairley out into the cold, grey morning, Miller and Hughes felt a sense of grim satisfaction settle over their bodies. The nightmare was over. But the scars - the fear and the trauma - would linger long after The Fox had been put away. And as the rain began to pour in earnest, the officers knew one thing for certain: darkness like this never truly disappeared. It only hid in the shadows, waiting for the next moment to strike.

And so, as the officers breathed a huge sigh of relief, Malcolm Fairley was detained and driven to Dunstable police station for questioning.

Chapter 30

Malcolm Fairley - The Fox - was finally in handcuffs.

The weight of the manhunt lifted, but there was no victory to savour. The dark clouds above Herts, Beds and Bucks wept tears of joy. The flickering lights of the squad car sliced through the darkness, casting long, twisted shadows that danced and wavered across the slick pavement. It was as if the day itself was reluctant to bear witness to the end of this grim chapter.

Malcolm Fairley arrived at Dunstable police station and was greeted by Detective Chief Superintendent Mark Talbot. A stern look addressed Fairley, Talbot took no pleasure in seeing the man he had chased for many months. As Fairley was led toward the building by Detective Sergeant Jake Miller and Detective Constable Tom Hughes, Talbot followed a few paces behind.

The tension was clear, a heavy, oppressive atmosphere filled with anticipation and anxiety. Talbot's chest heaved with each breath, a testament to the gruelling pursuit that had worn him down to the bone. His truncheon felt like an anchor, every step felt heavy.

Fairley's face showed a look of pure defiance. Even now, with his hands shackled behind his back and a drizzling rain soaking through his clothes, he wore a twisted smile. It was as if he found some perverse satisfaction in the spectacle of his own downfall. As the officers nudged him toward the building, his sneer seemed to mock not only them but the entire effort that had gone into capturing him.

"Keep him steady," Talbot barked to the two officers flanking Fairley. His voice was rough, edged with the strain of a long and bitter hunt. "I want him breathing when we get him inside."

Detective Sergeant Jake Miller drenched to the bone and his face as grey as the rain-drenched sky, approached Talbot. His eyes, though tired, remained sharp and focused. He was the epitome of fatigue and resolve, but even he couldn't hide the tremor of doubt in his voice. "Is that it, then? Is it really over?"

Talbot turned to Miller, his stern expression not faltering for a moment, despite the weight of the question hanging over him. Rain dripped from the brim of his hat, and for a brief second, he let out a sigh, deep and laced with uncertainty.

"Over?" Talbot echoed, his gaze fixed on Fairley, who was being ushered into the station. "Not yet. It's only over when we know why, and he's behind bars."

Miller nodded, his throat tight. It was supposed to feel like a victory - the end of an exhausting, relentless pursuit. But as the grim-faced detectives made their way into the station, the anticipated satisfaction was nowhere to be found. Malcolm Fairley, the monster they had dubbed The Fox, had been caught, but the damage he had done left a deep wound that no arrest could heal.

Inside Dunstable police station, the atmosphere was charged. Officers who had spent countless nights chasing leads and dead ends now looked at Fairley with a mixture of relief and disgust. His presence was an uncomfortable reminder of the terror he had wrought, and no one wanted to be too close to him.

Fairley was seated in a small, dimly lit interrogation room. His twisted smile had faded, replaced by a steely indifference as the cuffs were removed from his wrists and his wet jacket was peeled off. His hands, now free, twitched slightly, but there was no sign of panic or fear. He leaned back in the chair, his eyes scanning the room with the cool detachment of a man who believed he still had control.

Miller stood just outside the door, staring through the one-way glass at Fairley. Hughes joined him, shaking rain from his coat, his face a picture of exhaustion.

"He doesn't look worried," Hughes muttered.

"He's not," Miller replied. "Not yet at least. He still thinks he's got the upper hand."

Hughes' brows furrowed. "After everything? After what he did? He thinks we're the ones losing?"

Miller glanced sideways at his partner. "Men like him…they thrive on the game. It's not just the crime, Tom. It's the chase. He's been playing us for months, and now he's in here, he's still playing."

Hughes leaned against the wall, shaking his head. "I don't understand it. After all that…how can he still think there's something to win?"

Miller didn't answer immediately. He was too focused on Fairley, on the slight upturn of his mouth and the way his hands rested, unnervingly calm, on the table in front of him.

"We'll find out soon enough," Miller said. "We've got him in a box now."

Inside the interrogation room, Talbot sat across from Fairley, his face stony. A pile of case files sat to his right, documents full of evidence, testimonies, and crime scene photos that painted the picture of Malcolm Fairley's reign of terror. But it wasn't the paperwork that would break Fairley - it was the weight of truth, the relentless exposure of his cruelty that Talbot was prepared to unleash.

Fairley leaned forward slightly, his eyes locking on Talbot. "You look tired," he said with a casual smirk. "Was it hard catching me?"

Talbot didn't respond immediately. He simply stared at Fairley, his hands clasped tightly in front of him on the table.

"You've spent months terrorising innocent people," Talbot finally said, his voice cold and sharp. "Breaking into their homes. Stealing their lives, their safety. For what? For power? For fun?"

Fairley's smile widened. "It wasn't personal. Not really. They just…got in the way."

Talbot clenched his jaw, his anger barely contained. "They were families. Husbands and wives. Mothers and fathers. You left them broken."

Fairley's gaze didn't waver. "Like I said, it wasn't personal."

Miller and Hughes, still watching from behind the glass, exchanged glances. They could feel the unease mounting in the room, the delicate balance between Fairley's twisted calm and Talbot's growing fury.

"He's baiting him," Hughes whispered.

"Talbot knows what he's doing," Miller replied, though his own doubts were creeping in.

Inside, Talbot pushed the stack of files across the table toward Fairley, opening the first one. Photos of Fairley's victims stared up from the pages - blurred snapshots of faces contorted in fear, hands bound, eyes wide with terror, covered in bruises and blood. It was the raw evidence of his crimes, laid out in excruciating detail.

Fairley glanced at the photos, his expression unchanged. He leaned back in his chair, crossing his arms casually, as if he were above it all.

"You don't even care, do you?" Talbot asked, his voice low and full of disgust. "About the people whose lives you've destroyed. You don't care about anything."

Fairley's smirk returned. "Care?" he repeated. "I'm just very…good at what I do."

Talbot slammed his fist down on the table, the sound echoing through the small room. "You're nothing but a coward. A sick, pathetic coward who hides behind a mask. And now, we've got you. There's nowhere left to run."

Fairley didn't flinch. "Do you think this is a victory? You may have caught me, but you'll never understand."

"Understand what?" Talbot asked, his voice ice-cold.

"The thrill," Fairley said, leaning in, his voice dropping to a whisper. "Of being in control. Of knowing that when I walk into a room, everyone's life changes. I owned them, Talbot. I owned their fear."

Talbot stared at Fairley for a long, intense moment. But then, slowly, a hard, determined look crossed his face. "You don't own anything anymore. Not your freedom, not your control, not even your fear."

With that, Talbot stood and walked out of the room, leaving Fairley sitting there, alone, his smirk fading slightly. The door clicked shut behind him, and Talbot rejoined Miller and Hughes outside.

"Well?" Miller asked, his voice tense.

Talbot sighed, rubbing the back of his neck. "He thinks he's still in control, but that's the thing about men like him - they're only powerful when they're on the outside. In here, he's just another prisoner."

Hughes nodded slowly. "Do you think we'll ever understand why he did it? Why he hurt all those people?"

Talbot shook his head. "There's no real understanding it, Hughes. Men like Fairley - there's something broken inside them. Something we can't fix. All we can do is make sure they can't hurt anyone else."

Miller glanced through the glass at Fairley, who now sat in silence, his hands twitching slightly as he stared down at the table. "And what now?" he asked.

"Now," Talbot said, "we let him stew. He's got nowhere left to hide. Sooner or later, he'll crack. They always do."

As they stood there, the rain continued to tap against the windows, a steady, unrelenting rhythm. Outside, the storm raged on, but inside Dunstable police station, for the first time in months, there was a sense of finality.

Malcolm Fairley - the man who had haunted their every waking moment, the monster they had called The Fox - was no longer a menace to society. He was just a man, stripped of his power, trapped by his own arrogance.

The hunt was over. Now came the reckoning.

Later that day, Detective Chief Superintendent Mark Talbot stood behind the podium at the Dunstable police station, his heart pounding in his chest. Reporters jostled for position as they aimed their cameras and notepads toward him. The buzzing of conversations filled the space, a cacophony of voices blending together in an excited zing.

As he glanced down at the array of microphones positioned in front of him, Talbot felt a wave of pressure wash over him. It was a moment he had envisioned countless times during the relentless months of the manhunt for The Fox. He had imagined it would feel triumphant, a celebration of justice. Instead, a sense of sombre duty gripped him.

He cleared his throat, and the noise subsided, the room falling into a tense silence. Talbot straightened his back, adopting a stance that spoke of authority tempered with fatigue.

"Good afternoon, everyone. Thank you for being here," he began, his voice steady but firm. "I stand before you today to announce that the man responsible for a string of violent home invasions and assaults across Hertfordshire, Bedfordshire, Buckinghamshire and beyond has been apprehended. Malcolm Fairley, known to the public as The Fox, is now in police custody."

A flurry of cameras flashed, capturing the moment. Talbot felt a flash of irritation at the bright lights momentarily blinding him, but he pushed it aside. This was bigger than him; it was about the victims, the families whose lives had been shattered by Fairley's actions.

Talbot continued, "The arrest follows a meticulous investigation that has involved many dedicated officers from various departments. I want to take this moment to commend Detective Sergeant Jake Miller and Detective Constable Tom Hughes for their tireless efforts in bringing this case to a close."

He paused as the two officers, standing in the back, nodded slightly, their expressions a mix of exhaustion and relief.

"Malcolm Fairley has been charged with three counts of rape, two counts of indecent assault, three counts of aggravated burglary, five counts of burglary and also for the possession of a firearm."

"Malcolm Fairley has been a figure of fear for many in our communities. His criminal activities have left scars on countless individuals and families, and I assure you, the police force remains committed to seeking justice for every one of his victims." He held their gazes, the seriousness of his words resonating in the room.

"Fairley's capture was not without challenges. His ability to evade law enforcement for so long speaks to the tenacity with which he operated. However, through collaboration and perseverance, we were able to gather the evidence necessary to locate and apprehend him."

A reporter in the front row raised a hand, and Talbot gestured for her to speak. "Detective Chief Superintendent Talbot, can you provide any details about the circumstances of the arrest? Was it a violent confrontation?"

Talbot took a breath, noting the curiosity in her tone. "The arrest was conducted without incident. Fairley was taken into custody at his residence in Kentish Town after a thorough investigation into his whereabouts. I assure you, there was no threat to public safety at the time of his arrest."

Another hand shot up. "Can you tell us if Fairley has cooperated with police since his arrest? What do you expect will happen next?"

Talbot's brow furrowed slightly. He knew the media would want to dissect every detail, but he had to be cautious. "As of now, we are still in the early stages of our interrogation with Fairley. He has shown a certain level of cooperation, but we are prepared for a lengthy process. Our primary focus is to build a strong case against him and to ensure that the victims receive the justice they deserve."

A reporter shouted, "What can you say about the charges made against him, why aren't there more charges?"

Talbot nodded, acknowledging the urgency of the question. "Fairley faces multiple charges, including burglary, assault, and other related offenses. We will ensure that every crime he has committed is accounted for in the charges brought against him."

The questions came rapid-fire, each one probing deeper into the case and the man behind the mask of The Fox. Talbot felt a familiar weight settle on his shoulders, the responsibility of not just delivering news, but representing the countless lives affected by Fairley's actions.

"Are you concerned about Fairley's potential for a plea deal?" another reporter inquired, her voice sharp.

Talbot steeled himself. "That is something we will have to address as the case develops. I am more focused on ensuring that justice is served and that the victims' voices are heard throughout the legal process."

With each question, the atmosphere in the room shifted slightly. The reporters, initially buzzing with excitement, began to realise the complexity of the situation. The nuances of a criminal case, especially one as harrowing as this, were not lost on them.

Talbot continued, "I want to take a moment to acknowledge the victims and their families. Their courage in coming forward and sharing their stories has been instrumental in this investigation. It's important to remember that behind every statistic is a person, a life impacted by this man's actions."

A hushed silence fell over the room as Talbot's words sank in. He could see the cameras shifting, the reporters exchanging glances. The gravity of the situation was becoming intense.

"Going forward, I encourage anyone who has information or has been affected by Fairley's actions to reach out to the police. We are here to support you, and we will do everything in our power to ensure your safety and well-being."

As Talbot finished his statement, he took a moment to scan the room, his eyes resting on the faces in the crowd. Some looked sceptical, others hungry for more information, and a few appeared genuinely moved. He felt the weight of their expectations, the hopes and fears of a community that had lived under a blanket of fear for too long.

With a final nod, Talbot stepped back slightly from the podium. "Thank you for your time. I'll take a few more questions, but please understand that some details are still under investigation."

The room erupted once more into a frenzy of raised hands and shouted questions, each voice vying for his attention. He answered a few more inquiries, but his mind was already racing ahead, thinking about the next steps in the investigation and the task of helping the victims find closure.

As the press conference drew to a close, Talbot stepped away from the podium, wiping the sweat from his brow. He felt an overwhelming mix of relief and anxiety; they had caught Fairley, yes, but the battle was far from over.

Later that evening, in the quiet of his office, Talbot leaned back in his chair, staring at the framed photographs on the wall - moments from his career that now felt like a lifetime ago. The weight of the day settled heavily on him, and he rubbed his temples, trying to ease the stress that had built up over the previous few months.

The phone rang, breaking the silence. Talbot picked it up, his heart racing slightly, half-expecting it to be a reporter or a colleague needing something urgent. Instead, it was his wife, Claire.
"Mark," she said, her voice warm and familiar. "How did it go?"

"Exhausting," he admitted, sinking back into his chair. "But we caught him. The Fox is in custody."

"That's incredible news. I can't imagine how you must be feeling," she replied, a note of pride evident in her voice.

"It feels like a relief, but…it's complicated. There's still so much to do. The victims deserve to have their stories told, and I need to ensure we do right by them."

"I know you will," she said softly. "You always do. But don't forget to take care of yourself, too."

He chuckled lightly, despite the fatigue weighing him down. "I'll try, but it's hard to switch off when the job feels like it's never really done."

They talked for a few more minutes, the mundane details of their day grounding him, reminding him that life still existed outside the walls of the station. After hanging up, Talbot felt a flicker of warmth in his chest, a reminder of why he did this job - why he fought for justice every day. His Press Officer Katie McGee entered his office.

"Well, that went better than I expected. The press seemed satisfied. You handled their questions perfectly," sighed a relieved McGee.

Talbot nodded with a hint of a smile. "I've had plenty of practice. Although, it helps to have a good press officer steering the show."

"Flattery noted. But seriously, this is a huge win. The Fox has been a thorn in our side for months. The media's been relentless, and now that he's in custody, they'll finally ease off...for a little while, at least."

Talbot rubbed his temples. "For a little while. I'll take any reprieve I can get, though I suspect they'll be back as soon as they catch a scent of the trial. Still, the team deserves the praise they're getting."

McGee agreed. "This case was...personal for a lot of people. It's not every day we get to tell a story with a satisfying end."

Talbot nodded thoughtfully. "True. Capturing him took everything we had and then some. If it weren't for you keeping the press at bay and managing the narrative, we'd have been hounded at every turn."

McGee smiled softly. "All part of the job. And with someone like The Fox, we had to be careful. The public pressure was intense, but I think today helped show people how hard everyone worked."

"Let's hope it reminds them we're here to protect, even when it's messy and...slow-going. And Katie - thanks for everything. It wouldn't have been this smooth without you," replied a very grateful Talbot.

McGee nodded feeling touched. "Just doing my part. Now, let's enjoy the peace while it lasts."

The following days were a whirlwind of activity. Talbot's team worked tirelessly, sorting through evidence and gathering testimonies from the victims.

Talbot spent countless hours in the interrogation room, meticulously peeling back the layers of Fairley's defences. Each session revealed snippets of his twisted mindset.

Talbot made a silent vow to the victims: he would seek the truth, no matter where it led. The stakes had never been higher, and as he prepared to delve deeper into the twisted world of Malcolm Fairley, he felt the weight of their expectations settle firmly on his shoulders once again.

This was not just about catching a criminal; it was about unearthing the darkness that had haunted his community for too long. And he would see it through.

Part Five: The Aftermath

Chapter 31

On the twelfth of February 1985, Malcolm Fairley went on trial at St Albans Crown Court.

On day one of the trial, the courtroom was packed to the rafters. Reporters jostled for space in the gallery, their cameras trained on the dock where Malcolm Fairley - The Fox - sat like a stone statue. He wore a dark suit, his hands resting casually on the table in front of him, and his expression was unreadable. The trial of the decade had begun, and the room was charged with anticipation.

Detective Chief Superintendent Mark Talbot sat behind the prosecution's table, his eyes fixed on Fairley. Even in the controlled environment of the court, Talbot could feel the man's unsettling presence. It was as if a wild animal had been trapped in a cage, dangerous and unpredictable. Talbots face was lined with exhaustion, but his eye was steady. For months, he had chased this monster through fields, woods, and darkened streets. Now, he wanted to see justice served.

Judge Mary Crawley, a formidable woman with silver hair pulled into a severe bun, banged her gavel. "Order in the court," she commanded, her voice slicing through the murmurs.

"Ladies and gentlemen of the court, today we gather in pursuit of justice - justice for a summer dominated by violence, a community haunted by acts of terror, and a truth that lies tangled in shadows. At the heart of this trial stands a figure who has captivated and divided us, a man known as The Fox. A name that evokes cunning and survival, but also secrecy and suspicion. Yet we must remind ourselves that this courtroom is not the forest, and the laws we uphold demand evidence, reason, and fairness, not instinct or conjecture.

The defendant, Mr Malcolm Fairley, is entitled to the presumption of innocence. It is the solemn duty of the prosecution to prove their case beyond reasonable doubt. Likewise, the defence is here to ensure every detail is explored, every doubt magnified, so that justice may be served.

This case will ask us to confront uncomfortable truths, to look beyond appearances, and to weigh the facts without prejudice. The eyes of the country may be upon us, but our focus remains fixed on the evidence and the law.

This trial, like all trials, is not a spectacle nor a stage for personal agendas. It is a solemn process, guided by law and respect for justice. As we proceed, I will not tolerate interruptions, theatrics, or attempts to derail the pursuit of truth.

To the jury, your role is one of utmost importance. You are the impartial finders of fact, tasked with setting aside personal biases, preconceived notions, or sensational stories that may have reached you outside these walls. You will hear evidence - some of it straightforward, some of it complex, some of it upsetting, and it is your responsibility to weigh it carefully and decide what is credible.

To the prosecution, you have the burden of proving your case. Assertions alone will not suffice; you must present evidence that leaves no reasonable doubt. To the defence, your task is equally vital: to hold the prosecution to that standard and to advocate for your client with integrity and clarity.

This case, though extraordinary in its implications, is no different from any other in its core purpose - to seek justice, not vengeance.

Remember that this is not a trial of character, but of actions, facts, and law.

With these principles clear, we shall now proceed. Prosecution, you may make your opening statement."

And with that, the lead prosecutor, Mrs Harriet Whitman, rose with a calm authority.

"Ladies and gentlemen of the jury, today we begin a trial concerning a series of heinous and calculated crimes. The defendant, Mr Malcolm Fairley, stands accused of the following charges:

Five counts of burglary.

Three counts of aggravated burglary.

Three counts of rape.

Two counts of indecent assault.

One count of possession of a firearm with intent to cause fear of violence.

These charges are not mere allegations but are supported by compelling evidence, which I will now outline.

Firstly, let us consider the unique connection to Malcolm Fairley's vehicle. A key piece of evidence is a distinctive speck of yellow paint identified as seven-nine-one-nine Harvest Yellow. This paint was used exclusively on Austin Allegro cars, of which only fifteen hundred were manufactured in this country. It is an irrefutable fact that Malcolm Fairley owned one of these vehicles.

At a wooded area in Brampton-en-le-Morthen, connected to all the crimes, a branch bore traces of this same paint at the precise height of a scratch found on the defendant's car. This is not coincidence; it is direct evidence tying him to the scene.

In addition, we found at the same crime scene, a pair of gloves, a shotgun, a semen-stained bedsheet, all which link to many crimes committed by the same person, and some of which bear Malcolm Fairley's DNA.

Witnesses to these terrible crimes have provided a clear and consistent description of the perpetrator - a man with a northern accent, who was approximately five feet nine to five feet ten inches tall. He had brown curly hair and was of slim build. During many of his attacks, the assailant wielded a shotgun, holding it in a way that suggested he was his left-handed. During other attacks, he held a knife in his left hand.

Malcolm Fairley has the same appearance and is left-handed. During one attack, the victim bit the attacker's hand, drawing blood. Forensic analysis confirmed the blood was type O, matching Malcolm Fairley's blood group. Upon his arrest, Fairley bore a scar on his hand, consistent with a bite mark.

In another incident, the victim fought back, scratching the attacker's neck. When Fairley was apprehended, he had a scar on his neck that aligned with the victim's testimony.

Forensic analysis determined that a flathead screwdriver was used to break into the victims' homes. Upon Malcolm Fairley's arrest, officers recovered an identical tool from his car, matching the forensic evidence.

A pair of overalls with one leg missing was also found in Fairley's vehicle. One victim identified the fabric as identical to the material of the mask worn by "The Fox" during the attack.

Finally, and perhaps most damning of all, Malcolm Fairley confessed to his crimes during his initial arrest. While the defence may attempt to discredit this confession, we will demonstrate its reliability and truthfulness.

We anticipate that the defence may argue it was mistaken identity – suggesting that someone else committed these crimes and pointing to gaps in the timeline or evidence. Contamination or mishandling of evidence – questioning the integrity of forensic methods used to identify his DNA or the specks of paint. Coercion in obtaining the confession – claiming that Malcolm Fairley's confession was made under duress or was involuntary.

Ladies and gentlemen, we will demonstrate beyond a reasonable doubt that these arguments hold no weight against the overwhelming body of evidence. Malcolm Fairley is the perpetrator of these vile crimes, and justice demands a verdict of guilty.

The Crown calls its first witness, Mrs Lizzie Chambers."

A hush fell over the courtroom as Lizzie Chambers took the stand. She clutched a handkerchief as if it were a lifeline. She sat down, and the bailiff swore her in. The weight of what she was about to say settled over the room like a fog.

"Mrs Chambers," Whitman began, her voice gentle but clear, "can you tell the court what happened on the night of sixteenth of April 1984?"

Lizzie Chambers nodded, her eyes darting to Fairley for a split second before quickly looking away. "It was late," she said, her voice trembling. "My husband and I were asleep. I - I heard something downstairs. A creak on the floorboards. I thought it was just the house settling, but then...then I saw him."

"Who did you see, Mrs Chambers?"

Her eyes filled with tears. "Him," she said, her voice breaking. "The man they call The Fox."

The gallery erupted in murmurs. Judge Crawley rapped her gavel sharply. "Order!"

Lizzie Chambers continued, her voice gaining strength despite her fear. "He was wearing a mask. All in black. He...he had a knife, in his left-hand."

"And what did he do then?" Whitman asked, leaning in slightly, her eyes steady on Lizzie Chambers.

Lizzie Chambers' breath hitched. "He told us to be quiet, to not make a sound. He...he wanted us to know he could do anything, that no one would come to help us. I - I thought we were going to die."

Across the room, Fairley watched her with an eerie calm. There wasn't a flicker of emotion on his face, not even a twitch. Talbot stared at him, his blood simmering. This was the man who had stolen sleep and safety from countless families. And now, with the country watching, he didn't even have the decency to flinch.

"And can you please describe the appearance of the person who broke into your home," asked Whitman.

"Well, he looked like him, the man seated over there, Malcolm Fairley. He was the same height, same build, same curly brown hair sticking out of his mask. And his voice. It was a Geordie accent," replied Lizzie Chambers, while wiping away tears from her eyes.

Whitman guided Lizzie Chambers through the rest of her testimony, detailing the terror, the threats, and the psychological games Fairley had played. Each word tightened the grip of horror in the courtroom. Faces turned pale; eyes were wide. When Lizzie Chambers was finally excused, she left the stand as if she'd been carrying a great weight, her shoulders sagging with exhaustion.

One by one, the survivors took the stand: Markus Longman - the man who was beaten to a pulp, Clare and Nigel – the brother and sister who were forced to grope one another, Michael and Louise Stamp – the elderly couple who were sexually assaulted. Each testimony painted a clearer picture of the violence Fairley had inflicted, the lives he had shattered.

The courtroom grew colder with every word, but Fairley remained unyielding. His eyes were flat, his lips a thin line, his demeanour almost bored. When the court broke for lunch, Talbot could hardly eat. He leaned against the railing outside, the bitter wind whipping around him.

"He doesn't care," Detective Sergeant Sarah Kendrick said, coming to stand beside him. "Not a flicker of remorse. It's like he's proud of it all."

"That's because he is," Talbot replied. "To him, this is all a game. And he thinks he's still winning."

The afternoon session saw a harrowing procession of victims take the stand, their numbers overwhelming. Testimonies filled the courtroom with raw emotion, bringing tears to many in the gallery. The accounts painted a chilling picture of senseless violence, lingering nightmares, and the enduring trauma inflicted by The Fox. One by one, these courageous individuals recounted how Malcolm Fairley had broken into their homes and shattered their lives. They all confirmed that Fairley's accent and appearance perfectly matched those of The Fox.

Throughout, Fairley sat unmoving, his expression cold and devoid of emotion.

As Judge Mary Crawley adjourned for the day, the weight of the proceedings was palpable. Whitman and her team exchanged weary glances, releasing deep breaths of strain. They knew this was just the beginning - an uphill battle lay ahead to ensure Fairley would never harm another soul again.

Day two began, with the prosecution calling forensic experts to the stand.

The courtroom was tense as Dr Evelyn Carter, a seasoned forensic expert, adjusted her glasses and leaned into the microphone. The lead prosecutor, Harriet Whitman, paced deliberately.

"Dr Carter," she began, "is it your professional opinion that the yellow paint particles found embedded on a branch near the crime scene in Brampton-en-le-Morthen match the paint on Mr Malcolm Fairley's car?"

"Yes," Dr Carter replied, her voice steady. "The chemical composition and shade are consistent with the factory-standard paint used on Mr Fairley's vehicle."

Whitman nodded. "And the scratch on his car - would you say it aligns with the height and width of that very branch?"

Dr Carter hesitated for a moment, choosing her words carefully. "The dimensions are consistent, yes. The scratch appears to have been caused by a similar object, and the height aligns with the branch recovered from the scene."

The defence counsel, Ms Clara Lane, rose swiftly, her tone sharp.

"Dr Carter, would you agree that paint transfer could occur in many situations? For example, if Mr Fairley's car had been parked near a wooded area, could the branch have fallen naturally?"

Dr Carter frowned slightly. "It is possible for paint transfer to occur in other circumstances, but-"

Lane interrupted. "And regarding the height of the scratch, could it not have been caused by something else? A different branch, or even vandalism?"

Dr Carter glanced toward the jury. "While those scenarios are possible, the evidence strongly suggests-"

"Suggests, Dr Carter?" Lane pressed. "Not proves?"

The courtroom murmured as Lane sat down, leaving an air of doubt lingering over the forensic testimony.

Whitman leaned on the witness stand, a quiet confidence in her tone. "Dr Carter let's address the sequence of events. The paint transfer on the branch - does its placement suggest that it was stationary when struck by the vehicle or when it was moving?"

Dr Carter clasped her hands in her lap. "Yes, the pattern of transfer and the indentation on the bark indicate the vehicle made contact with the branch while it was reversing."

"And does this match the reported location of the branch found near the scene of the attack?" Whitman asked, her gaze fixed on the jury.

Dr Carter nodded. "Yes. The branch was positioned approximately forty-five inches above ground level, which is consistent with the height of the scratch on the rear of Mr Fairley's car."

Lane, stood abruptly, a sly smile creeping onto her face. "Dr Carter, forgive me, but isn't it true that branches of that size and shape could be found in almost any wooded area within the area in question?"

Dr Carter tilted her head slightly. "Branches of a similar size could exist, but the paint transfer and its specific location are what make this one relevant."

Lane stepped closer to the jury box, her voice dropping into a conversational tone. "Ah, but relevance isn't proof, is it? A fallen branch - perhaps carried by the wind - could have made contact with the vehicle. Or even a different car entirely might have brushed against it before."

Whitman interjected. "Your Honour, the evidence presented by Dr Carter is consistent with-"

Lane raised her hand. "Let the witness answer, please."

Dr Carter sighed, her professionalism intact. "Yes, theoretically, there could be alternative explanations, but the totality of evidence, including the specific chemical composition of the paint, strongly implicates Mr Fairley's vehicle."

Lane seized on the opening. "So, you admit there's room for doubt. And in the absence of direct evidence - like a witness who saw Mr Fairley at the scene, or his car strike the branch - this remains just an interpretation, doesn't it?"

Dr Carter hesitated, glancing at the jury. "That is for the court to decide."

A murmur rippled through the courtroom, the tension between prosecution and defence evident as Lane returned to her seat, her expression triumphant.

The room seemed to hold its breath as Whitman resumed her questioning. "Dr Carter, earlier you mentioned that the branch was found embedded with paint transfer. Were you able to determine the precise force required to cause such an imprint?"

Dr Carter adjusted her glasses, her calm demeanour unshaken. "Yes. Based on the analysis, the force was consistent with a vehicle travelling at a slow speed - approximately five to ten miles per hour."

"Interesting," Whitman said, her voice cool and deliberate. "And if this force occurred, would there not also be damage to the branch? Perhaps broken or splintered wood?"

Dr Carter straightened. "The branch was partially splintered, yes. But the paint was found only on the intact portion, which indicates direct contact without full breakage."

Lane stood up. "But you cannot definitively say the vehicle in question was Mr Fairley's, can you? After all, paint transfer could occur from other vehicles with similar colours and chemical compositions."

Whitman interrupted; her frustration barely concealed. "Objection, Your Honour. The evidence ties the defendant's vehicle to the scene."

The judge raised a hand. "Sustained. Please keep your argument focused, Ms Lane."

She smiled, unbothered. "Of course, Your Honour," she replied as she sat back down.

"Dr Carter, one last question," commenced Whitman. "Would you say the condition of the branch could have been influenced by weather, perhaps strong winds or heavy rainfall, prior to the alleged contact?"

Dr Carter's composure wavered for the first time. "Weather can alter physical evidence, yes. But in this case, it was summer, there were no strong winds or heavy rainfall that day-"

Before she could finish, Lane cut in, her voice rising. "So, we're not only dealing with uncertainties about the vehicle but also possible environmental interference! Members of the jury, is this the kind of evidence you'd bet a man's life on?"

A sudden voice broke through the tension. "I'd like to hear her finish that thought." It was Judge Crawley, her tone sharp, silencing the defence.

Dr Carter inhaled deeply. "What I was going to say is that while weather can influence evidence, the timeline and specific conditions of this case make it highly unlikely that wind or rain caused the branch to break. The alignment is simply too precise." Whitman seized the moment, stepping forward. "Thank you, Dr Carter. Your expert analysis has clarified the facts."

But Lane wasn't done. Leaning back in her chair, she smirked. "Clarified? Or muddied? I'll leave that for the jury to decide."

The courtroom buzzed with whispered speculation as Judge Crawley banged her gavel, calling for order. "The jury will disregard the speculative tone of the counsel's remarks," she said, her voice commanding. "This court will base its judgement on evidence, not conjecture."

Dr Carter exhaled quietly and returned to her seat, her testimony complete. Whitman and Lane exchanged glances - both knowing the battle for credibility was far from over.

The courtroom was silent as Dr Rachel Morgan, a forensic scientist from the same team as Dr Evelyn Carter, stepped up to the witness stand. She adjusted her jacket, her sharp eyes scanning the room as she prepared to testify. The prosecution lead, Harriet Whitman was the first to approach.

"Dr Morgan," Whitman began, holding up two clear evidence bags for the jury to see. "Can you confirm the items in these bags?"

"Yes," Dr Morgan said, her voice steady. "The first is a leather glove found in a field near the crime scene in Brampton-en-le-Morthen. The second is a matching glove discovered buried in a wooded area nearby."

Whitman nodded, pacing slightly. "You conducted a forensic examination of these items, correct?"

"That's correct," Dr Morgan replied. "We identified traces of rabbit fur lining inside both gloves. The fibres are consistent with rabbit fur found at several crime scenes linked to The Fox."

"Could you explain how this fur matches?" Whitman pressed.

Dr Morgan leaned forward slightly. "Using microscopic analysis and DNA testing, we confirmed the rabbit fur lining in the gloves shares identical characteristics - both structurally and genetically - with fur found on the upholstery and carpets of several victims' homes. This strongly suggests the gloves were present at those locations."

Whitman smiled faintly, turning to the jury. "In other words, Dr Morgan, these gloves are not only linked to the crime scenes - but they're also linked to each other?"

"Yes," Dr Morgan replied firmly.

The defence counsel, Clara Lane, stood abruptly. "Objection, Your Honour! The prosecution is leading the witness."

The judge waved her off. "Sustained. Proceed."

"No further questions at this time, Your Honour," replied Whitman. Lane approached, her heels clicking against the floor, her expression sharp. "Dr Morgan, you mentioned DNA testing. Are you suggesting that the presence of rabbit fur definitively links these gloves to Mr Fairley?"

Dr Morgan held her ground. "I'm suggesting that the evidence strongly supports a connection."

Lane smirked. "Strongly supports? Or implies? Rabbit fur is not exactly a rare material in the countryside, is it?"

"No, but the specific genetic markers in this fur are an uncommon match," Dr Morgan countered.

Lane seized the point. "And yet, no DNA from Mr Fairley was found on either glove, correct?"

"That's correct," Dr Morgan admitted, though her voice remained steady.

Lane turned to the jury, her voice tinged with mockery. "So, we're supposed to believe these gloves - lacking a single shred of DNA evidence tying them to my client - are somehow crucial to this case? Or could it be that they're just gloves discarded by someone else entirely?"

Dr Morgan opened her mouth to respond, but Lane cut her off, whirling back to the jury. "The rabbit fur might tell a story, but it's far from proof of guilt."

Whitman, unfazed, rose to make a counter point. "Dr Morgan, isn't it true that the buried glove had soil residue consistent with the same type found embedded in boots we recovered from Mr Fairley's home?"

Dr Morgan nodded. "Yes, that is correct."

Lane's face darkened, and a ripple of tension filled the courtroom. "Can you tell us about the condition it was in when recovered?"

Dr Morgan adjusted her seat and leaned into the microphone. "The glove was buried approximately eight inches below the surface. Despite its condition, forensic analysis revealed traces of the same rabbit fur lining as the glove found in the field. Additionally, the exterior contained faint but detectable fragments of the same soil composition present on the soles of Mr Fairley's boots."

"And this soil composition," Whitman continued, "was it unique to the area where the glove was buried?"

Dr Morgan nodded. "Yes. The soil contained a specific mix of chalk and clay minerals found only in that field and a handful of nearby locations."

Whitman turned to the jury. "So, not only do we have matching gloves with the same rare rabbit fur, but one of them was buried in a location that can be tied to the defendant's footwear." She paused for effect. "In your expert opinion, Dr Morgan, is it reasonable to conclude that these gloves were handled by Mr Fairley?"

Before Dr Morgan could answer, Lane was on her feet. "Objection, Your Honour! The question calls for speculation."

The judge raised an eyebrow. "Sustained. Rephrase your question."

Whitman nodded. "Dr Morgan, does the evidence you've presented suggest a connection between Mr Fairley and the gloves?"

"Yes," Dr Morgan replied firmly. "The combination of soil, fur, and location strongly supports that conclusion."

Lane was already rising, her voice sharp. "Strongly supports? Dr Morgan, isn't it true that no fingerprints, DNA, or other direct identifiers were found on the gloves?"

"That's correct," Dr Morgan admitted. "The gloves were slightly degraded, likely due to exposure to the elements and burial."

"And yet," Lane said, pacing before the jury, "we're expected to believe these gloves are crucial evidence in this case? Gloves that could have been discarded by anyone, at any time?"

Dr Morgan's eyes narrowed slightly. "The timeline of the burial, based on soil analysis, places the second glove at that location and is consistent with the timeline of the crimes."

Lane raised a hand dramatically. "But without DNA or fingerprints, you cannot definitively tie them to my client, can you?"

"No, we cannot," Morgan admitted, her tone calm but firm.

Lane turned to the jury with a triumphant smile. "Exactly. This is all conjecture, not proof. And in a case like this, where a man's life is on the line, conjecture simply isn't good enough."

The courtroom murmured softly, the sound of uncertainty filling the air.

Whitman, unwilling to let the point drop, stepped forward again. "Dr Morgan, one final question. Can you again explain the significance of the rabbit fur found in these gloves?"

Morgan straightened. "The rabbit fur is a unique link. It was found at multiple crime scenes - places where The Fox entered homes undetected. The fact that this fur is present in both gloves suggests that they were used repeatedly by the same individual, and the soil ties one glove to the area where Mr Fairley's boots once trod the ground."

Whitman turned to the jury. "Ladies and gentlemen, while the defence may argue otherwise, the evidence doesn't lie. These gloves were tools of a predator - and every piece of evidence ties them closer to the defendant."

Lane shook her head, but the seed of doubt had been planted. Dr Morgan stepped down from the witness stand. Judge Crawley called a break for lunch.

The courtroom felt stifling as Dr Morgan returned to the witness stand. The prosecutor, Harriet Whitman, approached her with a measured stride, holding an evidence bag containing a sheet of fabric.

"Dr Morgan," Whitman began, her voice steady and authoritative, "let's address the stained sheet recovered from the burial site in Brampton-en-le-Morthen. Can you describe what your analysis revealed?"

Dr Morgan cleared her throat. "The sheet was heavily soiled, but forensic testing confirmed the presence of semen stains. Further DNA analysis determined that the semen matched the DNA profile of the defendant, Malcolm Fairley."

Whitman nodded, her gaze sweeping over the jury. "How certain is this match?"

Dr Morgan replied confidently, "The DNA match probability is greater than one in a billion. There is no reasonable doubt that the semen came from Mr Fairley."

Whitman continued, her voice gaining intensity. "And was this sheet connected to any of the crime scenes?"

"Yes," Morgan said. "The size of the sheet and the fibres were consistent with a bedsheet found at the victim's home in Brampton-en-le-Morthen, with a hole cut out of it."

The jury exchanged glances, the weight of the evidence clearly sinking in.

The defence counsel, Clara Lane, rose, her tone piercing. "Dr Morgan, let's talk about contamination. This sheet was buried in the ground, exposed to soil, moisture, and who knows what else. Isn't it possible that external factors could have compromised the DNA results?"

Dr Morgan remained composed. "Contamination is always a consideration, but the DNA profile extracted was clear and uncontaminated. The soil or other environmental factors did not affect the validity of the match."

Lane smirked. "So you say. But were there any other DNA profiles found on the sheet? Perhaps from third parties?"

Morgan hesitated briefly. "No, only Mr Fairley's DNA was present in the semen stains."

Lane seized the moment. "Only his? Curious, isn't it? A single sheet supposedly linked to a crime and the home of two people, yet we're left with just one DNA profile. Couldn't this sheet have been planted to incriminate my client?"

Dr Morgan frowned. "There is no evidence to suggest the sheet was planted."

Lane leaned closer to the jury, her voice laced with scepticism. "No evidence. That seems to be the recurring theme here, doesn't it? A buried glove, a shotgun, and now a sheet - no witnesses, no direct connection to the crimes, just circumstantial evidence tying my client to this so-called burial site."

Whitman stood abruptly. "Objection, Your Honour! The defence is editorialising."

Judge Crawley banged the gavel. "Sustained. Ms Lane, stick to questioning."

Lane shot a glance at Whitman, then turned back to Dr Morgan. "One final question. Can you definitively place this sheet at a crime scene prior to its burial?"

Dr Morgan's expression remained firm. "The fibres link it to a crime scene in Brampton-en-le-Morthen, and the DNA evidence ties it to Mr Fairley. That is the extent of the forensic findings."
Lane smiled thinly. "Thank you for your carefully worded response."

The courtroom buzzed with hushed whispers as Judge Crawley banged the gavel once more. "Court will resume after a short recess," she declared, but the weight of the testimony lingered as everyone left their seats, the implications of the evidence impossible to ignore.

The atmosphere in the courtroom was electric as Johnson Lamble, a forensics firearms scientist, took the witness stand. He looked unflinching under the scrutiny of the defence counsel, Clara Lane. Seated nearby, Ashton Hartwig, the key witness whose fingers were mutilated in an attack, awaited his turn.

Lane paced before the witness, holding an evidence bag containing a shotgun. "Mr Lamble, this shotgun was recovered buried near a crime scene, correct?"

"Yes," Lamble replied. "It was found alongside the glove and the semen-stained sheet in Brampton-en-le-Morthen."

Lane nodded. "And Mr Lamble, you've examined this shotgun extensively. Are you absolutely certain it's the same weapon used in the attack on a Mr Ashton Hartwig?"

Lamble adjusted his glasses. "Yes. The markings on the spent shell recovered from Mr Hartwig's property match the firing pin and breech markings unique to this shotgun. There is no doubt."

Lane raised her eyebrows. "No doubt, you say. Yet this gun was buried, exposed to elements that could degrade evidence. Isn't it possible the markings were compromised?"

Lamble shook his head. "The markings are etched into the metal by the firing mechanism. Environmental exposure would not alter them in any significant way."

"What about fingerprints or DNA? Was there any evidence tying my client, Malcolm Fairley, to the shotgun directly?"

Lamble kept his voice steady. "No fingerprints were recovered, but DNA consistent with Mr Fairley's was found on the trigger guard. It's likely the burial process and environmental conditions degraded other potential evidence."

Lane smirked, turning to the jury. "Convenient, isn't it? A gun buried just long enough to erase crucial evidence but still somehow ties itself to my client."

Lead prosecutor Harriet Whitman stood abruptly. "Objection, Your Honour. The defence is speculating."

"Sustained," Judge Crawley said sternly.

Whitman approached the stand. "Mr Lamble, let's clarify. You're saying the unique markings on this shotgun and the shell found at the crime scene are a perfect match?"

"Yes," he affirmed. "This is the gun used in the shooting."

"Mr Lamble, did you find any forensic evidence specifically tying this weapon to the crime scene other than the spent shell?" asked Whitman.

Lamble nodded. "Traces of wood and fabric consistent with debris from Mr Hartwig's home were found in the barrel and stock of the gun."

Whitman offered half a smile. "No further questions, Your Honour." Next up in the witness stand was Ashton Hartwig.

Whitman turned toward Ashton Hartwig. "Mr Hartwig, please tell the court about the night you were attacked."

Hartwig, his voice steady but emotional, recounted the events. "It was dark. The man – The Fox - slipped into the house unnoticed. He had the shotgun. When I tried to fight him off, he aimed it at my hand and pulled the trigger." He lifted his hand, to show his mutilated fingers.

Whitman gestured toward the shotgun presented as evidence. "Mr Hartwig, is this the weapon he used?"

Hartwig's eyes narrowed as he looked at the gun. "Yes. I'll never forget it. That's the shotgun."

Lane rose, her voice cutting through the heavy silence. "Mr Hartwig, it was dark, wasn't it? And you were under extreme duress. Are you absolutely certain this is the same weapon?" Hartwig didn't waver. "I know what I saw. That's the gun."

"And Mr Hartwig, please describe the characteristics of the person who attacked you in your home," asked Whitman.

"Well, despite the limited light, I would say he was the same height as me, five foot ten. He was slim. He spoke with a Geordie accent. And he was holding the gun left-handed. That's all I can remember really," replied Hartwig. Tears streaming down his face.

Whitman, sensing the defence was on her heels, made her final statement. "Thank you, Mr Hartwig. Ladies and gentlemen of the jury, you've heard it from multiple sources. The forensic evidence, the firearms analysis, and the eyewitness testimony all confirm one thing: this shotgun is not just a weapon. It's a tool of terror, wielded by the man seated right there." She pointed directly at Malcolm Fairley, who stared blankly ahead.

The judge's gavel struck once. "Court is adjourned until tomorrow."

As the room emptied, the air was thick with the certainty of guilt, leaving only the question of how much longer the defence could hold on.

"Talbot," Whitman said as she packed up her notes, "we've got him, but it's going to be a fight to make sure it sticks."

"He won't win," Talbot replied, his voice steady and his eyes hard as steel. "Not this time."

The courtroom emptied slowly, the atmosphere still full of gloom from what had been revealed. As Fairley was escorted out in handcuffs, his eyes locked on Talbot's. That twisted grin returned. "See you tomorrow, detective," he called out, his voice taunting, echoing off the walls.

Talbot didn't flinch. "Yeah, you will," he muttered under his breath. "And you'll see me every damn day until you rot in that cell."

He turned away, the faces of the victims fresh in his mind. Justice wasn't just about the trial; it was about making sure the nightmares ended for good. Talbot and Whitman were prepared to see it through to the bitter end.

Day three commenced. It was the day everyone had been anticipating. Malcolm Fairley, the man accused of countless heinous crimes, took the witness stand.

As Judge Mary Crawley struck her gavel to open proceedings, the air in the courtroom crackled with tension.

Fairley, dressed in a stark black suit, sat motionless - his face expressionless, his eyes unblinking, betraying no hint of emotion. Leading the charge for the prosecution, Harriet Whitman rose to begin her questioning.

"Mr Fairley," Whitman began, her tone steady but pointed. "Let's revisit your whereabouts on the night of sixteenth of April 1984. You stated you were at home. Is that correct?"

"Yes, that's correct," Fairley replied, his voice measured.

"And you were alone?" Whitman pressed.

"I was in my bedroom. My brother was in his," he responded calmly.

"So, your brother can confirm you were home?" she asked.

"That's right," Fairley replied, maintaining his composure.

Whitman leaned forward slightly, her voice sharpening. "Interesting, because when your brother was interviewed by police, he stated you often went missing at night - a behaviour he considered routine since your teenage years."

Fairley shifted slightly but said nothing, and before he could respond, Whitman continued. "In fact, he told investigators that on the sixteenth of April 1984, you weren't home all day. He distinctly recalled hearing you return in the early hours of April seventeenth."

Fairley wiped a bead of sweat from his forehead, his confidence wavering. "I'm sorry, I don't recall being out that day," he muttered.

Whitman didn't miss a beat. "So, being out all day and night wasn't unusual for you?"

Fairley hesitated before answering, "No, not at all. I like to keep to myself."

Whitman thanked Fairley and returned to her seat.

The defence counsel, Clara Lane, stood with a measured calm. She adjusted her glasses and walked toward the witness stand, her demeanour soft yet purposeful.

"Mr Fairley," Lane began, her tone warm, "you've told the court you like to keep to yourself. Could you elaborate on that? What do you enjoy doing in your alone time?"

Fairley nodded, visibly relaxing. "I enjoy the quiet. I like walking, especially at night. It's peaceful - no one around, just me and the outdoors."

Lane smiled slightly. "That sounds quite tranquil. What do you do during these walks?"

Fairley leaned forward a bit, his voice gaining some animation. "Sometimes I just stroll, clear my head. Other times I stop to look at the stars. I've always been fascinated by the night sky. It's...calming."

"So, to clarify, these nighttime walks aren't unusual for you?" Lane asked.

"Not at all," Fairley replied. "I've been doing them for years. It's how I unwind."

Lane nodded. "And you mentioned earlier that your brother might not always know when you're out. Is that because these walks are a personal escape for you?"

"Exactly," Fairley said. "I don't always announce when I go out. Sometimes it's just a spur-of-the-moment thing."

Lane moved a step closer. "On the sixteenth of April 1984, you told the prosecution you don't recall being out. Could it be that you went on one of your nighttime walks and simply forgot?"

Fairley considered this, then nodded. "It's possible. I don't keep track of every walk I take. It's not something I think much about - it's just part of my routine."

"During these walks, do you often interact with people?" Lane asked.

"No," Fairley said firmly. "That's the whole point. I like the quiet. It's just me, the fresh air, and the stars."

Lane paused, letting his words settle with the jury before continuing. "Now, the prosecution has suggested that being out late is suspicious. Do you find it unusual to enjoy solitude and nighttime walks?"

"Not at all," Fairley replied confidently. "It's when I feel most at peace. Some people like the bustle of the day; I prefer the stillness of the night."

Lane smiled gently. "Thank you, Mr Fairley."

She turned back to the jury, her voice steady. "Let the record show that Mr Fairley's nighttime habits are neither unusual nor incriminating. He is simply a man who finds solace in solitude and the beauty of the night sky - a far cry from the villain the prosecution paints him to be."

She returned to her seat, her calm confidence echoing through the courtroom.

Whitman stood up, holding an evidence bag containing a screwdriver. Her tone was calm but deliberate. She leaned forward, her gaze fixed on Fairley. "Mr Fairley let's discuss a screwdriver recovered from your property. Forensic analysis confirms it matches tool marks left at multiple break-ins. Do you recognise this tool?"

Fairley glanced at the evidence bag, his expression unreadable. "Yeah, it looks like one from my toolbox."

"So, you admit this screwdriver is yours?" asked Whitman.

"I believe it is," he said carefully. "But I've lent my tools out before. It wouldn't be unusual if I have lent this one out."

Whitman's eyes narrowed. "You've lent tools out before. Do you recall lending this specific screwdriver to anyone?"

"No," Fairley replied, shifting in his seat. "Not specifically. But I've lent plenty of tools over the years. It could have been one of them."

Whitman's voice sharpened. "Are you suggesting that someone borrowed this screwdriver, used it in multiple break-ins, and then quietly returned it to your property without your knowledge?"

Fairley paused, wiping at the sweat forming on his brow. "I'm saying it's possible. I wouldn't know if someone did that."

Whitman let the silence hang for a moment, her eyes never leaving him. "Possible? Or convenient? Let's get specific, Mr Fairley. Tool marks left on the Chambers back door was an exact match to this screwdriver. Are you denying using that tool at their property?"

"I've never been to the Chambers' property," Fairley said quickly, his tone defensive. "I don't know how those marks got there."

Whitman's voice rose slightly, pressing the point. "So, you've never been there, yet your screwdriver left tool marks consistent with forced entry. How do you explain that?"

Fairley wiped his forehead again, his voice faltering. "I can't explain it. I've lent my tools to others - maybe someone else used it."

Whitman leaned closer, her tone cold and deliberate. "This isn't about one break-in, Mr Fairley. This screwdriver has been forensically linked to multiple crime scenes. At each one, the tool marks match perfectly. Are you asking this court to believe that all these crimes were committed by someone else using your tool without your knowledge, over a period of six months?"

Fairley's jaw tightened. "I don't know what else to tell you. I didn't do it. I can't control what people do with my tools."

Whitman straightened, her eyes glinting with satisfaction. "No further questions for now, Your Honour."
She returned to her seat, leaving the courtroom in a tense, uneasy silence as Fairley shifted uncomfortably under the weight of her words.

Lane, rose from her seat. "Mr Fairley," she began, "the prosecution claims this screwdriver was used in several break-ins. Who have you lent your tools to?"

"I've lent tools to neighbours, my brother, and people I've worked for." Fairley replied.

Lane nodded. "And when you lend tools, do you always get them back right away?"

"No, not always," Fairley admitted. "Sometimes I don't even realise I've lent something until someone returns it."

Lane stepped closer. "Would you recognise every tool you own if you saw it in someone else's possession?"

"Probably not," Fairley said with a shrug.

"Now, about this screwdriver," Lane continued, holding it up. "When was the last time you recall using it?"

"I honestly don't remember," Fairley replied. "It's been sitting in my toolbox for ages."

"So, it's possible someone could have borrowed it, used it, and returned it without your knowledge?" Lane asked.

"Yes, absolutely," Fairley confirmed.

Lane's voice sharpened slightly. "The prosecution suggests that you - and only you - could have left those tool marks on several victims' back doors, including the Chambers. But given that you've lent out your tools before, is it possible someone else could have used this screwdriver?"

"Yes, it's possible," Fairley replied firmly.

Lane paused briefly before asking, "Do you recall ever being at the Chambers' house?"

"No, I've never been there," Fairley said, shaking his head.

"So, to be clear, you're saying you have no connection to their property and no knowledge of how your screwdriver may have been involved?"

"That's correct," Fairley stated.

Lane turned to the jury. "Thank you, Mr Fairley. Let the record show that there is no direct evidence tying Mr Fairley to the scene - only the presence of a commonly used tool, which the defendant regularly lent to others."

Lane returned to her seat, her calm demeanour unwavering.

Whitman emerged from her seat, her sharp stare fixed on Fairley. She moved to the centre of the courtroom with the evidence table beside her.

"Mr Fairley," Whitman began, her voice careful and cautious. "Let's start with the paint fleck found in Brampton-en-le-Morthen. Forensic analysis confirms it matches the paint on your Austin Allegro. Have you driven near or through the woods in question?"

Fairley shifted slightly. "I've driven near there, yes, but I've never stopped or gone into the woods."

Whitman raised an eyebrow. "You've never stopped? Not once? Yet this particular fleck of paint - a rare colour, Harvest Yellow seven-nine-one-nine, found on only a limited number of Austin Allegros - is tied directly to your vehicle. How do you explain that?"

"I can't," Fairley replied, his voice low. "Like I said, I haven't been in the woods."

Whitman stepped closer, her tone hardening. "Let's talk about the scratch on the rear of your car. It aligns perfectly with the height of the branch where the paint fleck was found. Do you recall how your car got the scratch?"

Fairley hesitated. "Not exactly. I've had that car for years. It's been scratched before - parking, brushing against things."

Whitman nodded, her expression sceptical. "So, you expect this court to believe that the scratch - perfectly matching the height of the branch in Brampton-en-le-Morthen — both with the exact same paint - are a coincidence?"

Fairley wiped at his brow. "I don't know. Maybe."

Whitman's lips pressed into a thin line. "Let's move on. The gloves recovered near the crime scene. Do you recognise them?"

"No," Fairley replied quickly. "I've never seen them before."

Whitman picked up the evidence bag containing the gloves. "Forensic testing found rabbit fur contained within these gloves was consistent with fibres found at several crime scenes, where a screwdriver you own, was also used to break into. How do you explain that?"

"I - I don't know," Fairley stammered. "I've lent out gloves before. Maybe someone else used them."

Whitman's voice sharpened. "Lent them out? To whom?"
Fairley shifted uncomfortably. "I don't remember. It could've been anyone."

"Convenient," Whitman shot back, her voice cold. "The DNA found inside these gloves isn't incidental, Mr Fairley. Are you saying someone else borrowed these gloves, used them during the break-ins, and then left them in a location near the crime scene?"

"I'm saying it's possible," Fairley replied defensively.

"Possible," Whitman repeated, her tone cutting. "Or implausible?" She didn't wait for a response. "Let's discuss the shotgun found in Brampton-en-le-Morthen. Do you recognise this firearm?"

"No," Fairley said quickly, avoiding her gaze.

Whitman gestured to the weapon. "Forensic testing revealed your DNA on this shotgun. Have you ever handled it?"

"No," Fairley repeated firmly.

"Never?" Whitman pressed. "Then how does your DNA end up on a shotgun tied to multiple crimes?"

Fairley hesitated. "I've been hunting before, handled other shotguns. Maybe it transferred somehow."

Whitman's tone grew icy. "Transferred? From where? From whom?"

"I don't know," Fairley said quietly.

Whitman stepped closer, her eyes narrowing. "Let's address the bedsheet recovered in Brampton-en-le-Morthen - the one with your DNA on it. Can you explain that Mr Fairley?"

"No," he muttered. "I have no idea how it got there."

Whitman's voice rose, cutting through the tense courtroom. "This bedsheet didn't just happen to appear in Brampton-en-le-Morthen, Mr Fairley. Your DNA - your semen - was found on it. Are you still claiming you've never been there?"

"That's right," Fairley said quickly.

Whitman's expression was unyielding. "Then tell me, Mr Fairley, how does your DNA end up on a sheet buried in the woods, alongside evidence from other crimes? And how does soil from the same crime scene end up on your boots. Is the court supposed to believe all of this is coincidence?"

Fairley's face reddened. "I don't know how it happened. I didn't do it."

Whitman's tone turned steely. "So, the paint fleck, the gloves, the shotgun, the bedsheet, the soiled boots - all of these are accidents or misunderstandings? Mr Fairley, you claim to have no explanation for any of it, yet every piece of evidence ties you to the many crimes committed by The Fox."

Fairley sat silent, his hands gripping the edges of the witness stand.

Whitman turned to the jury, her voice resonant. "Ladies and gentlemen, the defendant's answers today were not explanations. They were evasions. The evidence is not circumstantial - it is conclusive. No further questions, Your Honour."

She returned to her seat, leaving the courtroom heavy with tension and unanswered questions.

Lane rose and approached the witness box with deliberate calm. She paused, letting the tension in the courtroom settle before addressing the defendant.

"Mr Fairley," Lane began, her voice steady and measured. "Let's discuss the paint fleck found in Brampton-en-le-Morthen, which the prosecution claims match the paint on your car. So, you have driven near Brampton-en-le-Morthen but not been in the woods nearby?"

Fairley sat up slightly, his hands resting on the stand. "Yes, that is correct."

Lane nodded, pacing a few steps before continuing. "And the scratch on your car – you do not recall how it occurred?"

Fairley shook his head. "No. I've had that car for years. It's been scratched a few times - parking in tight spots, brushing against bushes. Nothing unusual."

"So, it's entirely possible the scratch happened in a completely unrelated situation?" Lane asked, her voice calm.
"Yes," Fairley confirmed.

"And the paint - there's nothing unique about it, is there?"

"No," Fairley said. "It's just standard factory paint. Any car like mine would have it."

Lane turned to the jury. "So, the paint fleck found in the woods could have come from another car entirely, or been transferred by other means?"

Fairley nodded. "I suppose so."

Lane pivoted smoothly. "Let's move on to the gloves. So, you do not recognise these gloves, Mr Fairley?"

"No," he said, his expression neutral. "I've never seen them before."

"You mentioned earlier that you sometimes lend out tools and gloves?"

"Yeah," Fairley replied. "Sometimes."

"And you do not always get those items back?"

"Not always," he admitted.

"So, is it possible that someone else could have used gloves that you owned?"

"Yes," Fairley said firmly. "It's possible."

Lane let the answer hang for a moment before shifting. "Now, about the shotgun. So, you do not recognise the firearm presented in court?"

Fairley glanced at the evidence table, then back to Lane. "No, I don't."

"The prosecution claims your DNA was found on it. Have you ever handled firearms before?"
"Yes," Fairley said. "I've been hunting a few times."

"And where do you typically handle firearms?"

"At shooting ranges or on hunting trips," he said.

Lane's voice grew firmer. "Is it possible that your DNA transferred to a firearm through those activities?"

"Yes," Fairley admitted. "It's possible."

"To be clear, you've never seen this particular shotgun, but you acknowledge handling similar firearms in the past, which might explain the presence of your DNA?"

"That's correct," replied Fairley.

Lane moved a step closer to the stand. "Finally, let's address the bedsheet found in Brampton-en-le-Morthen. The prosecution has drawn attention to the fact that your DNA - specifically, your semen - was found on it. Can you explain how that sheet ended up in the woods?"

Fairley hesitated, his brow furrowing. "I have no idea how it got there."

"Have you ever had any relationship with the victims who were attacked nearby?"

"No," Fairley said emphatically. "Never."

"And do you know how a bedsheet with your DNA might have ended up buried in a wooded area in Brampton-en-le-Morthen?"

Fairley shook his head. "No. I can't explain it."

Lane's tone grew sharper, her words precise. "Is it possible the bedsheet - or your DNA - was stolen or planted?"

"Yes," Fairley said, his voice resolute. "That's the only thing that makes sense."

Lane faced the jury, her expression neutral but resolute. "Mr Fairley, you've been cooperative, yet all we've heard today are allegations tied to objects you cannot connect to personally. Do you believe someone might be trying to frame you?"

Fairley exhaled heavily. "I don't know why someone would, but it feels like that's what's happening."

Lane nodded. "Thank you, Mr Fairley." Turning to the judge, she added, "Let the record reflect that the defendant has consistently denied knowledge of or involvement in the crimes alleged, and that the evidence presented by the prosecution is circumstantial at best."

With that, she returned to her seat, leaving the courtroom buzzing with quiet mutters.

Whitman and Lane then probed Fairley over the scratches on his neck, the cut on his hand and the blood found at a crime scene which matched his DNA. Fairley remained consistent with his answers, claiming they were likely to be work related accidents, and he must have worked at the property where his blood was found.

By the end of the day, the courtroom was drained, the ambiance saturated with unspoken thoughts and unresolved tension.

All the evidence had been heard, the case was adjourned, the hostility in the courtroom evident as Judge Mary Crawley rose to deliver her final remarks. Her voice echoed through the chamber, firm and authoritative, as she reminded everyone present of the seriousness of the charges against Fairley. "This court will reconvene in one week to allow for closing statements from both the prosecution and defence. I urge the jury to reflect deeply on the evidence presented and the impact of the defendant's actions on his victims."

With that, the gavel struck decisively, marking the end of the day's proceedings. The room began to empty, but Talbot remained seated, taking a moment to collect his thoughts. He glanced over at the families of the victims, their expressions a mix of hope and anxiety, and felt a renewed resolve swelling within him.

Chapter 32

On the twenty-sixth of February 1985, the courtroom was a pressure cooker of anticipation. Every seat in the gallery was filled, every eye trained on the twelve men and women who now filed back into their places. Detective Chief Superintendent Mark Talbot could feel his pulse in his throat as he watched the jury foreman, an older man with a weary face, rise to deliver the verdict.

"All rise," the bailiff called out, and everyone stood, the tension thick enough to choke on. Judge Mary Crawley took her seat, her face stern and unreadable. She looked at the foreman and gave him a nod. "Have you reached a verdict?"

"Yes, Your Honour," the foreman said, his voice hoarse. He glanced at the slip of paper in his hands, then cleared his throat.

"On the three charges of aggravated burglary, we find the defendant, Malcolm Fairley, guilty.

On the five charges of burglary, we find the defendant, Malcolm Fairley, guilty.

On the three charges of rape, we find the defendant, Malcolm Fairley, guilty.

On the two charges of indecent assault, we find the defendant, Malcolm Fairley, guilty.

On the charge of possession of a firearm, we find the defendant, Malcolm Fairley, guilty."

Talbot didn't realise he'd been holding his breath until the final word was spoken. He exhaled slowly, a tight knot in his chest beginning to loosen. A murmur rippled through the room - relief, satisfaction, and a lingering unease. The heavy weight of months of working long hours and sleepless nights was finally coming to a head.

Malcolm Fairley - The Fox - stood in the dock, his expression impassive, though a faint smile played at the corner of his lips. Even now, he seemed to find some dark amusement in it all. He glanced around the room as if daring anyone to meet his gaze.

Judge Mary Crawley's voice was cold and clear as she spoke. "Malcolm Fairley, you have been found guilty on all counts. There are degrees of wickedness beyond condemnatory description. Your crimes fall within this category. You desecrated and defiled men and women in their own homes. You are a decadent advertisement for evil pornographers. The court hereby sentences you to six life imprisonments, with a minimum term of thirty years. You will be transferred to a maximum-security facility where you will remain until the end of your natural life."

There was a moment of silence, a collective breath held, and then the room erupted. Reporters jotted furiously onto their notepads, victims' families clutched each other, tears streaming down their faces. Talbot felt a wave of relief wash over him but knew it was a temporary reprieve.

"He got what he deserved," said a jubilant Detective Sergeant Sarah Kendrick, coming up beside Talbot, her voice a mix of satisfaction and weariness.

"Yeah," Talbot replied, eyes still locked on Fairley. "But it doesn't change what he did. Not for the people who'll never forget."

Fairley's eyes flicked to Talbot as he was led out by the guards. His smile widened, a mocking twist of his lips. "See you around, detective," he said, his voice low and venomous.

Talbot's face remained stoic, but inside, he felt the old anger stir. "Not if I can help it," he muttered. "Not if I can help it."

The courtroom slowly emptied.

Outside the courthouse, a crowd had gathered - victims, their families, curious onlookers, and, of course, the media. The moment the doors opened, cameras flashed, and microphones were thrust forward.

"Lizzie! Over here, Lizzie!" Claire Milford from the Leighton Buzzard Observer shouted. "Can you tell us how you feel knowing The Fox will spend the rest of his life behind bars"

Lizzie Chambers, the elderly woman who had testified with such courage, paused. Her face was drawn but determined.
"I'm glad it's over," she said, her voice trembling slightly. "But we'll never really be free of what he did to us. None of us will."

Across the steps, Selena King, a young mother who had faced Fairley and lived to talk about it, held her husband close. "He's gone," she whispered, though her own eyes remained haunted. "He can't hurt us anymore."

Yet the scars ran deep. For every family, every victim, this was a day of both justice and reckoning. Some stared into the cameras with defiance, while others looked away, unable to face the bright lights after months of darkness.

Inside, Talbot watched through the window. He knew that while Fairley might be behind bars, the true damage he'd done - the nights stolen by nightmares, the homes that no longer felt safe - would take years to heal, if ever.

"He's not a man," he muttered, almost to himself. "He's a disease. And it'll take time to clear him from their systems."

Harriet Whitman joined him. "You did good, Talbot," she said. "We all did."

"Yeah," he replied, his tone distant. "But it doesn't feel like enough. Not really."

She nodded, understanding all too well. "Justice doesn't always mean closure. You know that."

Talbot sighed, his eyes scanning the faces of the victims and their families. "Yeah, I know," he said quietly. "But it's a start."

The crowd began to disperse. Some of the victims found solace in the company of others who had lived the same nightmare. Ashton Hartwig spoke softly to Lizzie Chambers, the two of them finding a strange kinship in shared horror. Others, like Benjamin Young, stared off into the distance, still lost in a fog of disbelief.

Talbot finally stepped outside, feeling the weight of months begin to lift, if only a little. Claire Milford spotted him and hurried over. "Detective Chief Superintendent Mark Talbot!" she called. "What's next for you after this case?"

Talbot looked into the lens of her camera, feeling the eyes of the community on him. "For now, I think we all just need to breathe," he said. "It's been a long road, and there's still healing to be done."

Milford nodded, sensing there was more he wasn't saying, but she didn't press. Talbot turned away, walking down the courthouse steps, feeling the chill of the afternoon air cut through his coat.

As he reached the bottom, he paused and looked back. Fairley was gone, but his presence would linger. It would take time, and maybe it would never fully disappear. But today, they had taken a step - a small step toward something better.

Justice had been served. Now came the hard part - finding peace in the aftermath.

Chapter 33

Several weeks later, Detective Chief Superintendent Mark Talbot stood at the front of the briefing room in Dunstable police station, scanning the faces of the officers gathered before him. It was a typical spring afternoon, the sky outside bright blue, and inside, the mood was buoyant. The room hummed with a quiet sense of triumph, the kind of understated satisfaction that came after long hours of hard work had finally paid off.

At the centre of this achievement were two men - Detective Sergeant Jake Miller and Detective Constable Tom Hughes. They sat near the back of the room, trying to blend into the crowd, but today that would be impossible. Their efforts over the past few months had brought an elusive criminal to justice, and everyone in the department knew it.

Talbot straightened his posture and raised his hand for quiet. The chatter in the room died down, and all eyes turned to him.
"I won't keep you long," Talbot began, his voice calm but commanding, the mark of a man used to leading. "But I think it's important to acknowledge the work that's been done here, especially considering the circumstances."

He paused for a moment, letting his words settle in the room. "We're living in an age where technology is starting to take over much of what we do as police officers. But this case - this one - was solved without any of that."

There was a murmur of agreement from the crowd, and Talbot's eyes drifted to Miller and Hughes, who were sitting in the back row, clearly uncomfortable with the attention. He offered them a nod before continuing.

"What we had were lists - long, exhaustive lists - and two detectives who knew how to do good, old-fashioned police work."

"For most detectives, a list of fifteen hundred registered owners of yellow Austin Allegro's would have been a dead end. It was an overwhelming number of people to track down, a needle in a haystack. But for Miller and Hughes, it was just another challenge to be methodically worked through."

"It's easy to get lost in the glitz of modern policing," Talbot continued, his gaze still fixed on the two men in the back. "It's easy to think that with the new technology we have, the answers should come quicker. But technology doesn't solve cases - detectives do."

He allowed the weight of that statement to hang in the air for a moment. It was something he firmly believed. No matter how advanced their tools became, it was still the instincts, the patience, and the determination of his officers that made the difference between success and failure.

"And that's what we had here," Talbot said, pacing slowly across the front of the room. "Two detectives who refused to give up. They went through that list, person by person, knocking on doors, making calls, tracking down leads, following up on even the smallest details. It was painstaking work - days and nights spent combing through records, interviewing people, chasing down dead ends. But they stuck with it, and because of that, we caught our man."

Talbot turned to face Miller and Hughes directly, his expression softening.

"Jake, Tom," he said, his voice warm with appreciation. "You've both shown exactly what it means to be detectives. You didn't rely on shortcuts. You didn't wait for some piece of technology to hand you the answer. You went out there, you talked to people, you followed leads, and you put the pieces together. That's real police work. And for that, you have my respect and my gratitude."

There was a smattering of applause in the room. Miller and Hughes exchanged embarrassed glances. Neither man was particularly fond of the spotlight, but they both knew how much this case had meant to the department - and to Talbot, personally.

"You two proved that-" he said, nodding to Miller and Hughes. "You proved that no matter how much the job changes, some things stay the same. It's still about hard work. It's still about dedication. And it's still about knowing how to put the pieces together."

Talbot looked around the room, making eye contact with each officer. "Let that be a lesson to all of us. We should embrace the new tools we have at our disposal, but we should never forget what it means to be a detective. To follow the evidence, wherever it leads. To knock on doors, to ask the right questions, to listen to what people aren't saying as much as what they are."

There was a quiet rustle of agreement in the room. Talbot could feel the respect his team had for Miller and Hughes. It wasn't just about solving a case - it was about showing everyone that the fundamentals of policing still mattered, that the core skills of a detective were as relevant now as they had ever been.

Talbot returned to the podium, his voice becoming more formal once again. "In recognition of your hard work and dedication, I'm proud to present you both with commendations for outstanding detective work."

The room burst into applause once more as Talbot held out two certificates. Miller and Hughes reluctantly stood, making their way to the front of the room. Talbot shook their hands firmly, offering each of them a quiet word of thanks before handing them their awards. The applause continued as the two men stood side by side, clearly uncomfortable but honoured, nonetheless.

As the applause died down, Talbot stepped forward again. "This case was solved because of the determination of two detectives who refused to give up. But let's not forget that we all play a part in making this department what it is. Whether you're knocking on doors, analysing evidence, or managing the paperwork, every role is important. Every contribution matters."

He looked out at his team, his voice firm and resolute. "We're only as strong as the people who work here. And today, I'm proud of what we've accomplished."

The briefing concluded shortly after, and as the officers began to file out of the room, Talbot caught Miller and Hughes on their way out.

"Well done, both of you," he said quietly, his voice full of genuine appreciation. "You reminded all of us of what it means to be a detective."

Miller smiled sheepishly. "Just doing our job, sir."

Talbot clapped a hand on his shoulder. "Maybe so, but you did it damn well."

As they left the room, Talbot lingered for a moment, looking out the window at the blue sky beyond. He knew that the job was changing, evolving in ways that no one could have imagined even a decade ago. But today, at least, he felt a deep sense of pride in the work his team had done. No matter how much technology advanced, no matter how many new tools they were given, the essence of detective work - the persistence, the instincts, the dogged pursuit of the truth - would always remain the same. And that was something worth holding onto.

The operations room was eerily quiet, stripped of the frantic energy that had filled it for months. Desks that once overflowed with maps, notes, and coffee-stained files were now bare, ready to be reclaimed by the mundane routines of other cases. The whiteboard that had chronicled every lead, every theory, every dead end was wiped clean. It was as if The Fox had never existed, though the remnants of his crimes still clung to every corner.

Detective Chief Superintendent Mark Talbot stood alone. The task force had officially disbanded that morning - case closed, as they say. But for Talbot, it was anything but. He could still feel it - the chase, the failures, the sleepless nights replaying in his mind like a bad film reel on a loop.

Detective Sergeant Sarah Kendrick wandered in, breaking the silence. "So, this is it, huh?" she asked, her voice flat but tinged with something Talbot couldn't quite place. Relief? Resignation? "All that work, and it's like we were never here."

Talbot nodded, not tearing his gaze away from the window. "Feels strange, doesn't it? We spent months hunting him, and now - poof - everyone just goes back to their lives like nothing happened."

Kendrick snorted. "I don't know if 'back to their lives' is quite right. I mean, look at us. None of us are walking out of this the same way we walked in."

Talbot turned, studying Kendrick's face. The lines around his eyes seemed deeper, his posture more slumped. "Yeah," Talbot said quietly. "I suppose not."

A silence settled between them, both of them reflecting on what had been lost and what had been learned. Finally, Kendrick broke the quiet. "What about you, sir? You thinking about taking some time off?"

Talbot's lips curved into a humourless smile. "Time off? Christ, Kendrick, I wouldn't even know what to do with myself." He looked around the empty room, the emptiness suddenly feeling vast. "But maybe it's time I figure that out."

Kendrick nodded, understanding the weight behind those words. "You did good, Sir. You did what no one else could. Doesn't feel like much now, but...you caught him. You got the bastard."

"Yeah," Talbot replied. "But at what cost?"

He didn't wait for an answer. He wasn't sure there was one. Instead, he walked out of the room and down the hall, past the faces of his colleagues who'd been there with him through every twist and turn. He saw the exhaustion in their eyes, the haunted looks that would linger long after they filed away this case.

In his office, Talbot closed the door behind him and leaned against it. His desk was still cluttered with remnants of the investigation - photos of victims, reports, sketches of possible hideouts. A map of Fairley's attacks stared back at him from the wall, the ink of his own notes and theories now faded and redundant.

He crossed to his chair and sank into it, feeling the weight of every decision, every mistake. The manhunt had consumed him, made him question everything he believed about himself, about justice. He'd told himself he was prepared to catch a monster, but no one prepared you for the aftermath.

Talbot picked up a photo of a young woman - one of Fairley's victims Her face was smiling in the picture, but he knew she hadn't smiled like that since. He thought of an elderly woman who'd faced The Fox and survived but who'd never feel safe in her own home again. Faces like theirs haunted him, each one a reminder of what they'd lost. And what he couldn't give back.

A soft knock on the door pulled him from his thoughts. He looked up to see Harriet Whitman, the lead prosecutor, standing there. "Mind if I come in?" she asked, her voice gentle.

"Sure," Talbot said, waving her in. "But if you're here to ask me about next steps, I haven't got a bloody clue."

Whitman chuckled softly and sat down across from him. "No, I figured as much. Just wanted to check on you. See how you're holding up."

Talbot sighed, rubbing his temples. "Honestly? I feel like I'm still chasing him, even though he's locked away. Can't shake the feeling that I missed something, you know?"

"You didn't miss anything, Mark," Whitman said firmly. "You caught him. He's not blending in with the crowd anymore. You brought him into the light."

"Maybe," Talbot murmured. "But there's a part of me that wonders…if it was worth it. All those nights, all that…obsession."

Whitman leaned forward, her expression softening. "Listen, it's natural to feel that way. You were in deep, Mark. We all were. But it doesn't mean it was for nothing."

Talbot nodded slowly, but his mind drifted. He thought about his wife, and the nights he'd come home late, reeking of sweat and cigarettes, his eyes wild with exhaustion. How many dinners had he missed? How many mornings had he left before she woke up, a stranger in his own home? She'd stood by him through it all, but the strain was there. And it hadn't gone away.

"What now?" he muttered, more to himself than to her. "What does a man do when the monster's gone?"

Whitman smiled gently. "He learns to live again. He finds his way back to the things he loves, the people who matter. And maybe, just maybe, he figures out that there's more to him than the chase."

Talbot looked up, meeting her eyes. "You make it sound so easy."
"It's not," she replied. "But it's worth a shot, isn't it?"

For a moment, they sat in silence, two weary souls who'd stared into the darkness and come out the other side. Finally, Talbot stood, his eyes scanning the room one last time. He picked up his jacket, slung it over his shoulder, and looked back at Whitman.

"Maybe you're right," he said. "Maybe it's time to see what's left of me after all this."

She smiled, a real one this time. "Good luck, Mark. You've earned it."

As he left the police station, the sun began to dip below the horizon, stretching golden light across the pavement. Talbot stood there for a moment, feeling the cool breeze on his face. He took a deep breath, feeling the weight of the past months start to lift, if only just a little.

The Fox was behind bars. The hunt was over. But for Talbot, a different journey was just beginning. One that would take him back to the things that mattered to the parts of himself he'd left behind in the darkness.

He took a step forward, not entirely sure where he was headed, but knowing that for the first time in a long time, he was ready to find out.

Chapter 34

Benjamin Young's house was quiet - too quiet. He stood in the bathroom, staring into the mirror, his eyes vacant and hollow. His face looked like a stranger's, pale and drawn, with bruises blossoming along his cheek and neck. He could still feel the trace of his touch on his skin, and it made his stomach turn.

The faucet was running, water pooling in the sink. He'd been washing his hands for what felt like hours, scrubbing his skin raw, trying to erase the feeling of him. His breath came in ragged gasps, his chest heaving, but he couldn't stop. The water had long turned from warm to icy cold, but he barely noticed. He was numb, his body moving on autopilot.

"Get it off. Just get it off," he whispered to himself, his voice trembling, barely audible over the sound of the rushing water.

The clock on the wall ticked relentlessly, a cruel reminder of the minutes passing. How long had it been since he left? Minutes? Hours? Time had lost all meaning. He could still hear his voice in his ears, his breath hot against his skin. The way he'd smiled when he realised, he was too weak, too terrified to fight back.

A sob caught in his throat, strangling him. He sank to the floor, his back against the cold tile wall, pulling his knees to his chest. He wanted to scream, to rage, to tear the whole world apart, but all he could manage was a soft, broken whimper. He pressed his hands to his mouth, trying to stifle the sound, as if letting it out would make everything too real, too impossible to bear.

There were bruises all over his body, deep and angry, each one a mark of his cruelty. He'd fought, he'd tried to push him off, but he was stronger, relentless. He could still feel his weight pressing down on him, the cold metal of his belt buckle biting into his skin.

He squeezed his eyes shut, trying to block out the memories, but they played out behind his eyelids like a nightmare he couldn't wake up from.

In his mind, he was back there again. The room was dark, he could smell his sweat and feel his breath hot and ragged in his ear. His gloved hand was clamped over his mouth, muffling his screams, his voice a low, guttural growl. "No one's coming for you," he'd whispered, and he knew he was right. He was alone. Utterly alone.

The cold tile floor of his bathroom seeped into his bones, but he welcomed the chill. It was something – anything - to feel other than the terror still coursing through his veins. He had never felt so small, so powerless. Every muscle in his body ached from fighting, from struggling, but none of that mattered now. He'd lost. And the world felt darker for it.

He heard a knock at the door - a soft, tentative rapping that broke through the fog of his mind. His heart seized in his chest. Was it him? Had he come back to finish what he started? He could barely breathe, his pulse thundering in his ears. He stayed where he was, frozen on the floor, unable to move.

"Benjamin? It's Sara. Are you in there?" The voice on the other side was gentle, familiar. His sister.

Benjamin's breath came out in a shaky rush, relief flooding through him. He wanted to get up, to open the door, but his legs wouldn't cooperate. He felt like he was made of lead, every movement a monumental effort.

"Benjamin, please, talk to me. I'm worried about you."

His voice was a whisper, raw and broken. "I'm here...I'm here."

There was a pause, then the sound of the doorknob turning. Sara pushed the door open, stepping inside, her eyes widening at the sight of Benjamin crumpled on the bathroom floor. She was a petite woman, but at that moment, she seemed to fill the entire room with her presence, her concern palpable.

"Oh my God, Benjamin," she breathed, rushing to his side. "What happened? Who did this to you?"

Benjamin tried to speak, but the words wouldn't come. He shook his head, tears streaming down his cheeks, his whole-body trembling. He couldn't say it. He couldn't make it real.

Sara knelt beside him, wrapping her arms around him, pulling him close. "It's okay, it's okay," she murmured, rocking him gently. "You're safe now. You're safe."

But Benjamin didn't feel safe. He felt shattered, broken in ways he couldn't even begin to understand. He buried his face in Sara's shoulder, the sobs finally breaking free, racking his body with a force that took his breath away. He cried until there were no more tears left, his throat raw and his chest hollow.

Sara held him through it all, whispering soothing words, but Benjamin barely heard them. All he could hear was The Fox's voice, whispering in his ear, telling him he was his, that he'd never escape him. He knew those words would haunt him for the rest of his life.

VICTIM SUPPORT

If you've been impacted by crime or a traumatic event, please know that you're not alone. There are many support services available to offer guidance, emotional support, and medical assistance.

Victim Support is a national charity dedicated to helping people recover from their experiences, and they are here for you too. You can reach them at www.victimsupport.org.uk or call 08 08 16 89 111 for compassionate help whenever you need it.

Part Six: The Real Fox

Chapter 35

Malcolm Fairley, known as "The Fox", was born in 1952 in Silksworth, near Sunderland.

He was born to Hannah and Ambrose and was the youngest of nine children. He was often described as "shy and introverted" and had a difficult childhood. Bullied at school, he frequently played truant, unable to read and only able to sign his name. His severe stammer made him shy around strangers, and he left school at fifteen.

He often disappeared at night, taking his dog to camp in the nearby Tunstall Hills. Relatives described him as a quiet and lonely child who was close to his mother but distant from his father. He enjoyed cartoons as a child, but as he grew older, he began illegally importing violent pornographic films. His father passed away when he was still young. The only criminal record in the family was Ambrose keeping a dog without a license.

Fairley's first job was as a labourer at a dairy, but it lasted only a few months. He then worked for sixteen months at a coal washer plant before briefly trying his hand as a trainee welder. However, much of his time was spent unemployed.

But beneath that meek exterior lay something darker. As a teenager, he began his descent into crime with theft and burglary, early signs of what was to come.

Aged nineteen, Fairley met Joan Sinclair in a ballroom. Joan was impressed by his sharp appearance and dancing skills. Soon after, she became pregnant, and the two hastily married. Joan's mother had saved £100 for their wedding cake, but Fairley stole the money. After staying with Joan's parents for a while, the couple moved into their own place - though Joan later discovered that everything inside had been stolen. She even suspected that Fairley's nice shirts and ties were likely stolen as well. Fairley was violent toward Joan, and although she divorced him, he somehow managed to gain custody of their son. Despite his abusive nature, Joan's mother described him as a "dance floor Romeo" with a certain charm.

Fairley also stole cars but initially left fingerprints behind, which led him to start wearing gloves during his thefts.

Fairley later married Georgina Bell, whom he met at an ice-skating rink. They had two children and lived in County Durham, but their marriage was plagued by violence and Fairley's frequent unemployment. Georgina worked at Woolworths, but her income wasn't enough to support the family.

For the next decade, Fairley was a regular in and out of jail, unable or unwilling to break free from his pattern of crime. Fairley's roots trace back to the Fairley clan of Scotland, whose name means "beautiful woodland." Their motto, "I am prepared," was a fitting irony for Fairley, who meticulously planned his burglaries.

He often scouted hilltops to track potential victims and felt comfortable navigating through woodlands to evade capture.

In 1983, Fairley moved to Leighton Buzzard to live with his brother, hoping to find work. He took various labourer jobs in Hertfordshire, Bedfordshire, and Buckinghamshire, becoming familiar with the area.

His criminal resume grew steadily - burglary, theft, car crime - a persistent offender. But his crimes escalated in a disturbing new direction when he stumbled upon a shotgun. The chance theft of that weapon unlocked a new, twisted hunger within him - a need for power, control, and fear. And so began the reign of terror that would earn him his chilling nickname.

Nicknamed "The Fox" by the press and police alike, Fairley earned his moniker for his uncanny ability to evade capture, often slipping away into nearby woods after his attacks. More than that, he was known to build makeshift dens inside his victims' homes, like a predator setting up his lair. Throughout the sweltering summer of 1984, The Fox unleashed a campaign of terror that would shock the nation, committing over eighty crimes and sparking one of the largest manhunts in British history.

On the morning of the fourteenth of September 1984, Malcolm Fairley finally faced justice at Dunstable Magistrates' Court. The atmosphere outside the court was electric, bristling with rage and fear. A hostile crowd had gathered, their hatred unmistakable, their voices a chorus of condemnation. The police, fearing for his safety, had covered Fairley's head with a blanket, shielding him from the stones and insults hurled his way.

But that was just the beginning. On the twenty-sixth of February 1985, The Fox stood trial at St Albans Crown Court. The charges were staggering - three rapes, two indecent assaults, three aggravated burglaries, five burglaries and the possession of a firearm. In a chilling display of arrogance or perhaps a twisted attempt at repentance, Fairley asked the court to consider an additional sixty-eight cases. His crimes were not a series of unfortunate events; they were a calculated spree of violence and terror.

Standing before the court, Malcolm Fairley tried to explain himself. "I wanted to stop it," he said, his voice steady but devoid of remorse, "but I couldn't. When I got the gun, I felt I could get what I wanted." His words fell like stones in the courtroom. There was no empathy, no understanding. He was a man who had crossed the line into monstrosity. His claim that he had no experience with guns and had accidentally shot someone's hand only deepened the horror. The gun had been a catalyst, an enabler of his darkest desires.

Some of his crimes were too horrific to be made public. Many of the details remain known only to his victims, the police and the trial judge.

Mr Justice Caulfield presided over the trial with a heavy but unwavering hand. When it came time to deliver his sentence, his words were cold and final. "There are degrees of wickedness beyond condemnatory description. Your crimes fall within this category. You desecrated and defiled men and women in their own homes." With that, he handed down six life sentences. The Fox's reign of terror was over, but the scars he left on his victims and their communities would never heal.

Even in prison, Fairley remained a symbol of fear and danger. The Parole Board denied him parole in October 2023, declaring that he was still a "real risk to the public." Retired Superintendent Brian Prickett, who had led part of the investigation that finally captured Fairley, agreed. "He hasn't changed," Prickett said. "Men like Fairley don't change."

And he never did. On the twenty-eighth of May 2024, Malcolm Fairley died in his cell at HM Prison Hull. The news brought a grim sort of closure to those who had lived in fear of The Fox, the man who had hidden in their homes, watched them in their sleep, and violated the sanctity of their lives. His death marked the end of a dark chapter, but his legacy - a legacy of horror - would never be forgotten.

Meet The Author

Soren Lyman, a native of Bedfordshire, England, brings a fresh voice to the world of crime fiction with his debut novel, *The Fox: A Summer In The Dark*.

Born and raised in Leighton Buzzard, Soren developed a fascination with mystery and suspense, drawing inspiration from both real-life events and the hidden complexities of small-town life. This passion ultimately led him to pen his first novel, weaving dark, compelling narratives that explore the human psyche.

A lifelong reader of crime fiction, Soren combines this passion with a fresh, immersive style that explores themes of fear, control and the thin line between justice and vengeance.

The Fox: A Summer In The Dark marks the beginning of his journey as an author, with more suspenseful tales already on the horizon.

Printed in Great Britain
by Amazon